F
Dan

Daniel, John
Vanity Fire

DATE DUE

FEB 2 0 2007			
MAY 0 7 2007			
JAN 1 4 2008			

Vanity Fire

Also by John M. Daniel
The Poet's Funeral

Generous Helpings
The Woman by the Bridge
Play Melancholy Baby

Vanity Fire

John M. Daniel

Poisoned Pen Press

Poisoned Pen Press
6962 E. First Ave., Ste. 103
Scottsdale, AZ 85251
www.poisonedpenpress.com
info@poisonedpenpress.com

Printed in the United States of America

*For Susan, as always,
and for my heroes,
Morgan Daniel and Ben Daniel,
and for their families*

Acknowledgments

In the spirit of full disclosure, I must state that there is a city called Santa Barbara, California, and that I lived there for twenty years, during which time I was a small-press publisher. I also acknowledge that a few celebrities walk on and off these pages in cameo roles. But this is a work of fiction. All the other characters, including Guy Mallon and Carol Murphy, are entirely fictitious, and the events are entirely invented. Any similarity to real people or real events would be a big surprise to me.

Having said that, I'm safe in saying that without the partnership of Susan Daniel I would not have been a publisher, and without her companionship I would not have written this book. I thank Channing Bates for introducing me to Santa Barbara, Julie and Don Steele for introducing me to the Bay Islands of Honduras, and Meredith Phillips for introducing me to the pleasures of mystery fiction. I owe a great deal to the Great Intenders—Lance Hardie, Mary Wilbur, Dick Stull, Nancy Only, and Janine Volkmar—for their support, valuable constructive critique, and invaluable friendship while this novel was in progress. Thanks also to Robert Rosenwald and Barbara Peters and everyone else connected with Poisoned Pen Press.

—JMD

Then I saw in my dream, that, when they were got out of the wilderness, they presently saw a town before them, and the name of that town is Vanity; and at the town there is a fair kept, called Vanity Fair. It is kept all the year long....

Therefore at this fair are all such merchandise sold as houses, lands, trades, places, honors, preferments, titles, countries, kingdoms, lusts, pleasures, and delights of all sorts, as whores, bawds, wives, husbands, children, masters, servants, lives, blood, bodies, souls, silver, gold, pearls, precious stones, and what not.

And, moreover, at this fair there are at all times to be seen juggling, cheats, games, plays, fools, apes, knaves, and rogues, and that of every kind.

Here are to be seen, too, and that for nothing, thefts, murders, adulteries, false swearers, and that of a blood-red color.

—John Bunyan, *The Pilgrim's Progress*

Prologue

Saturday evening, no, actually it was Sunday morning, September 9-10, 1995. It was almost two in the morning when I got home. We lived on the East Side of Santa Barbara, a neighborhood of small houses and bungalows that was rapidly being munched by developers and turned into condos. Most of our neighbors spoke Spanish. The only Spanish the developers knew was the names of the streets in the neighborhoods they were destroying.

I parked on the street, even though I expected there was still room for my car in the garage. But the garage was Carol's space, and even though she'd been gone for a week, I still hoped she'd be back.

I got out of my car and stretched in the hot night. A Santa Ana wind had blown down from the mountains earlier that evening, raising the temperature twenty degrees and drying the air out. We get a lot of Santa Anas in the early fall, and that year they had been worse than ever. The town was a tinder box, too, whenever the Santa Anas blew through. People of Santa Barbara bragged about how long they'd lived there by remembering fires.

I locked my car and walked up the pathway to the front door. I let myself in as quietly as I could. I didn't want to wake Carol, on the off chance she had returned to our bed, to our house, to our business, to my life. And if she was home, I didn't want to wake her up and have to tell her where I'd been that night, and with whom, and what I'd been doing. I tiptoed back to our bedroom and peeked in. The bed was made and empty.

I walked out to the kitchen and switched on the light. Her note was still on the counter, where it had been for seven days.

Guy,

I've had it. I'm going for a drive. I'm going north, as far as I can get from this stupid city, this stupid business, and you. I love you, you little shmuck, but this time you really fucked up big.

C

She had me there. I had fucked up big.

I lay on our bed for an hour without getting any sleepier. I was stripped down to my undershorts on top of the bedspread. I was still wide awake shortly after three in the morning when the phone rang on the table next to Carol's side. I rolled over and picked up the receiver. "Hello? Carol?"

"Is this Guy Mallon?"

I sighed. "Speaking," I answered. "Who is this? You know, it's three in the morning."

"I'm very sorry, Mister Mallon. This is Detective Rosa Macdonald, Santa Barbara Police Department. I—"

"Oh no!" I said. "What happened? Is she all right?"

"Mister Mallon, I'm afraid I have some very serious news for you."

"What?"

"I'm sorry to tell you this, but there's been a major fire at the old DiClemente Avocado warehouse. As I understand it, you've been using that warehouse space for your business. Is that right?"

I breathed. "Thank God. I mean, is that all?"

"I'm afraid the fire damage was…complete," the detective said. "And I need to talk to you. We have a witness here who reports that your car was parked in the DiClemente warehouse lot from about nine till sometime after ten this evening."

"Nope," I said. "I've been with my car all evening, and I never was in the warehouse parking lot. Not tonight anyway."

"You weren't in the neighborhood at all?"

"Well, I was on that side of the freeway for a while, but not within half a mile of the warehouse. Who says I was there?"

"Just that your car was there," Detective Macdonald corrected me. "Red seventy-six Volvo, license plate GFA 096."

I gasped. "Where's that car now?" I asked. "Where is it? Still there?"

"No, sir. The parking lot's empty. But that is your station wagon?"

"No," I said. "It's my partner's car."

"I see," she said. "Can you tell me how I can reach your partner, sir?"

"No. I wish to hell I could." Then I asked, "Did you say police department? Is the fire department there?"

"Yes sir. They've done all they could. I'm afraid there wasn't much left to save. We believe the fire began about ten-thirty. Old wooden building. Took about three hours to burn."

"And you're with the police?" I asked again.

"Yes sir. I'm an arson investigator."

"Arson?"

"Mister Mallon, I'm stuck here for another couple of hours. Any chance you could come down here to the site and talk with me? I have a few questions—"

"That seventy-six Volvo," I asked. "It never showed up again?"

"No sir, not yet anyway. Can you get down here? I have to hang up now. I've got people waiting to speak to me."

"I'll be right there," I said. "Listen, if that red station wagon shows up again? Tell her to wait for me. I'll be right there."

Part One

Chapter One

I can tell you exactly when and where this mess began. Tuesday, June 28, 1994. Carol was out of the office on her morning rounds when the phone rang. I answered, "Guy Mallon Books."

"Is this Guy Mallon?" The voice was gravelly but friendly. *"The* Guy Mallon?"

"Speaking."

"Mister Mallon, my name is Fritz Marburger. I don't expect you've heard of me, but if you have the time I'd like to take you and your wife to lunch today to discuss an idea I have."

Oh right. Publisher beware. "Mister Marburger," I said, "I'm not married. I do have a business partner, but she's not my wife. I appreciate the offer, but we're busy today, and—"

"We could make it tomorrow," he said. "I'm free all week. One of the joys of being retired. Also one of the curses."

"Look, maybe I should cut to the chase and save us both some time. If you're looking to sell me stocks or real estate, I'm not interested. If you're a poet and you have a manuscript to show me, you're welcome to drop it off and I'll look at it when I can find the time. But it won't do you any good to take Carol and me to lunch, because—"

He cut me off with a jolly, gruff laugh. "Hey, Guy, I hear you, but let me cut to my own chase. Give me just a minute. I'm not selling a thing, and I'm not a poet. Jesus Christ, that's for sure. I'm a retired businessman. I had a long and successful career in mergers and acquisitions. Now I'm out of work and I'm bored.

I'm bored stiff. So I thought it would be fun to invest a little money in a small local business and see what might happen. I've been asking around, and some of the people here at Casa Dorinda are saying nice things about Guy Mallon Books. So I'd like to get to know you. I'm thinking of rolling the dice with maybe fifty grand, if I feel it's a good fit. If not, I'll keep looking. That's all. It's worth a lunch, especially since I'm buying. So if you have the time tomorrow, what say we meet at the El Encanto, say twelve-thirty?"

Casa Dorinda was a retirement home in Montecito for the wealthy. Residents there bought a lot of our poetry books from Tecolote Books, a nearby independent bookstore. So far, so good. Besides, lunch at El Encanto? "Well, tomorrow's busy, actually, but today's free after all."

"Grand." Wealthy people say *grand* a lot, I've found. "Twelve-thirty?"

"Swell," I answered.

I was hanging up just as Carol walked through the front door, carrying the day's mail. She plopped the pile of mail on my desk. "Guess what," I said. "We're having lunch at El Encanto today."

"How sweet of you!"

"Not me," I said. "Fritz Marburger's the sweet one."

"Who's he?"

"I don't know, but he's interested in our company. He has some money to invest and for some reason he wants to scout us out. I figure it won't do us any harm to—"

"Oh, shoot!" Carol said. "I'm getting my hair cut at one o'clock. Remember?"

"Damn, I forgot. Well, maybe I can call him back and reschedule."

"That's okay," she said. "You go on without me. You can tell me about it this afternoon."

"But it's a business deal," I said. "You're the business manager. I'm just an editor. What do I know about business?"

Carol chuckled. "You don't know squat. But you're a dreamer, Guy. And you know how to listen. See what he has to offer and we'll talk about it. But before you accept any money from this hotshot?"

"What?" I asked.

"I want to hear the string section."

"Look at that God damned view," Fritz Marburger remarked as we waited for our entrees to arrive. We sipped a local Chardonnay on the terrace of the El Encanto, a quiet and elegant restaurant high on the Santa Barbara Riviera, with the red-roofed city laid out below us like a bowl emptying into the harbor. Palm trees lined the beach and sailboats bobbed on the sapphire bay. Out on the horizon floated the Channel Islands; the air was so clear you could see, or at least imagine, the canyons on their hillsides.

Mr. Marburger was a tall, skinny man with a Walter Matthau grin, sparkling Sinatra eyes, and a forest of unruly gray hair, which he combed with his fingers throughout our conversation. He wore a tweed jacket and a plaid shirt. "I got to admit," he added, "Santa Barbara's easy on the eyes. I could get used to this town."

"How long have you been here, Mister Marburger?" I asked.

"Call me Fritz. Five years. The five slowest years of my life. Used to live in Chicago, but when I retired my wife insisted that we come out here and quote take it easy for a change unquote, move into that morgue in Montecito, play a little golf. Which was fine for her till she died two years ago, God damn her, and now here I am, twiddling my God damned thumbs, surrounded by beautiful scenery and beautiful rich widows."

"Too bad."

He laughed. "Just kidding. The widows leave me alone. I guess I'm too hot to handle. Actually, I've been seeing—I guess that's the way you say it—a younger lady lately, as you may know."

I shook my head. "Sorry, should I know?"

"You don't read the *Santa Barbara News-Press*?"

"Not the society page."

He chuckled. "Good man," he said. He reached into the breast pocket of his tweed jacket and handed me a small package wrapped in gold paper and tied up with a silver ribbon. "My lady friend wanted me to give you this." He handed the package to me.

"Feels like a CD," I said, pulling on the ribbon.

"Don't open it now," Fritz said. "Wait till you get back to the office. Ah, here's lunch." I slid the package into the side pocket of my jacket.

A uniformed waiter opened up a folding stand next to our table, where he placed a large tray. He proceeded to put plates before us: I had pumpkin soup and the crab melt with shoestring fries and Fritz had a huge Cobb salad showered with roquefort dressing. The waiter refilled our wineglasses, asked if we wanted anything more, and bowed when he was excused.

"Not bad," Fritz pronounced after a few bites. "I like this joint. I happen to know the maître d', personal friend of mine. So when did you come to Santa Barbara, or have you always had it this good?"

"I came here in nineteen seventy-seven," I answered. "I was just passing through. Bought a bookstore that was going out of business, then somehow got into the publishing business through the back door, almost by accident. Carol Murphy became my partner a few years later, and now we're working our butts off, doing what we love."

"Doing pretty well, from all I hear," he said.

I shrugged. "For a rinkydink little West Coast poetry publisher, I guess you could say we're doing all right. We pay the rent. We've had some good luck. One of our authors was Poet Laureate for a couple of years, and that helped. But it's not an easy way to make a living. We pay the rent and that's about it."

"Seems to me you could do better. I mean, publishing *poetry*, for God's sake? Does anybody *read* poetry anymore? I'll bet the bookstore's what's paying the rent."

"Nope. That was a total loss. We quit selling books years ago. It's all publishing now, and yes, there are a few readers left. We can sell a thousand copies of anything we publish. We're not getting rich, but we're having fun."

"You're not interested in growing?"

"Growing?"

"Hey, I don't mean anything personal. No offense, okay? How tall are you, anyway? Just curious."

"Five feet. No offense taken." I'm quite used to being the shortest man in any crowd. That doesn't bother me, but rude people give me a pain in the ass.

"Well, I'm talking business, is all. That's what I mean by growing. You may be stuck at five feet, but you could get a lot bigger in other ways." Fritz pointed at me with a forkful of lettuce. "Thousand copies? That's chickenshit, pardon my God damned French. You can actually live on that? What do you eat for dinner, pork and beans?" Then he glared and shook his head. "Sorry. It's just that numbers like that tend to make me sleepy, know what I mean?"

"I think I do," I said. "This crab melt is so good I'm going to finish it before I walk out. I hope you don't mind." I took a bite. Fuckin jerk.

But then he turned his glare into a grin and said, "Hey, Guy. Don't get me wrong. I'm just needling your ass. Thing is, I know you can do better. I've made a career out of recognizing talent, and you've got it. But a thousand copies? Poetry? Give me a break. You can do better." He poked his forkful of lettuce into his mouth and started chewing at me. "A lot better than a thousand copies. We're going to get you and your partner into play, my friend. And it ain't going to be with poetry. A thousand copies. Shit. Let's forget tiddlywinks, shall we? How much would it cost to publish a real book? A big book, couple of hundred pages, hardback, first class all the way, ten-twelve thousand copies. Huh? How much."

"Hell if I know," I said. "I've never done anything like that."

"But you're a publisher, right?"

"Tiddlywinks."

"You're a businessman, for Christ's sake. Come on. Let's have some numbers."

"Twenty thousand?" I guessed. "Twenty-five?"

Fritz Marburger grinned and nodded. He pulled a checkbook out of his jacket pocket.

"What the hell is this?" Carol asked, staring at the rectangle in her hand.

"A check for thirty thousand dollars. Your hair looks nice," I told her. "I like it that length." Actually I liked Carol's strawberry blond hair any length, because I like hair and because it's Carol's.

"I can see it's a check, Guy," she said. "I can see it's made out to Guy Mallon Books. What I don't know is who the hell's Fritz Marburger, and what the hell this is all about, and it's not about my hair. What's the deal?"

"Well, we don't have to cash it if we don't want to," I said. "That's the deal."

"What's this money for, Guy? Please don't make me beg."

I smiled. "It's in case we want to publish a novel," I said.

"We have to spend thirty thousand dollars publishing a novel? Is this man crazy? Are you crazy?"

"No. We publish the novel, and we get to do whatever we want with whatever money's left over. Publish more God damned little poetry books, as Fritz puts it—"

"I see we're already on a first-name basis," Carol remarked.

"—or, if we decide we like real publishing for a change, we can publish a couple more commercial novels. Anything we want. Our choice."

"Do we get to choose the first novel?" Carol asked.

"Well, that's the string section you were worried about."

"Let's hear it."

I pulled the small, square package out of my coat pocket and handed it to Carol. "Open it," I said.

Carol pulled the ribbon and tore away the gift wrap. *"I'll Be Seeing You,"* she read. "'Sweet Lorraine Evans Celebrates the Standards.'"

"Lorraine Evans?" I said. "She's my favorite singer. I didn't know she could write."

"You still don't," Carol pointed out.

"Come on, Carol. It might be a good book. Could be. We might like it. If we don't, we tear up the check."

"I'm not sure I like this idea, Guy," Carol said. "I love you to death, and whatever you say, we do. But damn it, we're not vanity publishers."

"Only if we like the book, Carol. Only if we love it."

"But even if we do," she reasoned, "even if it's the best book we ever read—"

"Yes?"

"We'd have to print ten, fifteen thousand copies to break even."

"Well? Now we can afford that."

"Yeah, but—"

"What?"

"Where would we store all those books?"

"Think big," I said.

"Of course," she said, kissing my forehead. "That's why I love you."

Chapter Two

We spent Fourth of July weekend out in the tiny backyard of our East Side bungalow. Carol did some gardening while I sat on the deck under a bougainvillea reading the Lorraine Evans manuscript. The first sentence caught my interest. The first paragraph had me hooked. The first page had me in love, and by the end of the first chapter I was out of my chair over and over, following Carol around the flower beds, reading aloud to her as she buried her hands in the soil.

Finally she put down her trowel and begged me, "Don't read me any more. Let me garden. Then let me read for myself. You're spoiling all the surprises, and besides, I'm getting a little bit jealous here."

That was on Saturday. That evening, during cocktails, I had a hard time keeping my mouth shut and a harder time trying to talk about anything other than the novel I had just finished reading.

Carol gave me the smiling Irish eyes over her gin glass and said, "Okay, okay, tell me all about it."

"Nope," I said. "You'll read it for yourself. Soon, I hope."

"Tomorrow. Otherwise we'll have nothing to talk about. And I don't want you hovering over me while I turn the pages. Tomorrow you're doing the laundry, the shopping, and the vacuuming, while I get to put my feet up and read."

"I vacuumed last weekend," I reminded her.

"I just want you to stay out of my hair while I read Miss Glamorpuss."

"Why do you call her that?"

"Because she flounces," Carol answered. "And because of the title of her so-called novel."

I grinned at her. She was in for a surprise.

So maybe Lorraine Evans wore hoop earrings and too much makeup when she delivered the manuscript to our office, including pancake on her cleavage. So maybe the novel was titled *Naming Names.* Carol was in for a surprise, and our publishing company was in for a new set of wings.

"God damn it, this is a fine book!" Carol admitted the next evening at cocktails. "I was ready to give it the once-over and hand it back to you. But shit, I *like* this book. I figured it was going to be a tell-all thing, with thinly disguised celebrities misbehaving in each others' beds. It's not that at all."

In fact, Lorraine's novel was a sensitive story about a penniless, schizophrenic old woman living in a Santa Cruz charity hotel, who, when she went off her meds, would undress in public and rant about how she had been sexually molested by both Allen and John Foster Dulles when she was a child.

I grinned. "Too bad we publish only poetry."

"Oh shut up, Guy. You know you want to publish this book, and I know we can afford to do it now. Call the lady and tell her to come in and sign a contract."

"You're not jealous anymore?" I asked. Just to make sure.

"Huh? You mean jealous of Miz Flounce? Don't be silly. Oh, you mean what I said yesterday? I was just jealous because you got to read a book in the shade while I had to strain my back and break all my fingernails in the dirt."

"I vacuumed today," I reminded her. "And folded laundry."

"Lorraine's number's on the manuscript. Call her up."

Lorraine Evans came into the office Tuesday afternoon, and she didn't come alone. She brought with her, or vice versa, her boyfriend, her sugar-daddy. Wearing a big, proud grin she said, "Carol, Guy, I'd like you to meet my agent. This is Fritz Marburger."

Fritz gave us his rubber-faced grin and extended his left hand; Lorraine was holding onto the right.

I said, "We've actually—," but a slight shake of the head and a wink from Fritz told me to can it. "We've actually heard of Mister Marburger," I said.

"Call me Fritz," he said in his jovial bass rumble. He turned to Carol and said, "I understand you're the brains of this organization. That's what Lorrie tells me."

"I control the purse strings," Carol said. "Strings are my specialty."

"Good girl." Fritz extricated his right hand from Lorraine's grasp and started moving around the office, looking at the bookshelves on the walls. "You published all these books?" he asked.

"No," I said. "Those are my collection. I collect postwar western American poets. First editions."

He looked at all four walls of the office, as if mentally calculating how many books I owned. "Lot of poets," he observed. "How much is this collection worth?"

"It's priceless," I said.

"Right, but if you were to sell it," he persisted.

"Not for sale."

"Okay, okay. Not like I want to buy it, you understand. I don't read poetry. I read the *Wall Street Journal* and that's about it. But this collection, how much is it insured for?"

Lorraine stepped in and said, "Don't answer that. Don't mind Fritz. He's got a one-track mind. Let's do business!"

So we sat at the round conference table and I passed around copies of a two-page contract I had drawn up that morning. Carol plopped down a yellow pad so she could take notes on the negotiations. Lorraine put on a pair of red-rimmed reading glasses and got to work. Fritz sprawled forward with his elbows on the table, humming and grunting as he went through the document. He nodded, he shook his head, he tapped the table, he ran fingers through his thicket of gray hair.

Lorraine looked up and smiled, then folded her hands on top of the contract.

Fritz looked up and said, "That's it? That's the contract?"

"That's it," I said. "That's the contract."

Fritz shook his head. "You can do better than this. This is fine as far as it goes, but I mean give me a break. Doesn't say anything about foreign rights, paperback rights, movie rights, greeting card rights, tee shirt rights, blah blah blah. Doesn't say how many copies of the book you're going to publish. Doesn't even name the God damned territory, for Christ's sake. And ten percent royalty? You gotta be kidding me. I think you could also throw in a few promotion guarantees, tour, advertising, we want a review in *Publishers Weekly*, yada yada. I want you to get Lorraine on 'Oprah.' And what's this horseshit about holding back royalties as a reserve against returns? There aren't going to be any returns. And another thing. Sales reports twice a year? Forget it. We get a sales report every month, and we get paid every month for that month's sales. The check's to be made out to Marburger Enterprises. I'll keep my agent's fee and pass the rest along to Lorraine. I want that written into the contract: an agency clause. Let me see what else—"

"Hold on," Carol said, her facial expression friendly. I know that expression. "It sounds as if you know quite a bit about the publishing business. Have you worked in publishing?"

Fritz raised his eyebrows. "I know a lot about business, and I know a lot about contracts. And as Lorrie's agent—"

Lorraine said, "Fritzy, be nice."

"You're the nice one. But somebody's got to play hardball. That's where business gets fun, right? Without back-and-forth, no give-and-take, there's no sex, pardon my French. Okay, let's roll up our sleeves." He moistened his thumb and forefinger, laid the pages of the contract side by side on the table before him, and said, "Paragraph one..."

It took us all afternoon, but the four of us hammered out a contract that suited us all. Fritz insisted that the territory be defined as the entire universe, which was fine with me and made

Lorraine squeal with pleasure. The contract named Marburger Enterprises as the agent, but Carol inserted a clause stating that Fritz Marburger have no decision-making power with respect to *Naming Names* or any other part of our publishing business.

That one was a little sticky. "Look, I don't see why you wouldn't want me to give you some advice from time to time, for Christ's sake," he said. "I mean I'm retired and I don't have all that much to do these days, so—"

"So play golf," Carol said.

Fritz brought a laugh out of his lungs that sounded like fifty years of unfiltered Chesterfields. "God," he said. "Missus Mallon, I like your style!"

"My name's Murphy. The clause stays."

Fritz gave us all a splendid slow-motion shrug, a grin, a nod.

We shook hands all around, Carol promised to have the revised contract ready to sign the next day, Lorraine kissed Fritz, and I went to the storage closet and came out with a bottle of wine, a corkscrew, and four glasses.

The next day Fritz called me and said, "Listen, Guy, I know we have a contract and all that, but you and I have to have a separate agreement that I get something more out of this than my fifteen percent of Lorraine's ten percent. I mean since I'm invested so heavily in this project, how about you put me on the payroll as an advisor or something?"

"Why didn't you bring this up yesterday?" I asked.

"I didn't want Lorrie to know I'd paid for this book to be published. I mean she's pretty sensitive, and frankly I don't want her to cut me off or kill me."

"Well," I answered, "I don't want Carol to kill me either, and we don't have a payroll."

"Then how about you give me some stock in your company. Not a controlling amount, just some equity. After all—"

"We're not a corporation," I told him. "Look, Fritz, if you don't like the agreement we agreed on, it's not too late to back out. Nobody's signed anything yet."

His sigh was like a resigned growl. "Forget it, he said. "We'll sign."

◇◇◇

Pre-press production took six months. In late January, we sent the book off to the printer in Michigan and called Lorraine and Fritz in for a conference on marketing.

"We've sent out the bound galleys," Carol told them. "Guy's writing the press release. Here's a list of places we plan to send review copies, everything from *People* to the *Santa Cruz Sentinel*. We've got a publication party scheduled at the Earthling Bookstore for Friday, April fifteenth. If you give us your mailing list—do you have a mailing list?"

Lorraine said, "Natch."

"And I want this girl on 'Oprah,'" Fritz interjected.

"Uh—we'll try," Carol said. "Remember, we don't have a lot of clout."

"I do," Lorraine reminded us. "Don't worry about 'Oprah,' my publicist will take care of her."

"If you get on 'Oprah,' we're going to have to be ready to reorder books. A lot more books," Carol said.

"That reminds me," I said. "We still don't have a place to store the books we're getting. I've got to look into warehouse space."

"Where are you storing your books now?" Fritz asked.

"We have a couple of units at Budget U-Stor, other side of the freeway," Carol told him.

"Shit. You guys really are amateurs, aren't you. No offense."

"Wait a minute," I said, my voice getting high and loud. "You can't get away with that, say 'no offense' after you do your best to offend us."

Fritz grinned at Carol, then at me. "Look," he said. "I'm here to help you grow. Work with me, okay? I'm going to put you on the map."

"We're already on the map," Carol muttered.

"Map of Santa Barbara, maybe. That's not enough for me, and it shouldn't be enough for you."

I thought about that. Yes, I had to admit having my name on a bigger map sounded good. "Go on," I said.

Fritz said, "I've had my eye on a piece of commercial real estate. I'll buy it as an investment and we'll move the books in there. You can pay rent to me, which is the least you could do, come to think of it."

"What do you mean by that?" Lorraine asked.

"Nothing, sweetheart."

"You paid them to publish my book," she said. I watched those big whole-note eyes of hers narrow to murderous slits.

"At least it's getting published," he fumbled. "Nobody else would touch it."

"You're really in trouble now, Fritzo."

"Baby, listen—"

"I'm not talking to you," she told him. Then she turned to Carol and me. "It's not true, you know. A lot of publishers would have been glad to have this book, I know that. But Fritz wanted to work with you, and I'm glad he did. I love you guys." She turned back to her agent and repeated, "Love you to death."

In mid-March, a week before ten thousand copies of *Naming Names* was scheduled for delivery, Fritz Marburger walked Carol and me through the DiClemente Avocado warehouse, which he had just purchased. It was run-down and dusty, a dimly lit cavern next to the railroad tracks on the ocean side of the freeway. And it was big. It was huge. It was made of wood that looked stained by the weather, but Fritz assured me that the cement floor was dry and the roof was new. It had a loud mechanized rolling door big enough to drive a truck into.

"You'll be paying rent to Marburger Enterprises," Fritz said. "Fifteen hundred a month."

"That's outrageous," Carol said.

"What can I say?" Fritz countered. "Rents are outrageous in this town. Get over it. How much would it cost you to store ten thousand hardback books at Budget Fucking U-Stor?"

"Okay," she said. "Since it's too late for us to shop around."

"Oh, and you'll have a roommate," Fritz added. "I'm renting the back third of this place to somebody else. Otherwise I'd have to charge you more."

"You have anybody in mind?" I asked.

"Yeah, we signed a lease yesterday. He'll be moving in next week. Another publisher, as a matter of fact. You guys should get along just fine. Name's Herndon. Roger Herndon. Great guy. Knows a lot about publishing. He's going to have his offices in the back, along with his printing equipment."

"Roger Herndon," I said. "Never heard of him."

"He's new in town. You'll like him."

"What does he publish?"

"Books."

"What kind of books?"

"How do I know? Good books. Books that sell. No poetry. You'll like him. You'll get along just fine."

"Is he paying fifteen hundred a month too?" Carol asked.

"That's between him and me," Fritz said. "But I'll tell you this much. I'm going to get my thirty thousand dollars back one way or another. Now that Sweet Lorraine Evans has shown me the gate, I'm going to be a lot more businesslike."

"You and Lorraine are—"

"Kaput. Finito. History City. But I'm still her God damned agent, and the royalty checks still come to Marburger Enterprises. I still own a piece of her ass, pardon my God damned French."

For a moment I detected a sadness I had never seen before in Fritz Marburger's eyes, but the expression quickly turned to steel.

Chapter Three

Ten thousand copies of Lorraine's book were already on a truck somewhere between Ann Arbor and Santa Barbara, and we had to get the warehouse ready to receive them.

It was filthy. Lit by a sprinkling of fifty-watt bulbs, I guess it had a romantic look, but the dust on the floor was thick enough to leave deep tracks in.

I phoned Fritz Marburger and asked him to get the place cleaned up for us right away and he said it would be less expensive for us and less trouble for him if we did the work ourselves. I told him it was customary for landlords to rent property in clean condition. He told me the property in question was a warehouse on the south side of town, not a condo on the Riviera for Christ's sake. I told him it was a lot of work, and I wanted some help. He advised me to get help from Roger Herndon, and get Herndon to pay half. I asked when Herndon would be showing up, and he said, "Guy, I'm not my tenant's keeper."

Ooooo-kay. At least we didn't have to worry about cleaning any windows.

I changed the bulbs to 125-watters, making the space look even dirtier, and I strung a lot more bulbs around the rafters. Now we could see it all: dust, rusty nails, scraps of wood, rodent turds, spider webs, the works. Not to mention the bathroom from the Black Lagoon.

No Roger Herndon. Carol and I were on our own. We dressed down, way down, rented a small pickup truck, and went to Scolari's Market, where we bought a Styrofoam ice chest and filled it with ice, sodas, and bottled water. Then on to the Home Improvement Center, where we bought a battery of cleaning supplies.

We drove to the warehouse and got to work. It was ten in the morning.

We broke for lunch at one, with sandwiches and beer from Johnny's Greek and Italian Deli. We ate at a folding table I found against the wall, sitting on two cleaning buckets turned upside-down. After lunch we got right back to work.

It was dark outside long before we finished inside, so Carol drove off and returned with a couple pizzas from Rusty's and a sixpack of Bohemia. By the time she got back I had finished the job and was wiping off the folding table again. Only the bathroom remained to be cleaned. We'd tackle that after dinner.

She served and we dug in, too hungry, too exhausted to talk.

We were just starting on the second pizza and had drunk two of the beers when the squeaky warehouse door rolled up and in walked a strange man and a stranger woman. Strange in that we had never met them before. Strange in other ways as well.

"Hey hey *hey!*" said the man. "Pizza! Aw right!" He and his companion approached the table. He had the grossest smile I'd ever seen; she wore no expression whatsoever and I already liked her better than I liked him. "Name's Roger," he announced. "Roger Herndon. Mind if we join you?"

Carol made a certain sound, something like "rrrrrmmmm," which only I knew the meaning of, because she didn't change her facial expression as she rose to offer the young woman her seat. I offered my bucket to Roger Herndon.

I sat on the edge of the table. "I'm Guy Mallon," I said. "This is Carol Murphy."

"Figured as much," said Roger Herndon, his mouth full of pizza. In the bright light I watched him chew with his mouth open. He was a tall, beefy middle-aged man with a stringy red comb-over and freckles all over his face. He wore a crimson sweatshirt and a dark blue windbreaker, and he had a scarf around his neck. To hide wrinkles, I was willing to bet; it wasn't all that cold. Which was a good thing for the young woman, who was skimpily dressed in a sleeveless purple tee shirt with the words "Kountry Klub" across her chest in hot pink.

"So we're sharing this space, huh?" he said. "Looks good. Lot better than when I checked it out earlier. The landlord must've cleaned it up."

"We cleaned it up," Carol informed him. "It cost us—"

"Cool," Roger said. "Thanks a lot. I guess I'll be moving my stuff in here tomorrow morning. Lot of heavy equipment. I could sure use a hand. You guys doing anything tomorrow morning? That your truck out there?"

"Rental," I said.

"Good through tomorrow, I hope?"

The young woman turned to me and said, "Could we shut that door? I'm freezing in this miniskirt."

"I'll get it," I said. "What's your name, by the way?"

"That's Gracie," Roger said. "My right-hand man."

"By the way, Roger," I asked. "We still have a toilet to clean, if you want to pitch in."

Roger turned to his right-hand man. "What about it, Gracie?"

"Can't," she said. "I have to be at the club at nine o'clock."

Roger gave me a shrug. "Sorry," he said. "Give us a raincheck."

Max and Art were already at the warehouse when Carol and I got there early the next morning. Maxwell Black and Arthur Summers, two of America's most celebrated contemporary poets, whom we were lucky to have in our stable of authors. We were even luckier to have Art and Max as friends that foggy March morning, since we had a lot of heavy lifting to do and they had volunteered to help with the move.

They stood grinning in the open door to the warehouse, which meant Carol and I weren't the first tenants to arrive. We hopped out of the rental truck and approached them with smiles. Shook hands.

"Who's this guy Roger?" Art asked, pointing over his shoulder with his thumb. "Is he in charge here?"

"No," Carol said.

"Acts that way."

"He's renting the back third of the space," I said.

"That's what he told us," Max said. "That's why we have to move his stuff in here first. Makes more sense, he says. I didn't know we were working for him."

"He's an asshole," Art said. "I'll help him move his stuff, if that's what you two want, but I'm not taking direction from him. I'm too old to be bossed around by a stranger."

Carol and I walked into the warehouse and back to where Gracie and Roger were plotting out their office space with a tape measure and a stick of chalk. Roger looked up and said, "Hey, Guy. Ready to roll? I see we got some strong backs on board."

"Listen, Roger," I said. "Those guys, those strong backs, are friends of ours."

"Hey, any friends of yours are friends of mine. Friends in need, right?"

"They're good friends," Carol said. "They're also good poets."

"I got nothing against poets," Roger said, grinning. "Especially poets with strong backs. I'm not sure I get your point."

"Our point," I said, "is that they're doing this as a favor, for free, because they're friends. Don't go telling them what to do."

"I wasn't telling anybody what to do. I just suggested that we get my stuff moved in first. Makes sense, doesn't it? Since I'm in the back of the bus here?"

"Just what's coming in here?" I asked.

"Oh, the usual," he answered. "Couple of desks, filing cabinets, chairs, computers, bookcase, and a TV."

"TV?" Carol asked.

"Gracie likes to watch her soaps," Roger explained. "And a few cartons of books, inventory, and the DocuTech machine. And a shitload of paper."

"Where's all this stuff now?" I asked.

Roger grinned and clapped me on the shoulder. "That's the good part," he said. "It's all in storage units over there at Budget U-Stor."

"That's where we've been keeping our stock," I said.

"So Marburger told me. Convenient, no? Let's get cracking."

"How big is a DocuTech machine?" I asked. "And what's it do, exactly?"

"It makes books. On demand. And it's one big mutha. It'll fit in the back of the truck, though. I measured last night."

"Our truck, you mean," Carol said.

"Yeah. Our truck," he agreed.

"Our? You paying half the rental fee?"

"We got a lot of work to do," Roger Herndon said. "We can work out the details and settle up later."

One big mutha was right. We moved that first, and it took the whole pickup truck to do it. Good thing Max and Art were both strong, tall guys, because I'm neither, and Roger didn't seem to want to get his hands dirty. We backed the truck right into the warehouse and Roger showed us—us included Max and Art, Carol and Gracie, and me—where to set the components of the machine. It stretched across half the back of the warehouse.

"Great," Roger announced. "Gracie and Carol can hook all the pieces together and string the wiring, while us guys go and shlep the rest of the furniture and books and shit."

Carol asked Gracie, "You know how this thing fits together?"

"It'll be easy without Roger here helping us," Gracie replied.

So the guys and I went back out to the truck. The poets climbed into the back and the publishers sat in the cab. "So how does this DocuTech work?" I asked as we drove back to Budget U-Stor, which was only a few blocks away. "I'm still in the Stone Age."

"Simple," Roger answered. "Stick a disk in one end and books come out the other, all bound and everything. Like sex in the front and a dump in the back. Of course the disk has to be perfect, and that's Gracie's department. She knows about computers."

"What's your department?"

"Sales."

"Selling books?"

"Nah. Selling book contracts."

"How much did that machine cost you? The DocuTech."

"Not a cent. I'm leasing it." He grinned and gave me a wink. "Other people's money. That's what publishing's all about, right?"

It was twelve-thirty by the time we had moved all of his furniture.

"Anything else?" I asked.

"That's about it," Roger said. "There's a few cases of paper for the machine and a dozen cartons of *Freelance Reader.* You can bring those things over when you bring your stock. Here's a key to the unit they're in. Number eighty-seven."

"Okay," I said. "Carol and the boys and I are going to go get some lunch."

Roger said, "Want some company?"

Carol said, "Are you offering to take us to lunch?"

Roger said, "Come to think of it, Gracie and I better get this office set up. Just bring us back a sandwich or something."

◇◇◇

"So Guy, what I want to know," Carol said as we were eating fish 'n' chips at Castignola's, "is why the hell you let that asshole push you around all morning. Us around, I mean."

"Well, we're going to be neighbors with Roger a long time," I began.

"My point exactly. The relationship's off to a bad start."

"Well, I just figured it would be easier to avoid an argument and go along with his program, just this once."

"That guy's a sidewinder," Max said. "You better keep your eye on him or he'll steal all your books."

"I don't think so," Art said. "I don't think he can read."

"Maybe his publishing company's a cover for dealing drugs," I said.

Carol said, "Nope. He's a talent agent and filmmaker in the porn industry, Gracie told me. But he's getting out of that business. He's gone legit. Now he's a vanity publisher."

"Other people's money," I said. "Pass the vinegar."

"I'm going to make that man pay for half the truck," Carol said. "And he owes us two beers and four slices of pizza from last night."

"Good luck," Max said.

"I'm serious," she said. "If he messes with us, I'll put him out of business."

"Oh?" I asked. "How—"

"Today I learned how to hook up a DocuTech machine. I also know how to make it break down if I have to."

By about five in the afternoon we were finished. Poetry books were stacked in towers eight cartons high, in rows like an arrangement of dominoes covering most of the middle of the warehouse space. "Let's hope we don't have an earthquake," Carol said.

"It's like a cornfield," Max observed. "Feller could get lost in there."

"Like the columns at Chichen Itza," said Art. "Love among the ruins."

"You guys want some dinner?" I asked. "You worked twice as hard as you bargained for. We'll treat and then get Roger to pay us back." But they both had other plans, so we thanked them again. Carol hugged them both. They walked out into the darkening lot and climbed into Art's car.

Carol and I took another stroll through the aisles of our new warehouse, holding hands. "I don't know what we've got ourselves into," Carol said, "but I have to admit these last two days have been fun. Even Roger and Gracie and all. I'm glad it's over, though. I'm looking forward to a long hot bath and a big, cold martini."

"We can pick up some take-out from the Shanghai on the way home."

We kissed. My shoulders began to relax.

That's when we heard the high-pitched beep in the warehouse parking lot. We looked out through the gaping roll-up door at the back end of a Yellow Freight semi which was approaching us slowly and unstoppably.

The brakes sang and the truck stopped. The engine shut off, the cab door opened, and the driver climbed down and walked back to us, a clipboard in hand. "You Guy Mallon Books?"

"That's us," I sighed.

"I got twelve pallets for you. Sign here." He held out the clipboard.

Carol and I exchanged a look that was somewhere between despair and hilarity. I signed.

The driver walked into the warehouse and looked around, his hands in the pockets of his jeans. "You're not scheduled for an inside delivery, but looks like you're going to need it. Lucky for you this is my last stop of the day. Lucky for you I got a lift gate and a pallet jack. So. How do you want me to arrange these pallets? I guess you don't have much choice. You got just exactly enough room here. My name's Dennis, by the way." He held out a greasy hand. "So you guys are publishers?"

"We sure are," I said. As tired as I was, this truckload of books had given me back my spirit. *Naming Names* was going to put Guy Mallon Books on the map.

"So what kind of books do you publish?" Dennis asked.

"Well, poetry, mostly," Carol said. "But as of now—"

"No kidding," Dennis said. "Hey, great. I write a little poetry myself. You got a card I could have? I'd like to send you some of my work."

Chapter Four

Carol and I went to our office the morning after the shipment arrived and loaded her Volvo station wagon full of all our shipping equipment. Carol pulled the accordion folder of advance orders for *Naming Names*; it was already fat with orders—hundreds of orders—thanks to the favorable reviews in *Publishers Weekly, Library Journal, Booklist,* and *Kirkus Reviews.* We'd been stickering, stamping, and mailing brochures every day for two months, and the orders were flying back to us just as fast, while our toll-free order number rang furiously every day with credit card orders. The brochure had a box to check if the customer wanted an autographed copy, and every order that came back had a check mark in the box.

When we got to the warehouse we rolled up the big door and turned on the lights—Roger and Gracie hadn't shown up yet—so we could admire our phalanx of pallets stacked with cartons full of books. Then we got to work rearranging the cartons on the first row of pallets, creating three four-by-four work surfaces. Two shipping tables and a shorter pile to serve as a desk. Short stacks worked as desk chairs.

We brought our equipment in and set ourselves up in the shipping business. I started building cardboard boxes to get ready for the day's work while Carol began typing shipping labels.

"Too bad Roger wasn't here to help us move those cartons," I said.

"That reminds me. I have to create an invoice for him. Half the pizza, half the beer, half the truck, half the cleaning supplies. I won't charge him for our time and labor." She punched the calculator as she spoke, then announced, "Eighty-seven fifty." She rolled a piece of our letterhead into the typewriter, then looked up and said, "Speak of the devil."

I followed her glance out into the parking lot. There they were, climbing out of a hot pink Datsun. While Carol typed I watched them walk toward us, Gracie carrying what looked like two heavy briefcases, and Roger carrying nothing. They were dressed for the chilly March morning, Roger in a turtleneck sweater and Gracie in sweats.

When they got to the warehouse entrance they stopped and stared with wondrous eyes. Gracie said, "Whoa."

Roger said, "Hey hey *hey!* It's the North Pole."

"Come on in," I said. "Let me show you around."

Carol continued to type while I proudly showed them our shipping operation, the twelve pallets of *Naming Names,* and the piles of poetry.

"Not too shabby," Roger pronounced when we got back to the front. "Not bad at all. Looking good. What do you think, Grace?"

"Awesome."

Carol rolled the sheet of paper out of the typewriter, folded it, and handed it across the desk to Roger. "This is for you," she said. "Send it to Accounts Payable."

Roger said, "Thanks, doll." He handed the sheet to Gracie and said, "Well, we better get back to our office and get to work. You guys make us look like lazy bums."

At noon Carol and I took a break and drove to the post office, then had lunch at the Sojourner Restaurant. After that we went to our office to pick up phone messages. There were fourteen, and they were all orders for Lorraine's book. Carol sorted through the mail; it, too, was almost all orders for *Naming Names.*

"Jesus," I said. "I guess it's time to let Lorraine know her books have arrived."

"Do we have to?" Carol said. "Haven't we got enough to do without having to deal with an author?"

"We can't fill most of our orders till she signs the books," I pointed out.

Carol shook her head, then leaned forward and put her forehead on her desk. "It's not going to work, Guy," she said. "We're never going to get it all done."

"We'll get it done," I told her. "We'll get it all done."

"Okay, you call Sweet Lorraine," Carol said.

So I called Lorraine Evans. When I told her the news she squealed, "Oh God, sweetie, I'm so excited! You've made my day—you've made my *century!* We'll be there at your warehouse in about an hour."

We? "It could wait till tomorrow, Lorraine," I said, "if you—"

"Are you kidding? Oh God, I'm literally going to pee in my pants! Bye, honey."

"Wait, let me give you the address."

"No need. Fritz knows where it is."

"Fritz? He's back in the picture?"

"Strictly business," Lorraine said. "Don't let him tell you any different."

When we got back to the warehouse, Roger Herndon was there waiting for us, sitting on the short pile we used as a desk and tapping his knee with a folded sheet of paper. "Greetings, sports fans," he said through his shit-eating grin.

"Hey," I said.

Carol nodded to him and sat down in front of the typewriter. "We have an author coming in to sign books," she told him. "So we'll need that space your ass is parked on."

"Lorraine Evans, right? I'm a big fan. She probably never heard of me, but I was in show business myself for a few years, before I got into publishing."

"So we heard," Carol said.

"Yeah. Uh, Carol, about this invoice." He opened it up and laid it on the surface beside him. "I'm a little short right now, so any chance we could work it out in trade?"

"We're a bit short ourselves," Carol answered. "Having spent all this money on cleaning and moving—for your business as well as ours. We're just asking you to pay your fair share."

"What kind of trade do you have in mind?" I asked.

"Guy, stay out of this," Carol snapped.

"I'm just—"

"I'm trying to be businesslike here, if you don't mind," she said. "Give me a break. What's Roger got to offer? Free tickets to a strip club? A lifetime supply of *Freelance Reader*?"

"Roger has a printing press, Carol," I said.

"He has a DocuTech machine," Carol countered. "We don't do print on demand. What's the name of your publishing company, Roger?"

Got to hand it to Roger. He was still grinning. "Caslon Oldestyle Press," he answered. "The printing isn't all that bad, actually. But that's not what I had in mind."

"Okay," Carol said. "Sorry. I didn't mean to attack you. So. What?"

"Well," he said, "pardon me for being nosy, but it seems to me if that accordion file is full of orders—"

"How do you know what's in that file?" I asked.

Carol said, "Let the man talk."

"Wait a minute," I asked. "Just answer me, Roger. Were you poking your nose into our private files? Because if so—"

"Wait," Roger said. "No. But I have an accordion file just like that crammed full of orders for *Freelance Reader*. I'm just guessing you use your accordion file for the same purpose, and I can see it's bursting at the seams. If I'm right, seems to me you're going to need a little help filling those orders."

"You're offering to help us wrap books?" Carol asked.

"Well, I'm pretty busy myself, but Gracie has some extra time. Her and her friend Kitty are a dynamite shipping team.

They've shipped thousands of *Freelance Readers*. I could let you have them for a reduced rate."

"How much?"

"Tear up that invoice and you can have the two of them for the rest of the week. Three full days. After that you work out your own deal with them if you want to keep them on."

I saw a smile steal over Carol's face. "Will you pay Gracie and Kitty a decent wage for their work this week? I don't hire slave labor."

"That's between them and I," Roger said. "Don't worry about those girls. They owe me big-time."

Carol squinted.

"Done," I said. I'm not much of a businessman, but I know an auspicious coincidence when I see one. I shook Roger's hand while Carol tore up the invoice, and that's the moment Lorraine Evans and Fritz Marburger walked through the warehouse door.

◇◇◇

We'd had the hugs and handshakes, and now it was time for business. We cleared the low surface off and turned it into a conference table, with Roger, Gracie, and Fritz on one side and Lorraine, Carol, and me on the other. Kitty Katz, the new shipping clerk, sat at the end. Fritz clearly considered this a top-level meeting of his own publishing empire, and he was showing us he knew how to control the action.

"Okay, people, listen up," he said. "We got a success on our hands, and the thing we have to do is not get swallowed by it. Growth is good, but there's such a thing as growing too fast. This business is about to grow like a garden on steroids, and we have to keep it watered and weeded. You with me here? Huh? Carol?"

Carol nodded and grunted.

"Okay. Let's get started. I got a golf date at three o'clock. I want to talk about film rights for Lorraine's book. Guy, where are we at with that?"

"We've received about twenty-five requests for review copies from people in the industry," I said.

"Any big names?"

"Bette Midler's company wants to see a copy."

"Forget it," Lorraine said. "Don't send her a copy."

"Why not?" Fritz said. "She's a big star. She could play you."

"The book's not about me," Lorraine pointed out.

"I know that. It's about your mother, right?"

"You shut up about that," Lorraine said. "Bette's just trying to compete with me, as always."

"Send Bette's people a copy," Fritz told me. "And from now on all the inquiries get forwarded to me. I'm Lorraine's agent. I'll do the follow-up, and I'll tell you which ones to send review copies to. Okay. You all heard the good news about 'Oprah'?"

Carol said, "No. What?"

"We got Lorraine booked on 'Oprah' for sometime in May."

"*I* got me booked," Lorraine said. "My publicist. You had nothing to do with that." She turned to me and said, "Isn't it thrilling? And there will be a cover story in *People* the same week!"

I'm sure my grin was as big as hers, but I stole a look at Carol and saw a grimace instead. Absolute panic. I asked her, "You okay?"

"We don't have enough books," she said. "Talk about growing too fast. We're going to be getting all this publicity to die for, and it's going to kill us. We'll run out in two days. By which time Oprah will be touting a different book and we'll be dead in the water."

"Better get more books right away," Fritz said. "Order another ten thou."

"With what?" Carol asked. "We've blown our wad."

"The whole thirty thousand dollars?" Fritz shouted. "Christ's sake, Guy, you told me twenty thou would cover it."

"That was a guess."

"Shit. Amateur. What about income from the sale of the first ten thousand copies?" Fritz asked. "Surely that ought to pay for a reprint."

"Doesn't work that way," Carol said. "Printers expect to be paid in thirty days. Bookstores and wholesalers usually take ninety days."

Fritz nodded slowly and then said, "Jaysus. Okay, no prob. I'll loan you the cost of a reprint of ten thousand copies, to be paid back in ninety days with fifteen percent interest. Fair enough?"

"That's highway robbery," Carol said.

"Understand me, missy," Fritz said. "I only want what's best for you and for Guy and for Lorraine, and mainly for me. I'm a businessman, unlike my little friend here, and I'm fronting you all this money. I'm putting your little company on the God damned map, right? I want big sales."

Lorraine said, "Fritz, cool it. Quit being such an ape."

The silence washed around the makeshift table. I caught Kitty blowing a kiss to Gracie and Gracie winking back. Lorraine was studying her book, reading somewhere in the middle. Carol's face was tomato red, and her hair seemed to be growing snakes. Roger was picking wax out of his ear. I was getting a hard-on from the tension; don't ask me to explain that.

"Okay, listen up." It was Fritz who broke the silence. "Here's the deal. Cards-on-the-table time. I own this building, and you guys need this building. Frankly, I spent a lot of money on this building, but I was mainly buying the land. I could give a shit about the building itself.

"But I don't want to burn this place down so some asshole can build condos. Why? Because Santa Barbara doesn't need more condos? No. Because I want to be in the publishing business. Why? Hell if I know, but I'm that crazy. I want to be in the publishing business. That's why I hired Guy Mallon Books to publish Lorraine's book. That's why I put you guys together with Herndon's operation. You guys could all be part of something big here, and when the time comes I'll be your agent and sell the whole operation to that big German outfit who's buying all the publishing companies, and then you guys will be rich enough to go back to publishing dorky little poetry books for the rest of your lives for all I care. But for now, you guys—Guy, Carol, you, too, Roger—you guys want to keep me happy. Savvy? Fair enough? Just keep me happy."

I looked again at Lorraine's face, and I saw an old woman on the verge of tears.

"Stay on my side," Fritz went on. "I've got big plans for you. I have breakfast every morning with Jonathan Winters and Bob Mitchum. And Sam Welch claims he writes poetry, if you can believe that. They've all been asking me about Lorraine's book deal, and we're talking numbers, okay? You're onto something big. I'm a big part of that, like it or not. There's no reason we can't be a great team. I think even Carol would agree with that, right, honey? Now if you'll excuse me, I've got to run. Lorrie, I'll come back and pick you up at about five-thirty."

"Don't bother," Lorraine said. "I'll take a cab."

Things got a lot more relaxed after Fritz Marburger left the building. Lorraine got busy signing books, Carol typed labels, and Gracie and Kitty wrapped the packages, while I made boxes and manned the Pitney-Bowes machine. Nobody said much, although Kitty did a lot of giggling at whatever Gracie was whispering in her ear.

Kitty Katz was, I have to admit, a looker. She had boobs out to here, stretching her Kountry Klub tee shirt. Platinum hair streaked with neon blue and green. Vampire makeup, but friendly looking. Maybe more than friendly. Half my age, if that.

Toward the end of the day, Roger came out front and asked if he could take a few pictures. He photographed us at work, then took a shot of the famous author and glamorous song stylist Sweet Lorraine flanked by Gracie and Kitty, then a shot of Carol and me standing in front of the phalanx of inventory.

"Smile," Roger pleaded.

Carol obliged, the flash went off, the smile evaporated, and we got back to work.

That evening, as we were having cocktails, Carol remarked, "I wonder if Lorraine Evans is aware she had her picture taken between two porn stars."

"They're porn stars?" I asked. "Really?"

"Roger's clients. He has a part interest in the Kountry Klub, too, you know."

"I didn't know," I said. "This is really a trip."

Carol set down her martini. "You really like all this, don't you, Guy? *People Magazine,* 'Oprah,' your own shipping department. You like this, don't you?"

"A dream come true," I had to admit.

"That's the trouble with you, Guy. You don't know the difference between a dream and a nightmare. What did you think of Kitty, by the way? Miss Kitty Katz?"

"Um—"

"She was making eyes at you."

"No, she—"

"She's half your age, Guy. If that."

"I noticed that," I said. "That much I noticed."

"I noticed it, too," Carol said.

Chapter Five

The Earthling Bookshop had already sold three full cartons of *Naming Names* by the Friday evening of Lorraine's big book signing, which was the official publication date of the book. Carol and I showed up at seven-thirty, half an hour early, with two more cartons in hand and two more out in the trunk of my car, just in case.

Tonight's crowd was a mob scene, even at seven-thirty, and the crowd continued to grow in number and in volume as the hour approached. They looked as if they were from Montecito and Beverly Hills, decked out in tailored outfits, coifed toupees, and designer shades, chattering like an orchestra tuning up.

I wandered through the crowd until I reached a small circle gathered around Jonathan Winters, who was mugging and rattling off an account of his most recent trip to Pluto. Samuel Welch took my arm and led me over to the history section, where the crowd was thinner. He traveled in a cloud of cologne.

Welch smiled, loomed over me, and said, "I want you to read something. You publish poetry too, right?"

"Well, yes, but—"

"Here." He pulled a sheet of paper out of his shiny jacket pocket and placed it in my hand. "I'm Sam Welch, by the way."

Duh. Hollywood's favorite bad guy. He'd been in more westerns than John Wayne and Randolph Scott put together. "I know," I said. "But right now I—"

"Read it. I got a bunch of them. Make a nice little book."

I looked across the aisles of the store and saw Carol trying to smile at a dozen munchers and moochers at the same time. "Listen," I said, "I really have things I need to do right now. But with your permission, I'll just take this with me and get back to you."

Samuel Welch reached down and patted my shoulder. "You're going to love it. It's about Marilyn Monroe and me." He showed me his dentures and I escaped back to Carol's side.

Penny Davies, the owner of the store, joined us and said, "Guy, dear, did you bring more books? The stacks are gone, and we're starting to sell copies out of the window display."

"We have two cartons out in my car," I said. "In the parking lot."

Penny said, "I'll get Joe to go with you. He'll bring the dolly."

Out in the parking lot I transferred the two cartons from my trunk onto Joe's hand truck. "Thanks," Joe said. "Good crowd."

"Yeah," I agreed. "All we need is one more."

"You mean her?" Joe nodded to the next lane, where a well-dressed couple were standing next to a vintage Mercedes-Benz. The woman was sobbing into her hands and the man was leaning over her, whispering fiercely.

"You go on ahead," I told Joe. "I've got to get this cleared up."

I walked over to where they stood and said, "Evening, folks."

"What's good about it?" Fritz Marburger replied.

Lorraine sobbed, "Guy, I'm so sorry! I can't do it!"

"You're going to do it," Fritz stated.

"I can't!"

"Can't do what?" I asked.

She shook her head. Tears streamed down her cheeks, leaving tracks through the makeup. "People," she cried. "I can't deal with any more *people.*"

I turned to Fritz and he shrugged. "Stomach flu," he offered.

"My ass," Lorraine snapped. "It's just people. People, people, *people!* Fritz, take me home."

Fritz scratched his head. "Nope."

"You asshole!" Lorraine turned to me and pleaded, "Guy, honey, will you drive me home? Please, Guy?"

"But Lorraine, I'm needed inside. We've got over a hundred people in there—"

"Shit! The hell with both of you!" She turned and walked off toward Chapala Street.

"Where the Christ do you think you're going, Lorrie?" Fritz called after her.

"I'll get a cab. Fuck you!" she called back.

I looked up into Fritz's glowering face and said, "Okay. Spill. What happened?"

"People," Fritz answered.

"Fritz—"

"The magazine. She had her interview today and they upset her pretty bad. Call me tomorrow and I'll tell you about it. I'm going to go give the little princess a ride home." He turned and opened his car door.

"But—"

"You just get your ass back into that store and sell books. Handle the crowd."

"What do I say—"

"Stomach flu," he shouted. "How many times I got to tell you?" He got into his powder-blue Mercedes and slammed the door. He fired it up and streaked out of the parking lot, slowing down only briefly to pick up his passenger.

I turned around and saw Carol hurrying toward me. "What's going on?" she asked. "People are getting really antsy in there."

"We got a problem," I said. "I have to make an announcement."

"You want to announce it to me first? I want to know what's going on, Guy."

I told her about Lorraine's panic attack. "I guess the interview with *People* was a disaster. I hope she performs better on 'Oprah.'"

"She'd better," Carol said. "I heard from Ann Arbor this afternoon. The presses are already rolling and and ten thousand more copies are scheduled to ship next Wednesday."

◇◇◇

The next morning at the office, I told Carol I was going to call Marburger to find out where things stood. Carol said, "No. Call Lorraine. Let her explain for herself. Fritz just wants to control things. This is Lorraine's crisis, not his."

But when I called Lorraine's number, all I got was a recorded message telling me that Lorraine Evans was unavailable at this time. Click. No invitation to leave a message.

"I guess you'll have to call Fritz and hear his side of the story, for what it's worth," Carol said. "You do that while I walk over to the post office and get the mail. Want me to bring you a scone and a cup of coffee?"

"Sure."

She kissed my forehead and left the office. I got up and paced around the office for a few minutes, then read the titles of the books on one of the shelves of my collection. Calm down, I told myself. Calm down.

The phone rang, and I picked it up. Fritz? Lorraine? "Guy Mallon Books," I said. "May I help you?"

"I want to get my poetry published," said a familiar voice. "How much will it cost me?"

"I'm sorry, sir, we don't work that way," I said. "Thanks for calling."

Before I could hang up he went on. "Says here in this brochure, 'We'll publish your book for you. How would you like to be the next best-selling author? Let us make your dreams come true!'"

"Who is this?" I asked. "Is this Sam Welch?"

"Sam Welch? That's a good one. In my dreams—I hear he packs a mighty mean six-shooter. No, pilgrim, this ain't Samuel Welch. I'm just a little old poet who wants to take advantage of your big offer. I want to be a best-selling author."

"I want to know who you are and what you're talking about, but even more than that I want to hang up, so—"

"This Caslon Oldestyle Press?"

"Absolutely not," I said. "We have nothing to do with that company."

"That's funny," Arthur Summers said—yes, Art Summers, that's who it was! "It sure looks like you."

"What are you talking about? This is Art, right?"

Art was laughing out loud now. "This brochure I got in the mail today," he answered. "Max Black got one too. And a couple of other guys in the English Department at UCSB. I don't know how big a mailing list Herndon's got, my friend, but your face is probably all over the country by now. You and Carol smiling in front of a stack of 'the next bestseller.'"

"Oh for God's sake," I groaned. "What a sleazeball. I remember when he took that picture."

"That warehouse of yours is going to be the center of a publishing empire, is all I can say. Judging from the brochure, you guys are big-time. You're going to put Alfred Knopf out of business. Or Vantage Press. Maybe both."

"Give me a break."

I hung up, just as Carol entered the office. She was not carrying scones and coffee. Just the mail and a faceload of fury. She slapped a brochure down hard on my desk and said, all business, "Call Channing. We're going to sue. Right now."

We walked into the warehouse twenty minutes later—Carol, myself, and Channing Bates, our attorney. Channing is a good friend to drink with and swap jokes with. He's also a no-nonsense lawyer who thinks clearly on his feet. And he's as big a man as I am small. The only legal work he had ever done for me was a simple business partnership with Carol, but I was glad to have him on my side that day as we marched to the back of the warehouse and saw the DocuTech machine spitting out a pile of evidence.

Channing picked up a brochure, turned the pages, and chuckled. "Good pictures," he said. He turned to Gracie, who was manning the DocuTech, and said, "I'd like you to turn the machine off, please."

Gracie raised her eyebrows and did as she was asked.

Roger Herndon came out of the small office he had built for himself. "Hey, Grace," he said, "what happened? How come you turned off the printer?" Then he looked at us and said, "Hey, Guy. Carol. How you guys doing?"

"Roger," I said, "I'd like you to meet our friend, Channing Bates."

The two men shook hands politely, with smiles, and Roger said, "What can I do for you, Channing? Want to have a book published?"

"Could we step into your office, Mister Herndon?" Channing asked. Channing has a very low voice when he wants to speak that way. You don't say no to such a voice.

Herndon nodded and led us into his cubicle. There was just room enough for the four of us, and Channing and Roger faced each other over a desk that looked like it had been hit by Hurricane Hugo.

Channing handed Roger a copy of the brochure and said, "I would like you to show me a signed release allowing you to use my clients in your advertisement."

Roger's eyes widened and then he broke out laughing. "Great brochure, huh?" he said. "How do you like it, Guy? Good shots of you and Carol, right?"

Channing shot us a look to tell us to keep quiet, which we did. I don't think Carol found that an easy thing to do, but she kept her mouth shut.

"If I read this brochure correctly, my clients now work for Caslon Oldestyle Press. Is that correct, Mister Herndon?"

"It doesn't say that. Hey, I just wanted a few pictures of my warehouse. These wonderful people are in my warehouse all the time, right Carol? And they're good-looking folks, wouldn't you agree, Channing? I never said these guys are the publishers or that they work for Caslon Oldestyle."

Carol couldn't hold it anymore. "This is *our* warehouse, and those are *our* books you photographed," she said. "This brochure says they're your books." She picked up a brochure and read, "'We keep our warehouse clean, neat, and dry, to protect all our books—your books, your best-selling books!'"

"The brochure doesn't claim—"

"Mister Herndon," Channing said, "you're right about that. So all you need to do is to show me that my clients signed releases allowing you to print their pictures in your advertisements. Show me that, and there's nothing more to complain about."

Roger's lips and nose twitched, but he managed to keep smiling. "Hey, man," he said. "I'm just a small-time one-man operation. I don't know all those legal mumbo-jumbo things you're talking about. I just took some pictures of my friends, here, and—"

"Well, in that case, this meeting isn't getting us anywhere." Channing rose to his feet and turned to Carol and me. "Shall we?"

Carol said, "But—"

Channing turned back to Herndon. "You'll hear from me before the end of the week. In the meantime I advise you that it's in your best interest to keep that printing press turned off and not to mail out any more brochures. Our claim will probably be figured on a per-unit basis."

Herndon frowned, then he laughed again. "Well, don't contact me. This isn't my business anymore. I was just doing what my boss told me to do."

"You're not the proprietor of Caslon Oldestyle Press?" Channing asked.

Roger pointed to the bottom of the brochure's front panel. *"Caslon Oldestyle Press is a division of Marburger Enterprises."*

"I was bought out three weeks ago," Roger said as we walked out of his office. "You'll have to deal with the man, Fritz Marburger. He knows a lot more about mumbo-jumbo anyway. So long, Guy, Carol. Gracie, turn that machine back on."

Chapter Six

I couldn't reach either Lorraine or Fritz on Tuesday. Lorraine's phone message hadn't changed, and Fritz wasn't returning my calls.

Same on Wednesday.

So after lunch on Thursday, while Carol stayed in the office sending out past-due reminders to stores and distributors, I went down to the warehouse to see how the shipping department was doing.

I found Kitty hard at work. She dropped her tape gun and walked up to me with a hungry grin, wrapped her arms around my shoulders, and planted a French kiss on my left ear. You're just going to have to take my word for it that getting hugged and kissed by a platinum blonde porn star half my age did not turn me on. Okay, so maybe it turned me on, but it was all a big flirt and we both knew it. "Guybaby," she cooed. "So how's it going?"

"Don't ever go into the publishing business," I said. "Stick with stripping, it's a lot less trouble."

"Aren't I in the publishing business, boss? Licking and sticking and stuffing and getting them off?" She held up a copy of *Naming Names* and rubbed it across her chest, then slid it slowly into a Jiffy Bag. "These little numbers work like Trojans. What exactly does that mean exactly, 'work like a Trojan'?"

"Beats me," I said.

She licked her lips.

Enough already. "So where's Gracie?" I asked.

"She's working for Roger today. Back there typesetting a book."

"Typesetting? What book?"

"It's called *Onward Christian Sailors,*" Kitty said. "The first book from Caslon Oldstyle Press. Roger got the contract and the check on Monday, and the book will be out tomorrow."

"That's fast," I commented.

Kitty said, "That's the way Gracie likes it. Nice and fast."

I walked to the back of the warehouse, and there was Gracie at her desk, her eyes glued to her monitor and her fingers dancing on the keyboard.

"Hi, Gracie, how's it going?" I asked.

"Hey," she answered.

"I understand you're typesetting today."

"All week. Don't worry, the wrapping will get done," she said.

"I'm not worried. So you're a typesetter, too?"

Gracie took her hands off the keyboard and took off her glasses. She looked at me without smiling and said, "I'm turning a piece-of-shit MacWrite document into a book. The author didn't even spellcheck. This is going to take all day, so if it's okay with you—"

"I'll leave you to your work," I said. "Where's the boss?"

"Fritz Marburger's in Rancho Mirage playing golf. If you want Roger, he's in his office selling more contracts. They're coming fast and furious." She put her glasses back on and returned to her computer, muttering, "Piece of shit."

I knocked on the open door of Roger's cubicle, and he waved me in and pointed to the metal folding chair. He was on the phone and he was turning over the pages of a manuscript on his desk. I sat down and listened to the sales spiel.

"Lillian, this looks like a winner, is all I can say. I mean look at this—romance, sex, love, tragedy, a happy ending, I mean what more do you need to have a bestseller? And that's the business we're in.…Yes, I can put this book on our schedule for fall, but if you want to pay the whole amount up front, I can move the project to the front of the line, in time to get review copies off to *The New*

York Times, The New Yorker, Cosmo, you know, all the big reviewers....Yes, twenty-two thousand dollars is a lot of money, but we're talking about an investment here. I mean read the contract I faxed you: it guarantees I'll print ten thousand books, as needed to fill orders. Ten thousand times twenty-four ninety-five is two hundred and forty-nine five, and you get twenty-five percent of that, which will triple your money, see what I mean?...Okay, dear, you think it over while I enjoy reading the rest of this wonderful novel....Oh, right. Memoir, that's what I meant. But let me know in a day or two, okay dear? I mean there are others waiting, and I'd like to get the presses rolling on your book....Good-bye, Lillian, I loved talking with you, too."

He hung up, swiveled his chair around, and placed the manuscript on a shelf behind his desk. The shelf was piled with manuscripts. He swiveled back to me and said, "Guy, my man. So how's it going?"

"Looks like that brochure mailing is paying off for you," I said.

He clapped his hands and whooped. "That mailing cost me twelve thou. They started going out less than three weeks ago, and I've already taken in four contracts, all of them over twenty thousand bucks apiece. Got their disks, their contracts, and their checks. And I've got a bunch more authors on the line, ready to be reeled in. Business is booming, my man. Booming!"

"And they're all paying up front?" I asked.

"So far. If they want to pay me half on deposit, that's okay, but I warn them there's a long waiting period."

"So how long will it take you to publish the first four books?"

"I'm starting out slow, till Gracie gets the routine down. I figure a week a book."

"You're going to turn out ten thousand copies in a week?"

"Hah. One copy for starters."

"But you told Lillian—"

"'As needed,' I told her. 'As needed to fill orders.' So, what can I do for you, Guy? I have to make a few more phone calls, so—"

"Where's Marburger?" I asked. "You know?"

"He's gone to Rancho Mirage, he told me," Roger said. "Took Lorraine Evans down there to give her the full spa treatment for a week—massages, mud baths, facials, saunas, and lots to drink. He'll be golfing and she'll be coming to her senses, or that's what he told me. I guess she's being difficult."

"We're going to sue his ass," Carol fumed.

"Roger?"

"No, I don't care about Roger anymore. Besides, within a few months he's going to be sued to death by disgruntled authors. No, I'm talking about Fritz Marburger. He's the one I want to sue."

"For what?"

"For getting us into this mess in the first place."

"We went along with him, Carol. I don't think there's much we can complain about."

"*You* went along with him."

"Listen," I said. "Don't piss off Fritz at this point. He told us he'd pay for the second printing, but we don't have that in writing. Let's get him to pay the printer's bill, and then we can let him know how we feel."

"By which time we'll be majorly in debt to him."

"I'd rather be in debt to him than to the printing company. We need to go on printing books."

"What books?"

"We're still publishers, Carol."

"More's the pity."

"I'm going back down to the warehouse," I said. "Are there any more orders to process?"

"A few," Carol said. "Fewer every day. And they need autographs. You might as well stay here and keep me company."

"The shipping department's shorthanded today," I said. "I'll see you later."

"So tell me, Kitty," I said as we wrapped books together across the work surface. "What's the deal with this *Freelance Reader* book?"

"*How to Earn Big Bucks at Home as a Freelance Reader,*" she answered. "It's a scheme Roger cooked up. It explains how publishers hire people to read manuscripts, right in their own homes. Roger charges fifty bucks a pop for these pamphlets, and they sell like hotcakes. He advertises in newspapers all over the country, and the orders come in every day. Gracie and I ship them out the next day."

"But publishers don't hire freelance readers."

Kitty shrugged. "That's probably why Roger is always changing the P.O. address of the company. When the orders come to us, they're forwarded from Indianapolis or Salt Lake City or Lake Worth, Florida, or Manchester, New Hampshire, places like that."

"Mail fraud," I said.

"That's Roger for you," Kitty agreed. "But then most males are frauds. Hey Guy, when are you going to come see me at the Kountry Klub?"

I chuckled. "Pass me the stapler."

"I'm serious, babe. Me and Grace do a sweet sister act. I mean sweet. It's a bondage thing, you know, handcuffs and feathers and stuff." She stuck a few Day-Glo strands of her hair between her pursed lips. "Hmmm?"

"I can't say I'm not tempted," I said. "Pass me the stapler."

"I already did, Guy. You're not paying attention."

When I got back to the office I found a sign on the front door in Carol's handwriting: "Gone for the day."

She must have walked home, I figured. Good. It was an easy mile-long stroll through the East Side of Santa Barbara, and I was glad she was working off some of that Irish steam among the springtime flowers and tree-lined streets. So I went into the office and straightened my desk as quickly as I could. I checked the phone messages—two people wanting to order *Naming Names* and no callback from Fritz. I pulled the blinds closed on the windows, then walked out and locked the office door behind me.

Then I heard the phone ringing in the office. On the chance that it might be Carol, wanting me to pick up something from the store or take care of some business on her desk, I fumbled with the key and let myself back in. I scurried across the office and picked up the phone on the fourth ring, just as the answering machine kicked in.

My mistress' voice: "You have reached the office of Guy Mallon Books. Our office hours are—"

"Hold on," I said, punching buttons in the dark until I found the one that cut off the recording. "This is Guy Mallon. May I help you?"

"You're Guy Mallon?" asked a familiar voice I couldn't quite place.

"That's right." What'd I just tell you, dummy?

"Yeah. Guy, this is Samuel Welch."

Oh right. "Oh right," I said. "Nice of you to call. How are you?"

"Dandy," he said. "Say, have you had a chance to read that poem I gave you?"

"Oh my God," I said. "I guess it's still in the pocket of my sport coat, hanging up in the closet. You know, Friday's event was such a disaster, I completely forgot." The truth was I had read the poem, essentially a love song to Sam Welch's legendary penis, as sung by Marilyn Monroe, supposedly. Dreadful in spades.

"Yeah, well that's okay," Sam Welch allowed. "I got a whole book full of them, and I'd like to drop them by your office. Tomorrow be okay?"

"Just a minute." I pretended to check my calendar while I tried to come up with excuses, but I couldn't think of anything, so I said, "How about ten tomorrow morning?"

"Gotcha. These little babies'll knock off your Argyles."

"Yeah. Okay. Listen, Mister Welch—"

"Mize well call me Sam, pal."

"I gotta hit the trail, Sam," I said. "My pardner's waiting on me back at the ranch."

"Adios. Hasta mañana."

◇◇◇

On the way home I stopped off at Riley's flower stand and bought Carol a bouquet of irises. I knew I'd been acting like an asshole, like a male fraud, as Kitty would say. Kitty. Another reason to buy Carol flowers.

Evening was rising from the streets of the *barrio*, a neighborhood of stately eucalypti and palms, gardens of bougainvillea, hibiscus, and star jasmine. It had been a long, stupid day, and I was glad to be almost home, even if the air there might be frosty at first.

Carol and I needed to do some fence mending. I realized at that moment that Carol was more important to me than business. More important than poetry. More important than books. That's saying a lot.

The house was dark. I parked on the street, because the garage was for Carol's car. Holding the irises carefully, I walked up to the front door and tried the knob. Locked. Let myself in with a key and turned on lights. Lights in the living room, lights in the dining room, lights in the kitchen, the bathroom, the bedroom and the other bedroom. Every light in the house, which made the house feel all the emptier.

There was a note on the dining room table:

Guy my dear,

I'm going up to Morro Bay for the weekend. All this crap we're getting from Marburger and Herndon has given me a sudden craving for abalone. Believe me, I'm not punishing you. I'm not mad at you. I just have to be by myself for a while, a couple of days.

I know I've been a bitch, and I'm still feeling bitchy, and I don't want to put you through that. I have to get away and cool down. I love you, and I'll be in a better mood soon, which is what you deserve. Forgive me for being such a shrew. I promise to get a better attitude.

*There's a chicken pie in the freezer, and some of the pasta
we had last night in the fridge. If you go to La Super Rica
for dinner, tell Isidoro hi for me. Have a good weekend. Try
to relax. We both need to relax. I'll be back Monday.*
   I love you.

Carol

I took a deep breath. It was true, we both needed to relax.
The Super Rica sounded like a good idea. Best Mexican food
in town. In any town. Fine. Fine, then.

I realized I was still holding onto that bouquet of irises.
I carried them into the kitchen so I could shorten the stems
and put them in water. I took a pair of scissors out of the junk
drawer and pulled the wastebasket out from under the sink. I
shortened the stems, then shortened them again, then shortened
and shortened and shortened them again and again and again,
then dropped the blossoms down on top of the stems and shoved
the wastebasket back under the sink.

Chapter Seven

"It's basically a tell-all type thing," Samuel Welch told me the next morning in the office. "It's my life story, of course, but who wants to hear all that boring crap about growing up in Boston and going to Andover and Princeton and being in the Air Force and doing a bunch of summer stock? All that's in there of course, but you know what people want to read as well as I do: they want to read about my sex life, right? I mean I've been on the cover of *National Enquirer* seventeen times, with fourteen different women. So that's what people want to read about, right? Am I right?"

I wasn't sure that question required an answer. I sat there and stared across my desk at the rugged, handsome face that had launched a thousand posses.

"It's all in there," Welch continued, tapping the manuscript on my desk. "Plus pictures. So what do you think? Do we have a best-seller on our hands or am I nuts?"

"Sam," I said, "I'm not a publisher of best-sellers. If that's what you're looking for—"

"What about Lorraine's book? From what I hear that's off to a great start. Gangbusters."

"It's too early to tell," I said. "We'll see." Thanks for reminding me, pardner, I thought.

"And I'll tell you another thing," he went on. "I'm going to promote the shit out of this book. I'm a way better promoter than Sweet Lorraine, know what I mean? I'm not temperamental, and I'm not proud. I'll get on the Limbaugh show, I'll go on 'Saturday Night Live,' whatever it takes. Because I believe in this book. This book is *me*."

"I expect it's a great book," I said. "But look, I'm just a poetry publisher. Lorraine's book is a fluke."

Sam Welch chuckled. "This book is flukier than hers by a long shot. *And* it's full of poetry. I've written a love poem for every one of the women in my life, and it's all in there. With pictures. Look, just read the manuscript, okay? That's all I ask."

I Wasn't Always a Bad Guy: My Life and Loves, by Samuel Welch. What a piece of crap. I read it that afternoon, figuring it would cheer me up to hear about the big man's big adventures among big stars. He had pictures of himself throughout the book, most of them movie stills and publicity photos, and each chapter also started off with a doggerel poem written for one of his legendary lovers, including Shelley Winters, Marie Wilson, Ava Gardner, Marilyn Monroe, Jayne Mansfield, Dagmar, a half sister and a cousin, his fourth-grade teacher (a nun), two stewardesses (same night, same bed), a Mexican prostitute, a duchess, three ex-wives, and a heifer.

I have to admit it gave me a laugh or two and took my mind off my loneliness and my fear of bankruptcy. But what in the world was I going to tell this cowboy come Monday? This legendary bad guy?

Easy, I decided. Sorry, I'd say. We've put all our cash flow into the Evans book and we have to wait to see how that plays out before we'll have any more capital to invest in another big book.

I called Fritz Marburger. Same announcement on his answering machine. I didn't bother to leave another message. Called Lorraine, and her message hadn't changed either.

Saturday morning I went down to the warehouse. I had the place to myself, and there was no wrapping to do, so I got out the dry mop and cleaned the place up. After I finished I noticed a hardbound book on the DocuTech machine: *Onward Christian Sailors,* by Commander Robert Worsham, USN, ret. The front cover depicted a battleship in a stormy sea. The back flap had a picture of the author, an elderly man in camouflage, with a gray crewcut and a Kirk Douglas grin. He looked like a very tall man. I put the book back where I'd found it.

As I was closing the warehouse door, Roger Herndon drove into the lot and parked his Datsun. I left the door unlocked and headed toward my car, but he headed me off at the pass. He gave me a toothy grin and pulled back the wings of his tan leather jacket. "Check it out," he said.

Check what? The paunch? I glanced at his gut and saw the new ornament, a dull silver metal belt buckle in the shape of one of those shapely silhouettes you see on the mud flaps of cross-country eighteen-wheelers.

"Class," I told him. "With a capital K."

"Always wanted one of these," he said. "It's made of Monel. You should see how you stick the other end of the belt—"

"Another time, Rog," I said.

I ate lunch at the Paradise Cafe, then went to the office and cleaned that too. Vacuumed and swept and dusted. I dusted every book in my collection. It was something to do. And it made me feel secure: no matter what else I might lose, I'd still have my books. My first editions.

I got home after dark. I baked a chicken pot pie and washed it down with three beers. I did the dishes; it took me less than a minute. Then went to the bedroom and lay on top of the covers, where I spent most of the night looking at the ceiling, which was dimly lit by the light from the bathroom.

Sunday I took a long walk on the beach, but I don't remember what I saw there. I went home and took a nap; I don't remember if I dreamed. While I waited around till dinnertime, I tried to read but couldn't stay focused on the page.

◇◇◇

She said she'd be back Monday. What did that mean, Monday?

What Monday meant was I had to go back to the office, which was fine with me. I didn't have that much work to do, just a whole lot of worrying. Besides, I had to call Samuel Welch and tell him gently that his book sucked out loud. No, just that it wasn't my cup of rotgut.

But even as I was reaching for the phone, it rang at me. So I picked up and said, "Guy Mallon Books."

"Guy, this is Fritz Marburger."

"Where have you been?" I asked. "I left four messages."

"Listen," he answered. "I'm afraid we have a situation on our hands. Our little friend, the so-called Sweet Lorraine, has lost touch with reality. So, uh—"

"What are you talking about, Fritz? Nice and slow, what are you talking about?"

"Well, we had something going with Bette Midler's people, but Lorraine told me to stuff it."

"That's too bad," I said. "Well, if she doesn't like Midler, maybe something else will turn up. The book's only just getting started. Let's see how reviews come in, and I'm sure we'll get other offers. So—"

"Hold on, Guy. Lorraine told me to stuff it, period. She doesn't want a movie deal. Period. No movie."

"Hmm. Okay, at least we got books," I said. "I mean, we got books. And once the *People* article hits the streets—"

"That's another thing," Fritz said. "Lorraine had her publicity person kill the *People* article. Took some doing, but she did it."

"She *what*?"

"And she's not going on 'Oprah.'"

I let that one sink in. Then, very quietly, I said, "What's this all about, Fritz? I don't want to have to put this together like a puzzle. I want you to tell me, in plain fucking English, what the fuck is going on."

He sighed through the phone. "The old lady in the book, that's her mother. She died in a flophouse hotel in San Jose back in eighty-nine. She was living on food stamps and meds, delusional, making weird accusations about having been sexually abused as a child, crazy as a loon."

"Well, I'm sorry about Lorraine's mother, but Lorraine wrote this book, and it's fiction or so she says, so what's the problem?"

"The problem is when *People* found out it was based on Lorraine's own family, that's all they wanted to talk about. Made a better story, they said. Well, that drove Lorraine over the edge, some kind of bullshit guilt trip, didn't want the world knowing her mother died crazy and penniless and abandoned."

"How did the *People* people find this secret out?"

"Huh?"

"You heard me."

"Well, I told them about it. I mean, it made a far better story. Personal experience. Look, that's what people want to read, real human problems of real celebrities, not some stupid novel about some crazy old lady who never existed. Jesus," Fritz said, "I was doing the woman a favor, for Christ's sake."

"My God," I said. "You really think that was a favor?"

"Well, shit. Maybe it was a mistake."

I paused and said, "Costly. You made a costly mistake, Fritz."

"What do you mean by that? It's not going to cost me a penny. I'm out one girlfriend, and my ego's bruised, and my heart's a bit beat up, but I'm done with the whole deal. She fired me as her agent. She doesn't want anything more to do with me, and the feeling is mutual. Dumb bitch."

Did he say "not going to cost me a penny"? "Let me remind you, Fritz, that we still have about five thousand books in the warehouse, and another ten thousand on the way, which you'll be paying for. It's going to take a lot longer to sell those books without the author's cooperation, which you pretty much flushed down the toilet. How are we going to move those books? Tell me that? And if the books stop selling, the returns start coming back. And there goes—"

"That's your problem," Fritz told me. "You're the publisher. And another thing that's your problem is that ten-thousand-copy reprint. I'm not paying for that. You think I'm a fool?"

Jesus. "Fritz," I said, "we had an agreement."

"Not in writing. And that agreement was based on conditions that no longer exist."

"Thanks to you."

"Whatever."

"You said you'd pay for this printing."

"Guy, I'm a businessman. Show me how it will be a good return on my investment, and I'll play ball. But you just told me the book's dead in the water. Why should I loan you money for that?"

"Are you trying to put me out of business?"

He did not answer for a long time, and then he said, "I suppose you want me to help you out of this problem you're in."

"I just want you to honor—"

"Shut up and listen, my little man. Sell the company to me, and you're not facing bankruptcy court, because I can keep the business going."

"You want to buy Guy Mallon Books?"

"Maybe I'm out of my mind, but I want to be a publisher. I told you that from the beginning. So I'm offering to take the company off your hands. It's a big headache for you and Carol, so why not just let me have the headache? I'll take over all your debts as well as all your assets."

"What are you offering for this company?" I asked. "Not that I'm interested in selling, but I'd be interested in hearing what you think the business is worth."

"I just told you. I pay all the debts. I bail you out."

"You want to bail me and Carol out of our jobs," I said.

"No, as a matter of fact, I'd expect you both to keep on working for me. On salary—more money than you're bringing home now. That's part of the deal. I'd expect a five-year commitment. Then after five years, you'd go your own way, but I'd get to keep the company name."

"What assets?" I asked. "Minimal office equipment, plus our inventory of poetry titles that sell a few hundred copies each every year? And Lorraine's book, which may turn out to be a dud."

"Plus other books I'll have you publish," he told me. "I'll be choosing the books to be published. Books that are going to sell a lot more than a couple of thousand chickenshit copies."

"Why do you want to do this?" I asked. "This is stupid, but I really am interested in knowing what's on your mind."

"I want you working for me, you and Carol, because you have a good reputation in the business and because you have already worked out distribution deals with wholesalers. And, I have to admit, you have a lot of charm, both of you, and I want that. And I want all your assets, let's make that clear."

What assets was this dodo talking about?

"So back to square one," I said. "You aren't going to pay the printer for the second printing?"

"They get thirty days?"

"That's right."

"I think you and I can work out the details in thirty days. The day you sign the company over to me, I'll pay every outstanding bill you've got. I'll give you thirty days to decide, but I'd rather hear your answer right now."

"Good-bye," I said.

"We'll talk," he replied.

I hung up, stood up and paced around the office, then sat back down at my desk and put my face into my hands. My mind was still full of little popping noises when the phone rang again.

"Guy Mallon Books."

"Guy, this is Dennis with Yellow Freight. I'm here at your warehouse. I got a delivery for you, eleven pallets. How soon can you be down here to sign for these babies?"

When I got to the warehouse the Yellow Freight truck had already left, and a crew of beautiful women was busy moving cartons of books off the pallets and into the warehouse, stacking them on top of the existing pallets.

Beautiful women: Kitty Katz, looking splendid in hotpants and a halter, her hair in bright pigtails. Gracie in her Kountry Klub tee shirt and jeans and a baseball cap from Disneyland.

And Carol.

Carol smiled at me shyly and walked into my hungry arms. "Come on in," she whispered. "We have work to do."

It took the three of us less than two hours to put the new books on top of the old books. When we were done the piles were like downtown Manhattan, daunting and enormous.

When the job was done and Gracie had gone back to her DocuTech and Kitty had left for the day, I finally spoke to Carol. "I have so much to tell you," I said.

"Good news or bad?"

"The good news is you're back."

"Shall we go to the office so you can tell me the bad news?"

"No," I said. "Let's go to Morro Bay."

"But Guy, I just—"

"I know," I said. "You just got back from there. But I need to get away for a couple of days. This town, this business, it's driving me nuts."

"Okay," she said. "Can we afford it?"

"We'll put it on the company card. Chances are we'll go bankrupt anyway. Either that or some kindly benefactor will come along and pay all our bills."

"Like that's ever going to happen."

"You never can tell," I said.

Then I stood on a carton of *Naming Names* and drew her into my arms. I kissed her long and hard. Our tongues played footsie while tears of relief rolled over all four cheeks.

Chapter Eight

We drove through the fresh, green Santa Ynez Valley, which glowed in the late afternoon light of springtime. I told Carol all about what had happened: Samuel Welch's miraculous staff of life, Lorraine Evans' latest freakout, Fritz Marburger's Mephistophelian offer to take all our troubles (and all our assets) off our hands, and Roger Herndon's belt buckle.

She said, "So you didn't have any fun while I was gone?"

"Fun?" I asked. "Did you have fun?"

"I asked you first."

We drove the rest of the way to Morro Bay in silence, holding hands. By the time we got there the sky behind the giant rock was bright apricot.

We don't actually stay in the town of Morro Bay, which is usually overrun with tourists and traffic. Instead, we stay in a cheap motel from yesteryear overlooking the muddy estuary of the south end of the bay in Baywood Park, a sleepy hamlet with one bar and a couple of good seafood restaurants.

As we drove into the parking lot of the Back Bay Inn, I asked Carol, "Is this where you stayed?"

"Of course not," she answered. "This is our place, Guy. I couldn't come here without you. I stayed at the Super 8 in San Luis Obispo," Carol said. "Cheap and clean."

"You stayed in San Luis all weekend?" I asked. "Doing what?"

We got out and I opened the trunk to get at our suitcase.

"I had a pretty good time," she said. "I went to every used bookstore from Cambria to Pismo Beach. But you know what I didn't do?"

"What?"

"I didn't have dinner at Cafe Roma." She grinned. It was our favorite restaurant in San Luis. Make that our favorite restaurant period.

I grinned back. "You're on. Let's register and get settled. You hungry?"

"Starved," she said.

After dinner we walked on the path beside the estuary. It was low tide, but there was still enough water to reflect the lights of Cuesta-by-the-Sea on the hillside across the bay. We stopped, wrapped our arms about each other, and kissed.

"So how come all the bookstores?" I asked her. "You went to all these used bookstores?"

"Within driving distance," she answered. "I love old books."

"So do I," I said.

"I kept thinking," she went on, "how much fun it was dealing in old books instead of trying to market new ones."

"Sounds lovely," I agreed.

"So you didn't tell me yet," Carol said. "Did you have any fun while I was away?"

I laughed. "You're kidding, right?"

"No," she said. "I really would like...I want to know, Guy: what did you do?"

"Nothing much," I answered. "Cleaned the warehouse."

"Was young Kitty there?"

"Kitty?"

"Kitty Katz. Your assistant in the shipping department."

"Kitty?"

"Guy, talk to me."

"I was by myself," I answered. "What's this about Kitty?"

"You like her."

"No I don't."

"You don't like Kitty?"

"Of course I like Kitty. I just don't—"

"I just don't trust her," Carol said.

"Oh for crying out—"

"She has the hots for you."

"Yeah, right," I said. "Hots for me."

Carol stopped walking and turned me around by the elbow. "Yes. Hots for you." She put her hands on my cheeks and drew my lips up to hers. "I got hots for you myself, Guy Mallon."

"You do?"

"Major hots. I'm slippery down to my knees."

I chuckled. "You're exaggerating."

"Maybe," she said. "Let's go back to the room and find out."

While Carol was in the bathroom I changed the light bulb in our bedside lamp. We had a special red bulb that we always brought to this room. Then I turned down the covers and stripped out of my clothes. I stood naked in front of the window, gazing out across the bay at the twinkling lights of Cuesta-by-the-Sea. The tide was coming in, filling the capillaries of the estuary, and I could feel myself start to grow.

Carol came out of the bathroom, turning off the light behind her. She wore a silk camisole that picked up the soft red from the bedside lamp. The light glowed on the smile that spread across her face as she looked me up and down across the room. I grew some more.

Even more when she peeled off the camisole and tossed it over her shoulder. She stuck out a hip and posed for me, lightly scratching the fiery blond curls of her thatch. More.

I continued to grow as she crossed the room, humming "I Cover the Waterfront," and by the time her pale pink-tipped handfuls touched my eager chest I was six foot two.

The next morning we strolled through the Sweet Springs Nature Reserve on the outskirts of Baywood Park. We held hands along the path under a canopy of eucalypti full of nesting herons, till we reached the shaded pond, which was busy with mallards and lazy with turtles. Then out of the grove to the marsh, where we sat on a warm bench and watched two egrets wading, silent and still between each careful step. Redwinged blackbirds flitted and twittered among the reeds.

I laughed.

"What?" she asked.

"You're not really jealous of Kitty Katz, are you?"

She laughed too. "Of course not. She does have the hots for you, and she may be a bisexual porn star, but I have something she doesn't have."

"Oh?"

"You."

One of the distant egrets bent forward, reached into the water and brought up something to eat, an eel or a fish, something long and brown. "Oh my God," I said. "I completely forgot to call Sam Welch back to tell him we can't publish his crappy book."

Carol groaned.

I said, "Carol, I'm sorry you're stuck with a job you hate."

She shook her head. "I don't hate it. It drives me crazy, but I can take it. It means we get to work together, and I know how much the business means to you. But I'll tell you this much: if Kitty Katz ever comes between you and me, I'll kill her."

"She won't, of course."

"No, of course she won't. But if the business ever comes between you and me, I'll kill it. I mean that."

"How would you kill a business?"

"I don't know. Burn down the warehouse?"

"That seems kind of risky," I said. "It would be cleaner just to let Fritz Marburger have the business. We'd have to work for him for five years, but we'd have to earn a living somehow anyway, so—"

"No," she said. "No fucking way. Number one, I'm not working for that creep. Number two, he expects to take over all our assets, you told me."

"Yeah, but what assets? Our bank account's running on fumes, our warehouse is full of backlist inventory that doesn't sell diddly, plus some fifteen thousand copies of a hardbound novel that even the author doesn't want anything to do with. Who needs it? And who needs all our payables?"

"Guy, listen to me. I'll say it one more time: Marburger wants all the company's assets. He doesn't give a rat's ass about being a publisher. He just wants the company's assets, which include, in case you don't remember, your priceless collection of first editions of postwar Western American poets. That's what he's after, Guy."

"Those aren't company assets," I said. "Those books belong to me."

She shook her head. "You've been buying them with the company credit card."

"But most of those books I've owned since before the company existed."

"And we listed the entire collection as one of our assets when we took out a bank loan to finance the last Arthur Summers omnibus."

I squirmed on the bench. "That loan's paid off," I tried.

"Fritz Marburger knows what he's doing, Guy."

"But why would he want a bunch of poetry books? He doesn't like poetry, or so he says."

"Money, babe. He'll sell them all. He'll make a killing, and meanwhile we'll be running a business that's broken our hearts." She rubbed my neck and said, "Or maybe he doesn't care about the money. Maybe he just likes to destroy people. Misses the action of cutthroat business. It doesn't matter. Guy, promise me you won't do this stupid thing."

"I promise," I said.

"I refuse to work for that asshole, and I don't want you to lose your books."

I stood up and faced her. "I could lose the books. I could live without them. But I can't live without you."

◇◇◇

We went back to the motel and packed our car. Before hitting the road we stopped at the mini-mart next door for a couple of coffees to go. Then the *Los Angeles Times* caught my eye. It wasn't the main headline, but it was right there on the front page, above the fold so I could read it in the rack: "LORRAINE EVANS IN INTENSIVE CARE." The subhead continued, "Overdose of sleeping pills blamed for singer's critical condition."

Chapter Nine

Luckily, Lorraine didn't succeed and the emergency room at Cottage Hospital saved her life. Unfortunately, *Naming Names* didn't fare so well. I hoped that Lorraine's misfortune would create some interest in her book, but on that score I got what I deserved. The book was dead in the water. Just as she wanted it to be.

"Tough luck about Lorraine, Good-Guy." Samuel Welch towered over me in Barnaby and Mary Conrads' backyard. It was the annual cocktail party, where the inner circle of the Santa Barbara Writers Conference gathered once a year to drink and shmooze on a late Monday afternoon. "I hear she couldn't take the heat, right? People giving her a hard time about her private life?"

"Right," I mumbled. I was out of Scotch.

"So I have a question for you, Good-Guy," he said. "And you know God damn well what it is."

"Let's go belly up to the bar," I said. "I'm gettin' powerful thirsty."

Me and the bad guy moseyed across the lawn, but even before we reached the outskirts of the drinking crowd, he draped his heavy arm down across my shoulders and said, "Did you read it? Did you read my manuscript? I know you been busy, but what did you think? Huh?"

I didn't even wait until I had a drink in my hand. "Sam," I said, "that is a truly beautiful collection of tales. Especially Rita Hayworth's."

"Dear Rita!" he sighed. "So? Are you going to publish my book?" he whispered. "That's all I want to know."

Cut bait. "Nope," I answered. "No can do."

"Why not?" He looked as if he'd been bonked on the bean with a beer bottle.

"Broke," I said. I faced him and turned my pants pockets inside out. "We spent all our cash flow on Lorraine Evans' novel. I can't afford to publish anything these days."

The world's highest-paid professional villain looked down at me and smiled. "Just tell me how much money you need, my friend, and we'll work out the rest of the details."

"What are you talking about?"

"Think about it, kiddo. Win-win situation."

I thought: *Don't call me "kiddo."* I said: "Are you serious?"

He nodded and smiled, one eyebrow cocked. "How much money are you in the hole?"

"You *what?*" Carol said that evening when I told her about the deal I had cut.

"Think about it, kiddo," I said. "Win-win situation."

"Don't call me 'kiddo,'" she retorted, picking up a wooden spoon and prodding me in the chest. "Don't ever call me 'kiddo,' okay?"

"Okay."

"Guy, aren't we in bed with enough assholes as it is? I mean Fritz Marburger and Roger Herndon, and now this two-bit heavy? What in the world were you thinking of?" She slammed the spoon down next to the sink.

I turned my back on her and rattled the martini shaker furiously, then poured her a cold cocktail that I hoped would help her see reason. I handed it to her and we walked together into the living room. "You're not having a drink?" she asked.

"I already had four scotches at the party," I said. "I'm good for now."

"That explains it," Carol said as she sat down. "And it's an out. Nobody can be held to a promise they made under the influence."

I plopped down in the other armchair and said, "Carol, I'm just trying to save the company is all. We need the money. It's as simple as that. Sam Welch is going to pay off our printer's bill. Without him, we'd lose everything."

"I could take out a second mortgage on this house," she offered.

"No. I'd rather turn the company and all my books over to Marburger Enterprises than to let you risk your house. Look, it's just one book we have to publish, and then we'll be back on our feet, okay?"

"And whose book will we have to publish to pay off the printing bill for Mister Welch's ego trip? Have you thought about that? And where are we going to store Welch's book? We don't have any room left in our warehouse. Have you thought about that? Jesus, Guy."

"It'll work out," I said. "Trust me," I told her. "No problem."

"My two least favorite phrases," Carol said. "Pour me another drink."

The day after the Fourth of July I went to the warehouse to process a few orders that had dribbled in. I opened the warehouse door all the way, because it was a hot day and I needed the air. I turned on the lights, put the orders on the work space, and sat down to type labels. I was disappointed but not surprised that nobody else was there; it would have been fun to swap a few jokes with Kitty. But the Caslon Oldestyle folks didn't keep regular hours. I was on my own to wrap books and stew about the stew I was in.

Not quite. "Guy?"

I stood up and saw Gracie's head poking out from behind a row of *Naming Names*.

"Hey, Gracie," I said. "I didn't know you were here."

"You alone?"

"I was till now."

"Can we shut the door?" she asked. She ventured out into the aisle. She was dressed for the weather, in cutoff jeans and a loose sleeveless tee shirt, pink as usual.

"Why? What's up?"

"There's some creep stalking me," she said. "Oh shit, here he comes now."

I turned and looked out the warehouse door into the parking lot, where I saw a tall man walking forcefully toward us, dressed in a tan suit and carrying a briefcase.

"Who is that person?" I asked.

"I don't have any idea who he is. I want you to stick by me, Guy. Don't let this guy do anything, okay?"

He was almost upon us. "You don't know him?"

"No."

"Seen him before?"

"Yes."

"At the Kountry Club?"

"No, at the post office, about an hour ago. I was on foot because it's such a nice day. I picked up Roger's mail, then started out of the P.O., and that's when saw this weirdo giving me this look, like he's seen me naked or something, but I don't remember him from the club. He followed me out of the P.O. and all the way to the Paseo Nuevo. It was like I could feel his eyes licking the backs of my legs. I lost him in Nordstrom's. But it looks like I didn't really lose him. Shit!"

"I'll handle him," I said. "Maybe you'd better go on back to the office till I get rid of him."

Too late. "No you don't, missy. You stay right where you are."

I turned around to face the man standing in the doorway, backlit by a bright sunny day, so I couldn't see much of his face. A tall man with a gray crewcut. He stepped into the warehouse, and his face came into focus. I'd seen that face before. "So," he said. He was talking to me, not to Gracie. "We finally meet. You can't hide from me anymore, Mister No Street Address. Your little Miss Priss here led me straight to your door." He took a few steps into the warehouse.

"Hold it right there," I told him. "Back off."

He stopped, but he didn't back off. "You don't answer my letters, you don't take my phone calls. Just who the heck do you think you are, Mister?" He set the briefcase down on my workspace, next to the typewriter.

"Mister," I replied, "just who are you and just who the heck do you think I am?"

"As if you didn't know," he answered, "my name is Bob Worsham. I'm the author of *Onward Christian Sailors,* and you're my darned publisher, or at least that's what the contract says. Ten thousand copies of my book. Where are they?" His gaze drifted back to the phalanx of pallets, all piled high with Lorraine Evans' disaster. "That them?"

I chuckled. "Look, Mister Worsham—"

"Commander Worsham."

"Okay, Commander. Look. You've made a mistake here. See—"

"I'm beginning to realize that," he thundered, back on the move now. He strode around the work space and stood two feet in front of me, so that I had to tilt my head far back to look him in the face. "A twenty-seven-thousand-dollar error. But let me tell you something, Mister Herndon—"

"See, there's your error, right there," I said. "I'm not Roger Herndon."

He took a step back and bent forward to look me straight in the eyeballs. Then he swirled around and opened up his briefcase, then swirled again and held a copy of the Caslon Oldestyle sales brochure six inches in front of my face.

"That's you, Sir. That's you, unless my eyes deceive me. Correct me if I'm wrong."

"That's my face all right," I said. It was the picture of me and Carol standing in front of piles and piles of our own books.

"But I have nothing to do with Caslon Oldestyle Press or with Roger Herndon."

"Oh yeah?" Commander Bob looked over at Gracie, who was twisting the bottom of her pink tee shirt in her hands. "And how about your little chippy here in her shorty-short pants? Is she Roger Herndon?"

"That's enough," I said. "Listen—"

"No, you listen to me, Mister Whatever Your Name Is. I don't care what your real name is. All's I want is to see my books. Every copy. Ten thousand of them. Show me those books, and I'll be on my way. Let's go. On the double."

"My name is not Roger Herndon," I told him once again. "I have nothing to do with Caslon Oldestyle Press. I don't have to show you a thing. You're trespassing here. Gracie, go phone the police."

But before Gracie could move, Worsham nailed her with a question. "Gracie, is it? Do you work for this man?"

Gracie nodded and whispered, "Sometimes." Her lip was trembling.

"And do you work for Caslon Oldestyle Press?"

"Gracie," I ordered, "get back inside the office and lock the door. Call nine-one-one."

Gracie skittered behind a row of pallets and disappeared.

Commander Bob Worsham picked up his briefcase and gave me a scowl and a nod. "I shall return," he said.

"Just get out of my warehouse," I told him.

"So you admit it is your warehouse?"

"Get out."

I went to the back of the warehouse and opened the office door. There I found not only Gracie but also the amazing Roger Herndon, who looked up from his desk and asked me, "Is he gone yet?"

"So you are here, after all," I said.

"I was catching up on a little work," he answered.

"Where were you when I first got to the warehouse, about fifteen minutes ago?"

"I was in the can, I guess."

"Hiding?"

He gave me a sheepish grin. "Well, Gracie told me some creep was following her, and I thought it might be Worsham. He's been leaving all kinds of messages on our phone, not to mention about twenty angry letters and a couple of telegrams. He called this morning and left a message saying he was in town. So, uh, when you opened the warehouse door—"

"He wanted to see his books, Roger."

"Why didn't you just show him some of yours and get rid of him?"

"Two reasons," I said. "Number one, those books aren't his. Number two, the problem's not mine."

"Aw shit," Roger whined. "God damn it. Fucking sailor-boy. Jesus."

"Relax," I said. "I got rid of him for now. But if I were you I'd run off another nine thousand, nine hundred, and ninety-nine copies of *Onward Christian Sailors* before he comes back."

"Don't be ridiculous," Roger said. "You realize how long that would take, and how much it would cost?"

"But your contract with the man—"

"Says diddly," Roger said. "It says I'll publish up to ten thousand copies, as needed to fill orders. There haven't been any orders. End of story. When he comes back, tell him to read the contract."

"I'm not telling him a thing," I said. "You tell him, Roger."

I spent the rest of the afternoon wrapping books, sweeping the warehouse floor, talking to myself, and selling what was left of my soul to the devil. When it was time to go back to my office and pick up Carol, I had come to a number of airtight conclusions:

Roger had done nothing illegal. That was true.

With very little trouble, and that trouble was Gracie's, he had published a book and had been paid twenty-seven thousand dollars for it.

He had what it took: the machinery and an employee who knew how to operate it.

I was in big trouble financially. So was Carol. So was our business. Carol and the business and I were intertwined. One problem, one solution, one size fits all.

Samuel Welch wanted a book published. A book.

Carol would not like the direction this logic was taking. But even she would admit I was planning nothing illegal. Sneaky, maybe, but that's business. Strictly legal, strictly business.

And I was doing it for her, right? For Carol? I didn't want her to have to mortgage her house, right?

Roger and I left the warehouse at the same time. The sun was still high and the parking lot was still hot. We walked together toward our cars. When we got to his, I said, "Roger there's something we need to talk about."

Chapter Ten

Carol didn't like it one bit, but the next day I phoned Samuel Welch and invited him to our office to sign a publishing contract with me. Carol said, "Guy, I just don't understand you. This Welch guy is going to bail you out of one printer's bill, but there will be another printer's bill when we do his book, and how're we going to pay that one?"

Tell her? No.

"Maybe by that time we will have sold enough copies of *Naming Names* to cover the bill?" I suggested.

She wrinkled her nose and gave me a "yeah, right."

"Think about it, Carol. We're going to be okay for now. Isn't that okay for now?"

"We're going to lose our reputation as publishers who care about what we publish. Is that okay for now?"

Sam Welch swaggered in fifteen minutes later. He gave Carol his devilish smile and he stunk up the office with expensive cologne. I showed him to the conference table, where he plopped down the manuscript and took a seat. We faced each other across the table, and I laid out the two copies of our contract, one in front of each of us. He took a pen out of his buckskin sport coat and said, "Where do I sign?"

"You'll probably want to read it first," I suggested.

"Hell with it," he said. "Let's pull the trigger."

"You realize, Mister Welch—"

"Call me Sam." He grinned at me. "I told you that already."

"Sam, listen. This contract says you'll pay me forty thousand dollars to publish this book. That's an awful lot of money."

Sam pulled his checkbook out of his pocket and slapped it down next to the contract. "To you, maybe," he said. "To me it's money well spent."

"But we may not be able to sell enough copies to earn you back even a fraction—"

"Don't talk numbers, Guy. If we get my agent or my accountant in on this, they'll tell me I can't do it. But screw them, know what I mean? I want my book published. Any fool can act. How many people can say they wrote a book, right?"

"But—"

"Listen, Good-Guy. I don't care if I don't make a dime off this book. I just want to hold a copy of my own book in my own hands. That's all I want. That and being published by Guy Mallon Books."

"I can't guarantee that you'll get good reviews," I continued. "Your book's controversial, all that gossip, all those poems, and who knows how the critics will react?"

Sam Welch chuckled and said, "Remember *The Poisoned Posse*? You see that picture?"

"I missed it, I'm afraid."

"Yeah, well Chuck Champlin of the *Los Angeles Times* said it was a misbegotten dog and Roger Ebert called it a Grade-B knockoff and *The New Yorker* said I ought not to be in pictures. All the critics gave me the finger. But you know what I got to say to them, when the dust settled and the smoke cleared and the chips were down? What I got to say to the whole damn world?"

"No, what?" I could see Carol across the room, behind Sam's back. She was staring at the ceiling, as if there might be a God up there somewhere who could be persuaded to strike us all with lightning.

Sam said, "I told them, 'I'd like to thank the members of the Academy.'" He grinned. "See what I mean? My book might be a hit, you never can tell. Okay, podnah. Where do I sign?"

◇◇◇

After he had left, Carol told me, "Well, you did a good job of covering your ass. I hope all those disclaimers were in the contract."

They weren't. "Carol," I said, "I write the contracts, okay?"

"Fine, fine," she said. "That's your department."

"Thank you."

"In fact, you can have the whole fucking book. You can acquire it, sign it, edit it, design it, typeset it, proofread it, correct it, register it with *Books in Print* and the Library of Congress, send out advance galleys to the industry journals, you can solicit blurbs from all your literary celebrity friends, you can design the cover and write jacket copy and you can send it to press. When it comes back from the printer, you can meet the truck and unload the whole shipment and stack them God knows where. Then you can write the press release and design the sales brochure, you can call stores and send out review copies, and arrange a party at the Earthling. It's your baby, Guy. Okay?"

"Okay," I answered.

"Okay. Oh, and another thing. You can write the check to pay the printer's bill when it's due. And you can figure out how to do that."

"Okay."

"Okay."

So that's what I did with the rest of the summer. Carol and I had called a truce, the one condition being that we never discuss *I Wasn't Always a Bad Guy,* Samuel Welch's book. I worked hard and I worked solo. Meanwhile, Carol paid the printer for the second printing of *Naming Names* and continued the good fight of trying to get that book noticed by the world. There wasn't much going on in the sales and marketing department of our business, and there were very few orders to fill, so she took some time off and stayed home a lot, working in her garden and battling with an overgrown bougainvillea that was threatening to eat us alive. More evenings than not I came home from the office like a hubby from the 'fifties, and Carol would meet me at the door with a kiss. We would have cocktails together, then dinner and a walk in the long, warm evening around our flower-covered neighborhood. We stayed in love because we were both careful not to bring up the one issue that was always on both of our minds. We approached that issue with different worries, of course. Carol worried about the financial future of our company. I worried about my eternal soul.

Meanwhile, Lorraine graduated from Psychiatric Rehab and reentered society on the arm of Fritz Marburger. The *Santa Barbara News-Press* considered them an item again, and although they maintained separate residences, they also rented a bunga-low together at the Biltmore Hotel, where they spent many of their nights during the rest of the summer. Lorraine sent me a letter of apology—not for crapping out on the *People* article or the "Oprah" show, but for getting me and Carol involved in her embarrassing, ill-conceived dream. Marburger did not communicate with us at all, although we still sent rent checks to Marburger Enterprises for our warehouse space.

Meanwhile Roger Herndon had dozens of books in the works. Gracie's work load was huge, and every week or so another couple of books were published by Caslon Oldestyle Press. One copy of each book would roll out of the DocuTech machine and Kitty would package it up and send it off to a proud published author somewhere. Roger was collecting well over twenty thou for each one of these titles, and if he kept going at this rate he'd be a millionaire before the end of the year, unless some irate author shot him first.

Meanwhile, I worked away at the same scam on a smaller scale.

I didn't thoroughly enjoy working on Sam Welch's book, but it wasn't that terrible. Well, I take it back; the poetry was terrible. But his life was somewhat interesting. What can I say? Maybe celebrity tell-alls aren't evil things. Sam left me alone, convinced that I knew what I was doing. Carol left me alone, nowhere near convinced, but we had our truce. I worked at the book steadily, and by September 1, the Sunday of Labor Day weekend, I had prepared the disk according to Gracie's instructions. It was ready to turn over to Caslon Oldestyle for a DocuTech birth. One book, coming right up, which would cost me nothing. Then more books as needed, if needed, at cost.

It was also time to tell Carol the rest of the story.

"Honey? I'm home...."

She stared at me with wide eyes full of dismay. Tears leaked to her cheeks. Her open mouth trembled. She dropped her martini glass to the redwood deck, where it shattered to smithereens. She turned her back on me and screamed into the bougainvillea, "No! NO!"

I reached out and touched her shoulder and she whirled back to me, slapping my hand away from her face. She looked very old and very young and not like any Carol I'd ever known before.

"Carol, I'm sorry."

"I thought you were just being stupid, Guy. I had no idea you were being dishonest."

"I'm sorry," I repeated.

"Guy, I can't live with this."

"I know how you feel," I said. "It's not easy for me, either."

"No, listen to me. I can't live with *you.* I've often doubted your wisdom, but I've never doubted your integrity before. Now there's not even a doubt about it: you're a cheat. You're going to have to leave. Out."

"Out?"

"Get out of my house."

"But this is where I live," I stammered. "You're the one I—"

"Go for a drive," she told me. "A long drive. Don't come back till tomorrow morning. I need some time to think."

She buried her face in her hands and sobbed, then turned back to the bougainvillea and rushed into its spiny embrace. When she turned around her face and arms were bloody. I reached out to her, and she snarled like a Gorgon.

"Out!"

I spent that night, Sunday night, at the Schooner Inn, a cheap hotel on Lower State Street. I have always had a fondness for that hotel, ever since I lived there in the late 1970s when I first arrived in Santa Barbara. I was even fonder of Joe's Cafe, across the street, and that's where I spent the evening, sitting at the bar and swigging Jim Beam as if it were soda pop.

"Hey, Guy, hiya dune?"

I swiveled on my stool and looked up into the happy, handsome face of Maxwell Black, my favorite cowboy poet. As always, he had a Budweiser bottle in his hand.

"Siddown," I said, pointing at the stool next to mine. "I have a number of very important things I can't tell you anything about. Max, can you keep a secret?"

He thought a long time about that one before saying, "Nope. I never have been any good at that."

"You're an honest man."

"Best policy." He took a pull from his Bud.

I said, "Oh shut up. You make me sick."

"I make you sick?"

"No, I make me sick." I climbed down off the barstool and watched Joe's Cafe whirl all over the universe. "Max," I said, "would you walk me across the street?"

◇◇◇

Monday morning I woke up early and ugly. My body felt like my mind, and my mind felt like the inside of a Dumpster. I went downstairs and checked out of the Schooner, then walked down to Esau's Coffee Shop for breakfast. God, that sun was bright. After breakfast I felt somewhat better, but not good enough to face the worst, so I decided not to go home, I mean to the house I'd called home for years. I also decided not to go to the office for fear Carol would be there. So I went to the warehouse instead. I had something to say to Gracie.

The man I least wanted to see in the entire world was standing there in front of the closed door of the warehouse, his arms crossed across his massive chest. He was dressed less formally this time: tan slacks and a baby blue golf shirt that appeared to be starched. I got out of my car and walked up to him. "Good morning, Commander," I said.

"I want you to open that door right now, sir," he replied. "I've been waiting here since eight-thirty this morning, and it is now ten-fifteen. Don't you have a business to run?"

I could have reminded him that it was Labor Day, for Christ's sake, but I ignored the question and opened the big rolling door, then walked into the warehouse and flipped on the lights, with Commander Worsham following close behind me. He was probably only a foot and a half taller than me, but I felt as if I were being shadowed by a giant.

"I expect you want to have a talk with your publisher," I said. "Mister Herndon is out of town at present."

"Don't give me that crock of bilge water, mister," Worsham snapped. "You and I are going right back to your office right now and we're going to sit down and talk business. I'll do the talking and you'll do the listening until I tell you to respond. Is that understood, sir? I expect a bit of common courtesy from the people I'm in business with. Common courtesy, honesty, respect. And results. And product. I want to see my books, Mister Herndon. And I want to see them now."

I scratched my head. "Commander Worsham, you are talking to the wrong man. How do I get you to understand this? My name is Guy Mallon. I am not Roger Herndon. I don't work for Roger Herndon and you and I are not in business together."

"I'll not have you try to make a fool of me, mister. I have returned, and I'm here in Santa Barbara to stay until I get satisfaction. I'm here on my boat this time, down in the marina, and I'm staying in Santa Barbara until I get satisfaction. Satisfaction. Is that understood, mister? Get used to that and be prepared to answer to my lawyer." His face was the color of rhubarb pie.

And my head hurt. And my life was a mess anyway. So I said, "Oh fuck you."

Commander Worsham stood at attention. "Sir, I will not allow you to take the Lord's name in vain."

Sheesh. I turned around and walked away from him, toward the back of the warehouse. I could hear his footsteps behind me. When I got to the poetry area, where the boxes were piled up in freestanding stacks instead of stacked on pallets, I turned to the right and ran to the end of the aisle, where I hid. I was grateful for once that I was short, shorter than the poetry stacks.

The commander was still coming, huffing and puffing.

I switched aisles, then darted down a third. I felt like Cary Grant hiding in the cornfield in *North by Northwest.* I could lose him in this maze, but for how long? And who was going to save me when he finally got his hands on my throat? Another aisle and then another until I was behind them all, back by the DocuTech. He was marching now, up one aisle and down the next, closer and closer.

"You can run, but you can't hide, you atheist, you cheater, you midget!"

Well, he had me there, on all three counts. "Okay," I called. "Just stay where you are, asshole."

"WHAT DID YOU CALL ME?"

Commander Bob Worsham roared and became an act of God, an earthquake, a calamity. In his fury he must have pushed into a row of poetry, a pile high enough to fall against a pile in the next row, which became three piles as they fell into the next, and the momentum grew all the way as the dominoes fell, with the rumble of a freight train, the force of the ocean, and before I could move out of the way the wall of boxes I was standing behind crashed down on me, knocking me to the floor, where my head bounced on the cement and cartons full of books covered my body.

Chapter Eleven

"Don't struggle."

I struggled.

"Don't struggle, Guy. I'm giving you an injection. I want you to relax."

"What the hell is what's why who are you what...."

That's as far as I could go with that one. I dropped back off the cliff.

I came to again inside the ambulance. The young man in green pajamas was taking my blood pressure. Gracie had her hand on my head. I opened my mouth.

"Don't struggle," the man said.

"Where are you taking me?" I squeaked.

"Emergency room, Cottage Hospital."

"Gracie?"

"I'm here, Guy. You're going to be all right."

"I'm already all right," I said.

"No you're not."

The young man in green pajamas said, "You'll live. You'll be back on the tennis courts in no time."

I rolled my eyes and saw that I was connected by a tube to a plastic sack of fluid. "What is that?" I asked, but I didn't stay awake long enough to hear the answer.

I don't know how long I was in the emergency room or how I got moved into a private room. They told me later I had a few hours in Intensive Care, but I don't remember that. I do remember a nurse in my private room asking me if I wanted to watch television. I told her I was in enough pain already, so she gave me another pill and left. There were other nurses, other pills. There was a catheter. There was an IV tube. I had enough pain in my body for a very large man. Another pill. I slept.

A doctor visited me the next morning. She looked at me and frowned, then looked at the paperwork on her clipboard. She tapped her clipboard with her ball-point pen, looked at me again, and smiled. "Buried alive, I understand," she said.

"So they tell me."

"And you feel—?"

"Like shit, but I expect I look okay?"

She chuckled. "Nope. You look a lot worse than you feel. But you're going to be okay."

"Lot you know about it," I mumbled.

"I'm a doctor, and I'm telling you you're going to be okay. Okay?"

"Tell me this, will I be able to tap-dance?"

"I've heard that one before," she said. "For now I just want you to practice walking. We have a PT coming in at ten o'clock. You're going to walk the halls. Go slowly at first."

"I can't walk."

"Yes, you can. How's your vision?"

"You look good to me," I said. "How long will I be here?"

"A couple more days," she said. "I want to make sure all your vitals are stable. You had a concussion, but no broken bones. Lab work indicates there's been no damage to any vital organs, and all your internal hemorrhaging has been at the surface level. I'll have you on Vicodin for a few days. You're going to be just fine. Stay away from mirrors; they're bad luck."

"That ugly?"

"Actually, it's quite lovely. Looks like you got in a paint fight with Paul Cézanne."

◇◇◇

The physical therapist came in and marched me around the halls, one step at a time, me slowly flashing my bruised butt through that peekaboo hospital gown. I used a walker and she strolled alongside me pushing the IV stand. She did not seem very friendly, but maybe she just didn't like little purple people. When we got back to my room I was exhausted. I stole a glance at the mirror over my sink. Lon Chaney's grandmother looked back at me and scowled.

◇◇◇

My next visitors were Gracie and Kitty, who brought roses and M&Ms.

Kitty started to tear up, but Gracie was all business. "I gave them your insurance card and Visa out of your wallet. I hope that's okay."

"Whatever."

"How did it happen, Guy?"

"Bunch of books fell on me."

"I know that much. I'm the one who called nine-one-one."

"Thanks. I suppose I owe you my life."

"Fuck that. How did it happen? Somebody pushed those books over on you, huh? Huh?"

I said, "Where's Carol? Why isn't she here?"

Kitty reached onto the bed and held my hand gently. "We can't find her, Guy. Nobody answers at your home or your office, and both places are locked up tight." She kissed my forehead, my raw purple cheek.

"Ow."

"Sorry."

"Do it again."

She did.

I took three more walks around the hospital halls that day, and I was able to walk without a walker, and then without crutches, and then without a cane. The next day I was walking without the IV or the PT. And the day after that, Thursday, I was wheeled to the lobby and set free to walk out the door on Gracie's arm, a bottle of painkillers in my pocket.

She drove me to the warehouse, where my car was still parked. She opened up the door and we both walked in, all the way to the back, where the lethal boxes were still strewn all over the floor. "Kitty and I are going to stack these up again," Gracie said. "But I thought maybe you'd like to see the scene of the crime. Maybe take a few pictures. Maybe call the police. Maybe tell me exactly what happened, Guy."

"I'll take care of all this," I said.

"Yeah right."

"I may not get to it for a couple of days. I'll get some help. I have friends."

"Me and Kitty are your friends. Get a couple more friends in and we'll have this mess cleaned up in no time. But Guy, come on. Tell me. Who did this to you?" She put her hand on my shoulder. That hurt but it felt good.

"Your boyfriend," I said. "The charming Commander Worsham."

"I'll kill that asshole."

"I've got to get home," I said.

"You sure you're okay to drive?"

"I'm in no condition to walk."

◇◇◇

The house felt cold and smelled stale. Was this still my home? It would have to be my home for a few days at least, until I was strong enough to pack a suitcase and find another place. For now I had to rest and heal, doctor's orders.

I walked into the kitchen and found the note:

Guy,

I've had it. I'm going for a drive. I'm going north, as far as I can get from this stupid city, this stupid business, and you. I love you, you little shmuck, but this time you really fucked up big.

C

I went to the refrigerator and took out a beer, then the ice pack from the freezer. I checked the phone messages: two from Gracie, both for Carol, telling her that I'd been in an accident, that I was at Cottage Hospital. That's all. I popped a pill and swigged my beer and phoned Arthur Summers, then Max Black. They both agreed to help me restore order in the universe, and we agreed to meet at the warehouse the next morning at nine. The beer tasted bitter, like tin, so I poured the rest of it out and opened a ginger ale.

The Vicodin made me sleep better than I expected, and it was almost seven-thirty by the time I woke up on Friday morning. It took me an hour to shower, shave, and dress. Every movement reminded me of my achy bones, my sore muscles, and fiery skin. My clothes felt like sandpaper. My head throbbed and every now and then I stopped moving and just stared into nowhere, thinking nothing. I had Vicodin and coffee for breakfast.

The poets were waiting for me at the warehouse when I arrived, which was about nine-thirty.

"Holy shit!" Arthur Summers said. "What in the hell happened to you?"

I shrugged. "A little accident," I explained.

"What ran over you, is what I want to know."

Max added, "That must hurt, huh?"

"Pain," I said, "is what connects my toe bone to my head bone."

"Any of those bones broken?" Art asked

"Just my funny bone."

The looks they gave me were more about frustration than sympathy. Max said, "I reckon we should go in and check out the damage." So we walked into the warehouse and went straight to the back.

"Mother of God," Art whispered. "Sweet Jesus. You got hit by all these?"

"Not all of them. Some of them missed me."

Max said, "Pal, I ain't lifting a finger till you tell us what this is all about. Did somebody do this to you? If so, who was it and what's his address?"

By this time I was feeling tired, so I sat on a box and said, "An angry author. I don't know if he knew what he was doing. But I had it coming."

"You're full of shit," Arthur Summers said. "What angry author, Guy? This certainly doesn't look like the work of a poet, especially now that Bukowski's dead."

"Not one of my authors," I said. "One of Herndon's."

"You keep strange company, dude," Max said. "I never did trust that old boy."

"I know," I said. "He's a slime bag, and the slime was rubbing off on me. That's what went wrong, see. I decided to pull a Roger Herndon on my newest author. Incidentally, Carol left me. The ironic thing is, I had come to the warehouse to tell Gracie the deal was off. I wasn't going to print that book on demand after all. Carol was right. I had decided to sell my poetry collection, fuck it. I didn't want to lose Carol, and I didn't want to be a creep like Roger, but the damage was already done, and so I got hit with a ton of bricks and Carol's gone and I'm a wreck and I haven't had breakfast, and I'm tired of whining. Okay?"

Art nodded. "Let's go to the Cajun Kitchen," he said. "I haven't eaten breakfast either. Max?"

"Yeah, I ate already, but I can always eat."

After breakfast I tried to help the boys lift some of the boxes, but it hurt me to bend over and my arms couldn't hold the weight of a single box. "Just sit down," Max told me. "We know how to do this. We put these books here in the first place, remember?"

So I pulled Gracie's chair around from her desk and sat down and talked to my friends while they did my work for me. I told them the whole story. I rambled and ranted and confessed for a solid hour until Art said, "That's enough, Guy. You're starting to repeat yourself."

"Yeah, I know, but—"

"But enough already. I'd like to tell you that Carol's just a woman and women aren't worth it, but women are worth it and Carol's not just a woman. You're in pain. I get it. Max gets it. But the self-pity thing is getting really, really old."

I looked from Art's face to Max's, and Max was nodding.

"I'm sorry."

"Oh shut up," Art answered. "You got a few problems, such as blue balls up to your forehead. But problems pass. Even women problems. Where do you want these three boxes of Charles Gullans? There's not enough for a stack."

"Hey, guys!"

Max and Art both turned and stood a little straighter and taller as we watched Gracie and Kitty stroll back into our work area. Gracie was in sweats, dressed down as usual, but she actually wore a bit of makeup on her face for a change. Kitty was, as usual, drop-dead gorgeous, wearing a tee shirt that looked like one coat of Day-Glo paint, her lavender-streaked platinum hair teased into a cloud around her face.

"Reinforcements," I said.

Art said, "Hello, ladies."

Max looked as if he wished he had a hat he could take off and hold over his heart.

Gracie and Kitty both kissed my cheeks, one on either side. "There," Kitty said. "Feel better?"

Gracie said, "Leave some of that work for us. We want to help."

"There's enough to keep us all busy for a couple of days," Max said. "If we wanted to drag it out a bit. How you gals doing?"

"Guy, you'll never guess who came to the club last night," Gracie said. "Knocked my socks off, except I didn't have any socks on, much less anything else. Shit. You'll never guess. Go ahead, guess."

"I give up. Samuel Welch?"

"I wish," Kitty said. "I hear he's a sight to behold. I'd like to give him a private."

I asked Gracie, "Who?"

"I'll give you a hint," she said. "Famous author, right-wing Christian, sailor boy."

"Bob Worsham? The Commander?"

She giggled. They both giggled. "Whoopin' and hollerin'," Kitty said. "He hired me for a personal, but I let Gracie take my place."

Gracie laughed. "Asshole didn't even recognize me. He wanted a private, but I wouldn't do that, not with that scum bag piece of shit. I gave him a quick personal and he tipped me ten bucks. Ten bucks! What a cheap dickhead."

"What are you people talking about," Max asked. "What club?"

"Gracie and Kitty both dance at the Kountry Klub," I explained. "Commander Worsham is the one who dropped the Berlin Wall on me. As for the rest of it, I don't know what they're talking about. What's the difference between a private and a personal, Gracie?"

"They're both lap dances," Kitty explained. "But a personal's out in the main room, and the G-string stays on. A private's in a private room, just the girl and the customer, and the girl's nude. Like anything can happen, right? You guys should come by the club some night. I'll give you a demonstration."

The two porn stars and the two poets worked all morning. I went out and brought back sandwiches and soda for lunch. Then I went home to take a nap. In the late afternoon I went back to the warehouse and got there just as the crew was finishing the job.

"Can I take everybody out to dinner?" I offered. "And Gracie and Kitty, I want to pay you for your time."

"That's okay," Gracie said. "We're just doing you a favor. And we have other plans for dinner. We gotta be at the club by seven. Friday and Saturday are our big nights. So we'll see you guys tomorrow night, right?"

"What's this?" I asked.

Arthur Summers said, "I won't turn down a free dinner. Max?"

"Shoot I reckon," he said. "Where we goin'?"

My poets and I ate dinner at Arnoldi's, a neighborhood bar and chophouse on the East Side. I didn't feel like drinking, and my jaw was still too sore to tackle their famous pork chops, but I made do with split pea soup and ravioli, while the boys wolfed down thick steaks.

"So what's this about tomorrow night?" I asked. "Are you two really going to the Kountry Klub?"

"All three of us," Art said. "You too, my friend. We're picking you up at nine o'clock."

"No way."

"Yes indeed. We don't like you feeling so small and looking so blue."

"Gracie and Miss Kitty are gonna fix you up," Max said.

"Can't do it," I insisted. "I appreciate the sentiment, but I'm a happily married man."

"You're not either one," Art pointed out.

"But what if Carol were to—"

"She won't. It'll be our secret. And the girls have already agreed to that."

I thought about it. "Max, you told me you can't keep a secret."

He grinned back. "This kind of a secret I can keep. We're buying you a private with both girls. They do this number with handcuffs."

"Please," I said. "My body can't handle the rough stuff these days."

"Okay," Art said. "We'll tell them to hold the handcuffs. This dinner's on me, by the way. Waiter!"

For some reason Gracie didn't show up the next night, but Kitty was the star of the show. Her stage name, I found out, was "Pussy Katz." A lot of the customers knew her well. Enchanted, they pounded their tables and chanted, "Puss-*ee!* Puss-*ee!* Puss-*ee!*" while she writhed on the stage like a boa in heat. My friends made me sit right up by the edge of the runway, my face inches from the action. She danced only for me. I still missed Carol, even in the midst of this undulating display, I still missed Carol, but I was hypnotized by the sight and the scent of someone who had been a small person, a friend, only the day before and now bloomed like a giant, fragrant, flower.

I refused to accept a private or even a personal, but there in the throbbing music, in the glistening pink light, I did get an up-close, in-depth look at home plate, the home of the brave, the holy grail, the pearly gates, the center of the universe, and what makes the world go 'round.

Yes, I felt guilty about it the minute we left the building and laughed our way across the Kountry Klub parking lot. But not during. Not one bit guilty, during. I was happy, high on Coca-Cola and Vicodin and testosterone and laughter.

I drove home and went to bed. Not long thereafter—at 3:07 a.m.—I received a phone call that took care of all my problems and handed me a whole new set. The old DiClemente Warehouse had burned to the ground.

Part Two

Chapter Twelve

Yellow tape kept me from entering the lot, so I parked on the street. I had to park two blocks away, because of all the cars that had come to the scene, and I had to weave my way through a throng of people in the parking lot to get close enough to see the damage. The scene was illuminated by klieg lights and flashing yellow warnings, which added a pulsating touch of green to the bluish glare.

What a mess. A few wooden beams still stood around the perimeter of what was once a warehouse, but most of what I could see and smell was a smoking, steaming mountain of soggy ashes and trash. I knew that underneath all that rubbish, what was left of my inventory of books still sat on the concrete foundation, but I also knew that whatever hadn't been consumed by fire had been ruined by water. Some of the best poetry books ever published, not to mention over fifteen thousand copies of a new hardback novel that had cost us a lot more money than we had in the bank.

Another barrier of yellow tape kept the crowd about twenty feet back from the action. I got down on all fours to crawl under the tape.

"Hey! You can't come in here!"

I stood up on the forbidden side and faced a cop a whole lot taller and at least a hundred pounds heavier than I. He pointed down to the asphalt. "Out."

"I'm Guy Mallon," I said. I had to bend my head way back to see his face against the black sky.

"So?"

"Detective Macdonald called me and said to come down, she wants to see me. This is my warehouse. My business is in there."

The cop's face softened and he nodded. "Was," he said. "I'm sorry. Come with me." Then he called into the cluster of uniforms and slickers gathered at the side of the foundation, "Hey, Rosie. Man here to see you."

A tall woman separated herself from the others and strode over to where I was standing with the cop. She wore a yellow slicker which was open in front, revealing a striped work shirt. She also wore rubber pants and rubber boots. She had a steno pad in one hand. She held out her other hand and said, "I'm Rosa Macdonald. You're Guy Mallon?"

"I am," I said as I shook her hand. "You must be hot in that suit."

"Comes with the job," she answered. "The worst fires are always on hot nights like these."

"Not in the daytime?"

"Not the ones I investigate."

"How did you get my name?" I asked.

"The night security watchman of the parking lot called in the fire. He told me your name, and also the name of another man." She checked her notes. "Mister Herndon? He also uses this building for his business? Used, I mean?"

"That's right. Roger Herndon."

"Do you have any idea how to get in touch with Mister Herndon? He doesn't seem to be listed in the phone book."

"I understand he's out of town on business," I said. "He's been gone for over a week, I don't know where. Somebody over at the Kountry Klub might know. He's a part owner, I think. I'm not sure about that."

Detective Macdonald revealed a bit of disgust in her face when she said, "That strip club? Are you involved with that place too?"

"Absolutely not," I said. "I'm a book publisher. Listen, what about my partner, Carol Murphy? That was her red Volvo. The night watchman saw that car?"

She nodded. "It was the only car in the lot when he drove by about nine o'clock, and it was still here when he drove by at ten. It wasn't here when he drove by again at eleven. By that time the fire had started. Her name again?" She took out a ball-point pen and opened the steno pad.

"She's not responsible for this fire," I said. "I can assure you of that. She hasn't returned since then, huh?"

"Her name, Mister Mallon?"

"Carol Murphy."

"And do you and Carol Murphy own this building, or did you?"

"No. It's owned by Fritz Marburger, Marburger Enterprises. You'll find that number in the phone book."

She took notes and then checked the watch on her wrist. "It's going to be light soon, and I'm done here for now. How about you and I go get an early breakfast at the Comeback Cafe? I have a bunch of questions I need to ask you."

◇◇◇

"So how are you so sure it was arson?" I asked. "Couldn't it have been faulty wiring or something?" I shook a Vicodin pill out of the bottle and downed it with orange juice.

"Yeah, or a mouse chewed on some Lucifer matches; I've heard that one before, too." Rosa Macdonald was a nice-looking woman in her mid-thirties. A big woman, looked Hispanic, which matched her first name. She had a pleasant smile with fleshy lips and big teeth, but she also had fierce Frida Kahlo eyebrows. By the way she shoveled down her fried eggs and gulped her coffee, it was clear that she was used to having her meals interrupted by emergencies. "No," she said, "this was a set fire. No question about it. Whoever torched that building wanted it to burn down in a big hurry. The structure was old and made of wood, and we have a Santa Ana condition, but still, when a building that big goes down in three hours, you know somebody did it on purpose, and did it right. Where were you this evening, Mister Mallon? Fire started about ten-thirty, we're pretty sure. Where were you at ten-thirty?"

"Surely you don't think—"

"Easy, easy. I'm just asking a few routine questions. It's my job."

"It's just that my whole business was tied up in that building. I've just lost hundreds of thousands of dollars' worth of inventory, so—"

"Insurance?" she asked.

"No."

"No?" Her dark eyes widened. "Why not?"

"I'm not much of a businessman," I said.

"Okay." She mopped up what was left of her egg yolk with what was left of her toast. "More coffee?" she asked, holding up her hand to summon our waitress. "By the way, what the hell happened to you? Looks like you got run over or something. That happen tonight?"

I shook my head. "Last Monday," I said. "Labor Day."

"You got worked over, all right. What happened?"

"Bunch of books fell on top of me."

"In your warehouse?"

I nodded.

She nodded back. "So can I call you Guy? I'm Rosa, by the way. Okay? Good? So tell me, Guy, where did you say you were last night about ten-thirty, eleven o'clock?"

"I'd rather not tell you," I said. "Not until I have to."

"You're going to have to eventually. Probably."

"There are other people involved," I explained.

She raised her brows: one strong, questioning line arched over those large brown eyes. "None of my business, I gather," she said.

"It wasn't what you're thinking."

"You don't know what I'm thinking. What I'm thinking is, if there are others involved, you'll have an alibi if you need one.

Okay, that's good enough for now. Let's try another approach." She opened her steno pad and laid it on the table beside her empty plate. "Know anybody who would be glad to see the old DiClemente Avocado warehouse burned to the ground?"

Oh brother. How was I supposed to answer a question like that? Tell nothing? Tell all?

"I see I hit a nerve," Rosa said.

"Okay. But what if I get sued for slander?"

"That's not an issue," she said. "Trust me."

"'Trust me' is an oxymoron."

Rosa tapped her pen on the steno pad and said, "Let's go. Who? And why? Go."

"Well," I began, "the owner of the building told us he wants out of the warehouse business. He wants to put up condos on that lot."

Rosa consulted her notes. "Fritz Marburger," she said. "Okay, who else? How about Roger Herndon?"

"I don't think so. He's got a gold mine in that business, I mean he had a gold mine in the business he ran out of that warehouse. Besides, he's out of town."

"So you told me. Anybody else?"

"I really feel bad about this," I said, "but one of my authors doesn't like her book anymore. She's ashamed of it. I can't imagine she'd do anything so destructive, though."

"What's her name?"

"Lorraine Evans."

Rosa looked up sharply. "The singer?"

I nodded. "But I'm sure she didn't do this. She's not that kind of person."

"How about your partner?" Rosa asked. "Carol Murphy. Did she have any reason to want to see the building burn down?"

Carol? Want the building burned down? Carol hated Herndon, she hated Fritz Marburger, she hated the publishing business, and I'm afraid she also hated me.

"None whatsoever," I replied.

Rosa balled up her paper napkin and dropped it onto her plate. "Okay, Guy. Let's go. I have to get back to the fire scene. I'll drop you at your car."

We left the Comeback and she let me into her squad car, which was parked in a yellow zone. I was glad to be done for the night.

But as we were driving through the State Street underpass below the 101, Rosa's shirt pocket jingled. She took out her cell phone and flipped it open with one hand, then used her teeth to pull out an antenna about four inches long. "Yo."

I watched her face in profile as she listened to this contraption the size of a blackboard eraser. I have no idea how those things work. Come to think of it, I don't know how real telephones work either. But as I watched her face turn dark I realized that the problem had just gotten far more complex.

"We'll be right there," she told the phone. She snapped it shut and stuffed it back into her shirt pocket. "Well, Guy," she said, "looks like I'm not done with you yet. I hope you have a strong stomach. We're going to see if you can identify what's left of a tall male."

◇◇◇

Any romance the crime scene might have held in the klieg lights had gone out with the dawn. Daylight made the remains of the building look just plain ugly. The crowd had been dispersed, but the yellow tape was still stretched across the entrance to the parking lot. A fireman let us through. We parked and got out of Rosa's squad car.

"Where's the crispy critter?" she asked.

"Behind. Medical will be here in a few minutes."

"Ready, Guy? You willing to do this?"

"Okay. I'm numb enough, I guess. I can take it."

She took a tube of goop out of her pocket and squeezed some onto her finger, then smeared it on her upper lip. She handed the tube to me and said, "Want some?"

I smeared goop on my upper lip and my nose filled with dizzying eucalyptus odor. "That's pretty foul."

"Wait till you smell the competition," she said. "You'll want to hold your nose."

We walked around to the back of the building, to the corner where Roger's office had once been. The crew had carefully removed the debris from the floor in the area between two melted filing cabinets and the carcass of an office chair, leaving a circle of bare concrete around the long black body. What was once a man was lying on what was once his back. I started to retch.

"I told you to hold your nose."

I did as I was told, but it wasn't the smell. I got control of myself and nodded.

"Look familiar?" Rosa asked.

I opened my mouth to speak but started to gag. A cop passed me a plastic bag, where I heaved my breakfast. Then he gave me his water bottle. I drank as much as I could, then heaved again, this time missing the plastic bag.

"Careful," Rosa said. "You're contaminating the scene."

I don't know why that made me laugh. Shit. Okay. I was up for it. "How do you expect me to recognize that?" I asked. "It's naked and it's so badly burned I have no idea how you know it's a male."

"Well, he's six-two and his hips are too narrow for a woman that tall. We'll be doing a dental check," Rosa said. "I was just hoping you could save us some time and some trouble." She turned to one of the firemen and said, "Find anything else we can work with?"

He picked up a plastic box and opened it for her. "We collected a few metal objects in the near vicinity of the body," he said.

"Set it down," she said. "Tongs."

He set the open box on the cement and Rosa squatted and peered inside. The fireman slapped a pair of tongs into her right hand and she gently dug around among the treasures. She pulled up a chain with two metal loops. "Handcuffs?" She looked up at me. "Ring any bells?"

I shook my head. She put the handcuffs back into the box. One by one she pulled out an assortment of scorched and mis-shapen screws, drawer handles, a stapler, a pair of scissors, and then something that puzzled us all. An odd shape, about three inches by two. "Gimme a rag," she said.

She rubbed the object clean and revealed a two-dimensional babe leaning back on her arms, her knees up and her breasts pointed at heaven. "What the Christ is this?" she wondered aloud.

Oh God. "It's a belt buckle," I told her. "It's made of Monel."

"No wonder it's in such good shape," Rosa said. "Monel has a very high melting point. What else can you tell me about this belt buckle? Whose, for example?"

"Herndon's," I answered. "Roger Herndon. This was his office. That was his belt buckle. And that thing was his body."

Rosa Macdonald walked me back to my car. We didn't talk until we were leaning against the car. I wiped what was left of the goop off my upper lip, but I couldn't erase the necrotic phantom of burnt flesh from inside my sinuses.

She spoke first. "So one suspect down. Now we're dealing with an arson murder. Double-header. So, Guy, who hated Herndon?"

I shrugged.

"Any enemies? He was in the strip club business, right?"

"Well, he was mainly a publisher. Or a printer. Or both. Actually neither, if you want to get technical."

"You're tired, aren't you?" she said.

"I'm a basket case," I confessed. "I just barfed my Vicodin, and I'm not supposed to have another one till about ten o'clock. I'm beat to shit. My warehouse is a roach. My business is toast. I'm sorry to babble."

Rosa patted my shoulder. "Go home and get some sleep, my friend," she said. "Take a shower. You stink. Here." She handed me a business card. "Come see me in my office first thing tomorrow morning. We have to talk. Meanwhile, don't talk to anybody about what you just saw. And don't leave town or you're in deep shit."

I got into my car and started the engine. She tapped a knuckle on my window, and I opened it.

"You okay to drive?"

"I don't have far to go. I'm okay."

"One more question," she said.

"Yes?"

"Where were you last night between ten and eleven o'clock?"

I drove away without answering her. I also didn't mention that I had a pretty good idea who murdered Roger Herndon.

Chapter Thirteen

I slept for five hours.

When I woke up, I padded into the bathroom and took a Vicodin. I stripped and took a long, hot shower. After I dried off, I wiped the steam from the mirror. My face was there all right, all purple and orange, but there was no soul behind it.

I flushed what was left of the Vicodin down the toilet.

It was after noon when I left the house. I drove along Cabrillo Boulevard, where Sunday tourists flock to Santa Barbara to beep and creep along the seaside street.

The marina parking lot was full, as it always was on Sunday mornings, but I found a place in front of Brophy Brothers' Restaurant. I went in and was offered a chance to go upstairs and wait in the bar forty-five minutes for a chance to eat lunch. I gave the hostess my name and said I'd wait outside. She told me I had to be back in the bar when she read my name or I'd get scratched. I told her I understood.

Forty-five minutes of free parking. I walked out of the restaurant lot and across the marina lot, where I noticed three old red Volvo station wagons, and one of them even had a strawberry blonde in the driver's seat, but the blonde wasn't Carol and the Volvo wasn't her car. I'd been spotting blondes and red station wagons all over town for a week, always the wrong ones.

The harbor was a forest of masts. Boats were squeezed in, tied up to berth after berth. Big working boats with tires hanging off the sides, fishing boats with giant spear guns in the bow, and pleasure boats—yachts, schooners, sloops, and dinghies. The colors of the craft and the tall reach of their masts were reflected in the still harbor. Seagulls swooped and scolded. The marina smelled deliciously of salt, fish, and spilled oil. Water calmly chuckled against the sides of the boats.

I went into the office, jingling the bell on the door. A young woman in jeans and a tee shirt stood up from her desk and came to the counter with a smile. "Help you?"

"Yes," I said. "I'm looking for my friend Bob Worsham. He's staying here in the marina. In his boat."

"Transient or liveaboard?"

"Transient, I guess. He's from Newport Beach, just up for a month or so."

"Transient. You know what berth he's in?"

"No. Can you tell me?"

She brought a wooden box up from below the counter and thumbed through it, then pulled out a yellow registration card. "Oh yeah," she said. "Him. He arrived September first. He's in J-18. Paid up to the end of the month. He's a friend of yours?"

"You sound dubious."

She shrugged. "Takes all kinds. Whoa, man, pardon me for mentioning it, but that's quite a shiner you got there. You get in an accident?"

"Your friend Bob Worsham did this to me," I said, grinning.

"Your friend, not mine. J-18."

"Thanks."

I jingled the bell again and went out into the hot afternoon. I walked along the main pier until I reached J, which stretched out to the left. I walked out onto pier J until I came to berth 18. It was vacant.

A wiry man was leaning over the side of the schooner in the next berth, painting the wooden paneling with marine varnish. I waited until he pulled himself back onto his deck, set down his brush and paint can and lit a cigarette. He sat on the railing, his back to me.

"Excuse me," I said.

He twisted around and looked down at me, then stood up, scratched his beard, and stretched. He wore cutoffs and a sleeveless gray tee shirt and an old sailor hat. Took a drag on his cigarette and said, "Tsup?" His face was lined and leathery from too much time in the sun, and he squinted like Popeye.

"The guy in this berth here," I said, pointing at the empty space. "You seen him today?"

"Shit. He a friend of yours?"

It didn't look as if this old salt wanted me to say yes to that one. "As a matter of fact, he beat me up in a bar last week. I came to collect."

"You got a lot of balls to come back for more," he told me. "You're lucky he ain't here, man. What an asshole."

"So he's gone sailing for the day, I guess. You know when he'll be back?"

The old salt flicked his cigarette butt into the water. "That asshole doesn't sail," he told me. "He's strictly motor, and he can't do that any good either."

"So you expect him back this afternoon?"

"Shit no. They left this morning about dawn."

"For good?"

"For good riddance, man. That sumbitch bumped my boat three times getting out of his berth. I yelled at him, told him I was calling the harbor police, and he told me to quiet down. 'Relax, man,' he tells me, 'don't wake everybody up. I'm leaving,' he says. 'I'm out of here. Going home,' he says."

"You know anything about him?"

"I know he's an asshole."

"Besides that? I mean you ever talk to him or anything?"

"I just got here last night, man," the sailor said. "I never seen that guy before this morning, and if I never see him again it'll be too soon, but if I do see him again I'll beat the shit out of him for knocking my boat and beating you up too, a little guy like you, that dude belongs behind bars. I gotta get back to work. But like I say, they're gone. Good riddance."

"They?"

"Him and his wife, I guess. Came on board at dawn, while I was having a cup of coffee. Then he fired the engine up like he had no idea what he was doing and bumped his way out of the marina. Must have hit three or four boats not counting mine. What an asshole. Probably drunk. Good riddance is all I can say."

◇◇◇

As long as I was on the ocean side of the freeway, I decided to go have another look at what used to be the DiClemente Avocado warehouse, or more recently the warehouse for Guy Mallon Books and Caslon Oldestyle Press. A crew was there with a steam shovel and two roll-up Dumpsters from BFI Waste Disposal. I crawled under the yellow tape and approached a man in a tan suit who was standing by himself, studying papers on a clipboard he held in his left hand. When he saw me coming, he took off his mirrored glasses and tapped them against the clipboard. He held out his right hand. "Hi. I'm Joe Robinson, city fire department. You must be Guy Mallon."

"How did you guess?" I shook his hand.

"Detective Macdonald described you."

"Short guy with a rainbow-colored face?"

The man grinned. "Something like that. Mister Mallon, I wonder if I could get you to fill out a couple of forms for me." He shuffled the papers on his clipboard and handed the bundle to me, with a ball-point pen clipped to the clasp. "Top three pages."

"What's it for?" I asked.

"Rough inventory and evaluation of what was destroyed. I understand you lost a lot of books."

"That's about it," I said. "As for a financial estimate of the loss, I'm afraid you'll have to ask my partner. She's the business part of the business."

"Where can I reach her?"

"I wish I knew."

"Well, I guess for now if you could just fill in the parts you know and also I need you to sign a release, on page three, saying we can clean up your part of the debris."

I took the clipboard to the short wall in the front of the lot, where I sat down and checked a bunch of boxes.

Insured? No.

Insurance company? N/A

Sole owner of the damaged property? In partnership with Carol Murphy.

Total value of goods lost: Sorry. I just don't know.

I signed off on the mess and authorized the fire department to shovel it all into landfill.

I walked the paperwork back to Joe Robinson and handed it to him. "Thank you, sir," he said. "I guess we're not going to get a signature out of the other proprietor."

"Dead," I said.

"Basically," he agreed. He consulted his papers and said, "Fritz Marburger, guy who owns this building. You know how to reach him?"

"He's in the phone book," I said. "Lives at Casa Dorinda in Montecito."

"Doesn't answer his phone," he said.

"Do you need him to fill out a form before you haul away what's left of his building?" I asked.

"Nothing much left to haul," he said. "But still." He handed me a card: Sergeant Joseph Robinson, SBFD. "If you see him, have him call me, okay?"

I nodded. "Is Detective Macdonald still here?"

"She left about an hour ago. She won't be back this afternoon. She didn't get any sleep last night. You want me to tell her—"

"It's okay," I said. "I have an appointment with her tomorrow morning."

◇◇◇

I went to my office, where I found the phone answering machine blinking, telling me I had eleven calls. I sat down at my desk, took out a yellow pad, and pressed play.

"Mister Mallon, this is Stephanie Roberts at the *Santa Barbara News-Press.* Please call me at—"

"Guy, this is Rosa Macdonald. I called your home, but no answer. I guess you're not at the office either. Okay, no biggie, I'll see you tomorrow. Bye."

"Mister Mallon, this is Stephanie at the *New-Press* again—"

"Congratulations! You have been selected to receive—"

"Guy, what the hell happened? This is Art Summers. Max told me he went by your warehouse this morning, and holy shit! Call me!"

"Mister Mallon, Stephanie again. Listen, I—"

"Mister Mallon, if you're there, please pick up—"

"Mister—"

"Hi, Stephanie again. You can call me on my cell phone, 555-3242. I'm on a deadline, so please call right away, as soon as you get this message."

Okay, so I called Stephanie Roberts, and I got, "Hi this is Stephanie. Leave me a message, bye."

I hung up and threw her number away.

No call from Carol.

I spent the rest of the afternoon dusting the books in my collection of first editions, taking them off the shelf, one by one, and blowing the dust off the tops of the pages. I opened each book and ran my fingers over the title pages, often feeling the bite of letterpress printing on soft rag paper. I published a few of these volumes, but most of them were published by other houses, large and small. Every one of these books was made with love.

My collection of post–World War II Western American poets was undisputedly the best private collection in the world in that limited field. Most of my books were in mint condition, a lot of them signed and numbered. Low numbers. Some even had uncut pages. Other book collectors envied me, and almost everybody else thought I was nuts. I didn't care. My poets made me feel proud and dusting my books made me feel calm.

Rosa Macdonald could wait until the next morning. By that time Bob Worsham would probably be back in Newport Beach. Open and shut case.

Chapter Fourteen

"You what?"

"I went down to the marina yesterday afternoon. I had this hunch, and I was right. I figured out who killed Roger Herndon and burned down the warehouse. But I wanted to check it out to be sure, so I went down to the marina and poked around."

"You *what?*"

"Poked around. See, I wanted to be sure I was right. I mean, I could have been prejudiced by the fact that Bob Worsham tried to kill me on Labor Day, dumped a bunch of book cartons on me, which I'm sure he did on purpose. I figured I'd better go have a talk with him."

"You what?"

"Relax, Rosa," I said. "I didn't get to talk to him, as it turned out. He skipped town at dawn, about the time you and I were eating breakfast. But he did it, all right. I mean, he was paid up to the end of September, but he left town just hours after the crimes. See what I mean? Now all you have to do is—"

"Listen, you little pissant," she said, "are you trying to ruin this investigation?"

"No, I'm trying to help," I said. "Maybe I should have talked to you first, but it was Sunday, and you needed a day off. So I—"

"I'm the detective," she told me. "Me. I am the detective, and this is my damn investigation. *I'm* the detective. *You're* the little pissant."

"Hey," I said. "What right do you have to bully me around? Don't you want me to cooperate?"

Then she softened her face and her tone of voice. "What's the matter. I hurt your feelings or something?"

"It's okay," I said. "I'm used to being reminded that I'm little."

"Awwww. Guy, I didn't mean 'little' as in *little*. I meant 'little' as in *little pissant*."

"Pissant."

"Look, you probably want to think I'm Good Cop, as in Good Cop/Bad Cop, right?"

I bit my lip and shook my head.

"Well I'm not."

"I just wanted to ask the man a few questions," I said. "But okay, I'll leave that to you. His name is Robert Worsham, and he lives in Newport Beach. He's probably home by now. You can get his address and phone number from the office at the Santa Barbara Marina. He's still registered there, even if he did skip town. Here's how I figure it—"

"I'm not Good Cop," she continued. "I'm not Bad Cop either. I'm a practical detective, which in my experience usually starts with being a friendly cop. I also happen to be the only member of the Santa Barbara Police Department who's on speaking terms with the Santa Barbara Fire Department. And I'm good at my job. I'm an arson investigator, but I've also brought several related murder suspects to trial. This DiClemente Warehouse case is in good hands. I'm telling you, and I mean it: don't fuck it up. Keep your damned mouth shut. Is that understood?"

"There's somebody at the *Santa Barbara News-Press* who's trying to get in touch with me," I said. "What do I tell her?"

Rosa rolled her eyes heavenward. "Stephanie Roberts?"

"That's right. If I'm supposed to keep my mouth shut—"

"You are unavailable for comment. Forget about getting your picture in the paper. If Stephanie needs to talk to somebody, tell her to call me. She knows my number."

"What will you tell her?"

"None of your business."

"Sorry."

"No. I mean I'll tell her it's none of *her* business."

"But the media has a right to inform—"

"Tell me something, Mister Mallon," Rosa said. "Will you tell me something?"

"Sure," I answered. "What do you want to know?"

"Where were you Saturday night about ten o'clock?"

"I can't tell you that," I said.

"You little pissant. You listen to me. Do you want me to arrest you on suspicion of arson and murder? Huh?"

"I didn't do it," I said. "I didn't do either one."

She wiggled a pencil between two fingers, then brought it down till it was drumming a tattoo on her linoleum desktop. "You're obstructing my investigation," she said. "That much is true, and it's a criminal offense. I can go through a lot of hoops to make you give up that information. But it would be much easier to just book your ass for murder."

I shook my head. "I promised a couple of friends I wouldn't tell anyone about that evening, and they promised me the same thing. I'm sorry. I could talk to them and see if it's okay with them if I—"

"You're not talking to anybody, remember? Keep your damn mouth shut. As far as you know there are no suspects, no known motives, no nothing. You never heard about a body, either, by the way. As far as you know, nobody was hurt in this fire. It was just a fire. Just a fire. Let me do the investigating. And don't leave town. I mean it. When I need to get the information out of you I'll bring you in and I'll have the Bad Cop talk to you with a rubber hose. Just kidding." She smiled, showing me for the first time that morning the gleam of her perfect big teeth.

Then she folded a page back on a yellow pad and brought down the tip of her ball-point pen. "Okay, what was the name of this guy who left the marina yesterday morning?"

◇◇◇

My emotions over the next few days darted between boredom and panic. I spent the rest of Monday, and all of Tuesday and Wednesday in my office, reading newspapers that had no news, sorting mail for a business that was out of business, and listening to the phone ring and get answered by a machine.

Stephanie Roberts called over and over until she finally announced, "Well, I guess you're not near either of your phones. The answering machine at your home number isn't working. You should get it fixed. What if somebody wanted to get in touch with you? Okay, okay. All I want is a little cooperation. Have a nice life."

Arthur Summers called a few more times, and then on Wednesday morning I decided to pick up while he was leaving another concerned message. "I'm here, Art."

"Jesus, Guy, where have you been? Is everything okay?"

"Not really."

"No, I guess that was a foolish question. But you, you're all right, other than the obvious?"

"Other than that, I'm afraid I can't tell you anything."

"Guy, what happened? How did the warehouse catch fire? The *News-Press* says arson's being investigated. Is that true?"

"Must be, if it's in the *News-Press*."

"Who did it?" Art asked. "Guy, who did this thing to you?"

"I have no idea."

"Yes, I see. But do you have any ideas?"

"I am unavailable for comment."

"Oh, that."

"That," I confirmed. "I'm sorry. Art, let me ask you something. Would you mind if I were to tell someone where we were last Saturday evening?"

"Gee, Guy. I hope it doesn't come to that. The university frowns on that sort of thing. I don't want to be uncooperative, but if you can avoid it, I'd rather—"

"Okay, skip it," I said. "Maybe Max can vouch for me."

"I've talked to Max," Art said. "I'm afraid he feels the same way. It's just that—"

"Never mind," I said. "I don't want anybody knowing about it either. Listen, I have a lot of things I have to take care of here. You wouldn't believe the mess on my desk."

"I can imagine," Arthur Summers said. "You know you have my support. You know that, right?"

We said good-bye and hung up.

Wednesday afternoon the phone rang, the machine picked up, and I heard the gravelly voice of Fritz Marburger, the former owner of the building that was no more: "Listen to me, Guy Mallon. If you can hear my voice, God damn it, *pick up the God damn phone,* excuse my French."

I did as I was told. "Okay, okay," I said. "Hello, Fritz."

"Answer me this, Mallon," he said. "Did you burn down my building?"

"Nope."

"Then who did?"

"Hell if I know," I told him.

"Shit."

"My sentiments exactly."

"Shit," he said again. "All you lost was a few books."

"Which were worth more than that sorry excuse for a building," I told him. "How's Lorraine?"

"She's back at Betty Ford. Stupid bitch."

"Does she know about the fire?" I asked. "That the books are gone?"

"Why do you think she's back at Betty Ford?" I heard a choke in his voice.

"Fritz, are you okay? You sound a little shaky."

"I'm okay, under the circumstances. I don't give a french-fried fart about that building. But I'm going to get the bastard who burned up Lorraine's books. I'm going to burn that bastard alive. It wasn't you? You sure about that?"

"Be reasonable," I said.

"Then who do you think it was?"

"I don't know."

"I know you don't *know*, Guy. I said who do you *think*?"

"I am unavailable for comment. The police—"

"Screw the police."

I wondered if he had met Rosa Macdonald. "I'm afraid I have nothing more to say to you, Fritz. Oh, except that I paid you rent for the whole month of September, so you owe me a refund. Do you want me to send you a bill?"

"Forget it," he answered. "If you hear any more on this fire thing, you call me right away. I mean it. You understand that?"

"I'm not an investigator," I reminded him. "Besides, you're hard to reach. You're never home."

"I realize that, but I pick up my messages. You can leave a message and I'll call you back."

I hung up.

I decided that Rosa Macdonald couldn't stop me from working, from being a publisher, someone with a business, even if the business was in the trash can. I had an obligation to take care of.

I called Samuel Welch.

"Guy," he said when I had given him my name on the phone. "Jesus, man, I read the story in the paper. I'm so sorry. What the hell happened? I mean how did it happen?"

"I don't know," I sang, a familiar tune by now. "Listen, Sam, we have a problem. I'm pretty much out of business for the foreseeable future."

"I hear you, man," he said. "Bad luck for both of us. I guess I'll have to look for another publisher."

"I can't even give you the disk that contained all my keyboarding, typesetting, and design. That was destroyed in the fire, too."

"You still have my manuscript? And the contract."

"Yes."

"Throw them both away. I've got lots of copies of the manuscript, and the contract's worthless. Just return that deposit, the money I paid you."

"That's the thing, Sam," I said. "I don't have that kind of money anymore. I used your deposit to pay a printer's bill, and

I was expecting to pay for your book with income from the sale of Lorraine Evans' book, and now there's no books to sell, and I'm afraid I don't know how to handle this."

"What about insurance?"

"*Nada.* I don't know how I can possibly pay you back."

Then I heard the famous Samuel Welch growl. "You'll think of something," he told me.

Thursday morning I heard a knock on the glass front door of my office. The working part of the office was in the back of the storefront, behind a door. But the banging was loud enough to get through the door, so I went out into the storefront, which is where I kept my poetry collection on the shelves of what had once been a bookstore.

I opened the Venetian blinds that covered the glass door and looked out. There stood my friend Kitty, wearing skimpy cutoffs, a bikini top, flip-flops, and nail polish, her lavender-streaked platinum hair down to her shoulders.

I opened the door and let her in. She rushed into my arms and I held her trembling body close to me. I stroked her hair and said, "It's going to be okay."

She pulled away from me and gave me a valiant attempt at a smile. Her sapphire eyes were glistening with tears. "Guy," she said, "have you seen Gracie?"

"Gracie? Not since last Friday afternoon," I said.

"She didn't come home on Saturday night," Kitty said. "And she hasn't been to the club. Nobody's seen her for almost a week."

I let out a huge breath of air. "This could get complicated," I said.

"What do you mean? Do you know where she is?"

"No idea," I said. "Sit down."

We pulled chairs away from the conference table and sat. Kitty put her elbows on the table and placed her face in her cupped hands. "And with Roger gone too," she mumbled, "I don't know what I'm supposed to do."

"Gone where? Any idea?"

"He's been out of town on business for a couple of weeks. I can't tell you what that's about, but he was making arrangements for a big change. He said he'd contact us, and we were going to join him. I'm not supposed to be telling you this, but I'm really worried. I mean, what if he got in touch with Gracie, and Gracie didn't tell me, just left me out of it?"

"Out of what?"

Kitty started sobbing, hiccupping. I went into the bathroom and came out with a box of Kleenex. She blew her nose. I tried again: "Left you out of what, Kitty?"

"I can't tell you. Guy, will you help me find them?"

"No," I said. "I can't."

"Why not, God damn it? Not like you have anything else to do these days. Shit." She blew her nose again. "You have to help me, Guy."

"You want a glass of wine?" I offered. "I have some good Cabernet in the closet for special occasions."

"No, I don't want a glass of fucking wine. I want Gracie!" The tears were flowing again. "Why won't you help me find her?"

"I'm not a detective, Kitty. You should go to the police."

"Yeah, right."

"Why not?" I asked.

"Of all the stupid questions."

"What do you mean?"

"It's not like everything they do is strictly legal."

"The police?"

Kitty gave me a look: get real. "Not the police. Roger and Gracie. You have to help me find them, Guy. If they're trying to leave me behind, I'll kill them both, I swear to God."

"I'm sorry, Kitty," I said. "I can't help you. I don't know anything, I can't leave town, I can't even talk to you. That's a fact."

Kitty stood up. "Fuck you, Guy," she said. "Just fuck you, okay?" She walked out of the office and onto the street, rattling the glass door behind her.

◇◇◇

Thursday passed. The phone rang a few times, and I let the machine do the answering. No call from Carol. No call from Rosa. Nothing more from Stephanie Roberts, Arthur Summers, Fritz Marburger, or Kitty Katz. *People* magazine called, but I didn't pick that one up either; they probably wanted to know what I knew about Lorraine Evans. I was unavailable for comment.

I worked on a card catalog I was developing for my collection of first editions, the Post–World War II Western American poets. My goal was to have a way to sort the collection by author, title, publisher, and date of publication. Eventually I'd enter the information into my computer. Maybe. I was still pretty fond of index cards. It took me the rest of the day to complete the listings for two shelves of books. I worked slowly. I had my favorite poems in each book, and I couldn't just record the data without rereading the poems. I had to find some sanity in the world, and that was the best I could do.

Friday morning I got to work early, after very little sleep. Another day, another....

My glass front door was smashed in. Not big enough to step through, but big enough to put an arm through and reach the lock on the inside, which is what I did. The door was unlocked.

I opened the door and walked in. A pool of glass shards sprinkled out across the hardwood floor, and a trail of scratches and slivers led to my back office, where the door was wide open. I always kept it shut when I was out of the office.

I went to my desk, sat down, and picked up the phone.

Detective Rosa Macdonald was at my office door in less than ten minutes. She had two uniformed policemen with her. I let them into the office, telling them to be careful stepping over the glass. Rosa was in uniform. As she strode in, I noticed again what a strong woman she was, with shoulders like a swimmer's and those dark, darting eyes. Rosa introduced me to the two cops, but I immediately forgot their names. One of the cops got busy gathering samples of the glass and taking measurements and photographs. The other cop and Rosa and I sat down at the conference table. The cop took notes as we talked.

"Any idea who did this?" she asked me.

"None whatsoever," I answered. I had a good idea, but I wasn't going to tell her about it. Marburger had a motive. But that was between him and me.

"Anything missing?"

I glanced over at my shelves of poetry books. "Everything seems to be in place," I said. I guessed he was just trying to scare me. Send me a message. Sell or else.

"Petty cash?"

"I don't keep any in the office."

"We're dusting the drawers just in case." She turned to her assistant, "Steve, go out and get the kit." The cop left and Rosa turned back to me. "I want you to tell me where Carol Murphy is."

"I've told you, Rosa, *I don't know.* I wish I did. I'm worried she may be in trouble, and I want you to—"

"She's in a lot of trouble. Damn right she is."

"What do you mean?" I asked. "What have you heard?"

"You already know what I've heard, Guy. Carol Murphy's vehicle was seen on the scene of the fire at the time that fire was started. Now the car's gone missing, and she's missing with it. She's our number-one suspect. I'm sorry. And if she's angry with you—"

"God damn it, Rosa, that's ridiculous. She wouldn't bust into her own office." I stood up and tried to look tall.

"Why?"

"Because she has a key! Somebody is out to ruin my business, and it wouldn't be her. She's part of the business. That means she's probably in trouble too. Look. I'm being threatened. My office has been vandalized. The books on those shelves out there are all I have left in the world. I want you to—"

"Hush. I'll have your front windows covered with plywood. Now sit back down."

"What for?"

"I'm the cop, remember? Do as I say."

I sat down.

"I want you to tell me where Carol Murphy is and what you were doing Saturday evening between ten and eleven o'clock."

I shook my head.

She shook her head back at me. "Do you have a phone?"

"Duh."

"You have a lawyer?"

"Channing Bates," I answered. "Esquire."

"He's a good man," Rosa said.

"I think so. What's going on here?"

"Guy Mallon, I am taking you in on suspicion of murder, arson, and obstructing justice. I'm going to read you your rights now, as soon as Steve gets back here to witness it. Then I want you to call Channing Bates and tell him to meet us at my office."

"Channing Bates? Your office? *Murder?*"

"I have a feeling Mister Bates will encourage you to cooperate with me fully and tell me everything you know. I'm sorry, Guy, but you leave me no choice."

Chapter Fifteen

"So that's where you were when the warehouse fire started?" Rosa Macdonald asked, her black eyes wide and fierce. "In a strip club?"

"Uh, yeah," I said. "What? That's so bad?"

She shook her head. "And you wonder why your honey skipped town?"

"She didn't skip town. Well, okay, so she skipped town, but that was before I ever went to a strip club."

"Maybe," Rosa said. "But if that's the way you feel about women, no wonder Carol Murphy doesn't think you're worth the effort."

"What are you, a therapist now? I thought you were a police inspector."

She smiled at me as if I were a bad boy and she were the teacher. "My line of work, I deal with crazies. So I guess I'm part therapist. Okay, back to business. So what you're saying is these two men,"—she consulted her notes—"Arthur Summers and Maxwell Black, can substantiate your whereabouts at the time of the warehouse fire. If that's the case, I can't hold you any longer."

"I'd rather you left them out of it," I said. "Call Kitty Katz. She'll vouch for me."

"I should take the word of a stripper?"

"Now who's putting down women?"

Rosa nodded and picked up her pencil. "What's Miss Katz's phone number?"

"I don't know," I said. "But you could go find her at the Kountry Klub."

Rosa drummed the pencil on her pad until the point broke. "You go find her," she said. "I'm releasing you, and I want you to go find this Katz person and have her get in touch with me." She smiled and added, "Your bruises hardly show at all now, by the way."

I ate dinner that night at the Super Rica taco stand on Milpas, then drove down under the freeway to the industrial part of the city. I didn't go to the warehouse, or where the warehouse had been. I went to the Kountry Klub.

It was only eight o'clock when I got there, the sky still full of evening light. I parked the car, walked across the parking lot, and pushed the door open. I stepped into a dark vestibule where a burly young bouncer sat behind a counter. "Tsup," he said. I remembered him from the time I'd been there before.

"I was just wondering," I began, "if—"

"Admission's twenty-five. Two-drink minimum, drinks are five each."

"Is Kitty here?" I asked.

"Who?"

"Pussy Katz," I said.

"She'll be here in about an hour," the bouncer said. He grinned. "You like her, huh? She's a hot chick."

"Yeah. Listen, I don't really want to see the show. I just have to ask Kitty a question. Could you ask her—"

"Doesn't work that way, dude." He stood up so I could see just how tall he was, as if I didn't already know. "You buy your ticket, you go in and buy your minimums, and then you can have a nice long chat with Miss Pussy. She's available for personal dances, private sessions, whatever you want. That's about it. But first...." He held out his hand.

"Aw shit," I said. "Okay, here."

But while I was reaching for my wallet I heard a voice from behind the inner curtain call, "Hey, Terry!"

The bouncer yelled back, "Yeah, just a minute." He turned back to me and said, "Let's go, dude. They want me in there."

"That was Kitty's voice," I said.

"Like I said—"

"Hey." The curtain swooshed back, and there she stood, wearing a sparkly floor-length cocktail dress. "Terry, we got a drunk prick passed out on his table and he's....Guy, that you?"

I nodded. "Hi, Kitty. I need to ask a favor of you."

"Oh, right," she said. "Like I owe you any favors. What?"

"Would you be willing to swear I was here a week ago last Saturday night?"

She looked at me like I was nuts. "Piss up a rope," she said. "Terry, you got to get in there. He's grossing everyone out. He barfed on the runway. You need to toss him out behind." With that she turned and drew the curtain behind her.

"You coming in or what?" Terry asked me.

"Terry, you were here that night," I said. "Remember me? Short guy?"

"You want a ticket? Hurry up, my man. I got a job to take care of in there."

"Would you be willing to say I was here?"

"To who?"

I decided not to say the word "police." "I don't know, to anyone who asked?"

"This place is discreet, man," he said. "We don't share that kind of information, company policy. It's for your own protection. There's the door, behind you. Come back when you're ready to pay your money and see a good show."

It was around ten o'clock the next morning when I left for my office, with a stop at the P.O., where I picked up my mail and bought a copy of the *News-Press* from the box outside. When I reached the office I found my glass windows were boarded over, but the door still accepted my key, and the inside was intact.

I sat down at my desk and began opening mail, most of which was for Carol. I sorted her mail by size, then put it in neat stacks on her desk, along with all the other business that had accumulated for her in her absence, which was now approaching three weeks' worth. There were only a few new phone messages on the machine, and they, too, concerned the business side of the business. I wondered if I'd eventually have to start taking charge of the sales and marketing.

Where the hell was my partner?

Was she safe?

If she was in trouble, was there anything I could do about it?

If I lost her, would I….

I quit thinking. I needed a beer.

I took care of the few pieces of mail that fell into my department, then stood up and tucked the newspaper under my arm. It was eleven-fifteen when I left for lunch.

I went to the Paradise Cafe, where I sat on the terrace, under an umbrella, sipping my Dos Equis and waiting for my burger and shoestrings. I opened the newspaper to see what the world had to offer.

Weather. The hell with the weather.

Sports. Screw sports.

Politics. Who cared.

Page seven:

BODY FOUND IN WAREHOUSE IDENTIFIED

Newport Beach retiree dies in Santa Barbara fire

The body of an Orange County resident was discovered in the debris of a warehouse fire that occurred Saturday, September 9. The man was said to be visiting Santa Barbara for the month of September, staying aboard his yacht in the marina. His yacht, however, has been missing since last Sunday morning, the morning after the fire that destroyed the old DiClemente Avocado warehouse on September 9th.

The victim, Robert Worsham, 72, was a retired naval officer, an avid sailor, an elder in the Orange County Pentecostal Church of Jesus Christ, and the author of a recently published religious novel, Onward Christian Sailors. He was identified by dental records, according to Santa Barbara Police Department arson inspector Detective Rosa Macdonald. Worsham's identity was withheld until yesterday, when Macdonald was able to contact Mr. Worsham's family.

The cause of the fire that destroyed the building, owned by Marburger Enterprises, Inc., is still unknown, Macdonald said...

I stood up and tucked the newspaper under my arm, then fished a twenty out of my wallet. I left the money weighted down by what was left of my beer and left the restaurant, running.

"Because, Mister Mallon, I don't have to tell you dick."

"But Rosa, for Christ's sake, I'm the one who told you who Robert Worsham was."

Rosa gave me a look that was half smile, half sneer. "Right," she said. "He was the murderer, if I remember correctly. And the arsonist."

"Okay, so I was wrong about that. How did you know to check his dental records, anyway?"

"Because, my friend, investigation is what I do. When a woman tells me her husband hasn't been heard from for five days and I have an unidentified body in the morgue, I tend to put two and two together."

"So," I said. "So you admit you called Worsham's wife, which you wouldn't have done if I hadn't told you about him. You were expecting to find him at home, right? I at least put you on the right track, right? Right?"

Rosa Macdonald sighed. "Okay, Guy. What else do you have to tell me? Any other hot tips? Let's have it, because I have a lot on my plate right now."

"Why are you so mad at me?" I asked.

"I'm not. But I'll tell you this: if you start your own investigation again, I'll be mad. I'll be more than mad. I'm running the investigation. So if you have anything for me, let's have it right now."

"First tell me—"

"No, no. Information flows this way. It's a one-way street. We're not swapping secrets. You're contributing to my investigation, and if you know something and don't tell me what it is, you're obstructing justice, and you know what happens when you do that."

"You don't seem to realize that the woman I love is missing, too," I said.

"I'm sorry."

"Don't expect me not to try to find out where she is. The arson investigation is your business. Carol's safety is my business. Don't you obstruct me, either."

She nodded. "Okay, I understand. If I find out anything about Carol Murphy, I'll certainly let you know. I promise. I have to tell you she's number three on the list of people I most want to locate myself."

"And the others?"

She shook her head.

"Roger Herndon?" I asked. "Now that he's among the living?"

"Lucky guess. Now—"

"Fritz Marburger."

She laughed. "Okay. Bingo. Now do you have anything to tell me?"

"No," I said. "Sorry. If anything turns up, I'll—"

"Guy," Rosa said, "be careful. Don't go looking for trouble."

"What are you doing about Herndon and Marburger, not that it's any of my business? Do you know where either of them is?"

"I'm working on it. Please get out of my office and let me work on it. Good-bye."

◇◇◇

I went back to my office. No new messages on the answering machine, but then I still hadn't erased all the messages that had built up since the previous Wednesday, the day before the break-in. So I hit Play and listened through a bunch of duds until I came to the gravelly voice of Fritz Marburger telling me, "Listen to me, Guy Mallon. If you can hear my voice, God damn it, *pick up the God damn phone,* excuse my French."

And the recording continued, a full record of my last conversation with Fritz, ending with *"...if you hear any more on this fire thing, you call me right away. I mean it. You understand that?"* That was Fritz.

"I'm not an investigator. Besides, you're hard to reach. You're never home." That was me.

"I realize that, but I pick up my messages. You can leave a message and I'll call you back."

Click.

The time had come. I had reasons of my own to talk to the man who was so interested in ruining me. A chance, maybe, to redeem myself, if it wasn't too late.

I called his home number, the one at Casa Dorinda, and got the same answering machine message I'd heard every other time I'd tried to reach him. Where, I wondered? Rancho Mirage? Or maybe that bungalow....

That bungalow. At the Biltmore Hotel. He and Lorraine had rented that bungalow for the summer.

A long shot, but if somebody at the Biltmore could tell me anything, anything at all....

I stood up from my desk and went to my production shelves, where I pulled out the original manuscript of Lorraine Evans' novel, *Naming Names.*

I walked into the dining room of the Four Seasons Biltmore with Lorraine's manuscript under my arm. The hostess said, "One for lunch?"

"I'm meeting someone," I said. "Fritz Marburger?"

She consulted a list on her podium. "Mister Marburger? He doesn't seem to have made a reservation. We haven't seen him for over a week. Oh well, no problem, there are plenty of tables. Come with me."

She led me across the restaurant and out onto the terrace. "He and Miss Evans usually like to sit outside," she told me. "Will this be okay?" She laid two menus down on one of the wrought-iron tables close to the garden.

"Fine," I said. I checked my watch. "He hasn't arrived yet, huh? He's usually prompt."

"As soon as he shows up I'll bring him right out," the hostess said.

A busboy filled my water glass.

A waiter offered to tell me the specials and I told him I'd wait for Mr. Marburger.

I let half an hour go by, drinking ice water and admiring the clipped lawn and the topiary camellia bushes. Time's up. I stood up and returned to the hostess' station. "I don't understand this," I said. "Maybe I'm supposed to go to his bungalow. Does he ever order his meals delivered over there?"

"Not usually," she said. "I could call his bungalow and see if—"

"That's okay," I said. "I'll just go on over. I have to deliver this manuscript to Lorraine Evans anyway. What's his bungalow number?"

"What's your name?" the hostess asked me.

"Guy Mallon," I told her. "Miss Evans' publisher."

"Just a minute." The hostess called the front desk and asked if there were any messages for Mr. Mallon from Mr. Marburger. No? What's his bungalow number? 107. Thank you.

"Thank you," I said. "Sorry I dirtied a water glass. This is for the wait staff." I laid a five-dollar bill on her podium and walked out into the tiled lobby, carrying the manuscript in my tight, nervous grip. I'm a lousy liar.

◇◇◇

A dusty DO NOT DISTURB sign hung on the doorknob of Bungalow 107. I saw a maid pushing a housekeeping cart along the tiled pathway and I approached her. "Excuse me," I said, pointing at 107. "Have those people been away long?"

The maid smiled nervously at me and shrugged.

"I mean, have you seen them? Mister Marburger or Miss Evans?"

She shrugged again and shook her head.

"No?" I asked. "When did you last see them?"

"No ingles," the maid told me.

Oh. I smiled at the maid, and then spotted a dark-skinned fellow weeding a flower bed in front of Bungalow 108. I motioned to the maid to wait right where she was, then walked over to the gardener and said, "Excuse me, sir. Do you speak English?"

He looked up, smiled, and said, "Yup."

"I wonder if you could help me out. I'm trying to ask that chambermaid a few questions, and I wonder if you'd be willing to translate for me?"

"Can't," he said.

"Why not?"

"I don't speak Spanish."

Oh. "Sorry," I said.

"That's okay." The gardener stood up and took off his gloves. "What kind of questions?"

"The man in Bungalow 107," I began.

"Mister Marburger?"

"That's right," I said. "He told me to put this package inside his bungalow, but I see there's a 'Do Not Disturb' sign on his door."

"He's not around, far as I know," the gardener said. "Haven't seen him for several days."

"Right. So I was wondering if somebody could let me in for just a second."

He shook his head. "I don't have a key. And you don't want to get the maid in trouble. You could leave it at the front desk."

"No, has to be inside the room. He was very clear about that."

"Have you tried the door?"

"That's a thought," I said. "Thanks." I checked my watch. Two-fifteen, and I still hadn't had anything to eat since my breakfast doughnut.

Yeah, right. Just open the door. But what the hell.

And I did. And it opened.

Nobody home, but Fritz still occupied the place. A pair of slacks over one chair, a shirt on the back of another. A couple of video cassettes on the bed.

I walked across the room and laid Lorraine's manuscript on the teak desk. Next to the phone was a courtesy notepad and ball-point pen. The letterhead on the notepad and the logo on the pen were not from the Biltmore. They were both from The Missing Links Golf Resort and Luxury Spa in Rancho Mirage. I tore a sheet off the pad, folded it, and put it in my shirt pocket.

Then, before leaving the bungalow, I took a closer look at the video tapes on the bed. Two of them.

IN THE BUFF AND IN THE CUFFS!
Starring Amazing Grace, the Bondage Queen

THE ISLAND OF LESBO'S
Starring Pussy Katz as Helen of Troy
Love Goddess of the Ancient World!!

Beautiful packaging. Well, no. Sleazy, but the women were beautiful, or maybe they just seemed to be beautiful because they were friends of mine. And on the back, next to the barcode, the name of the film company: "XXX-Tra Credits. A Division of Caslon Oldestyle Publishing."

Which, if I remembered correctly, was a division of Marburger Enterprises.

Chapter Sixteen

I got to Rancho Mirage the next morning a little before eleven. I'd never been there before, but I had no trouble finding the Missing Links Golf Resort and Luxury Spa; it had the grandest stone gateway on Frank Sinatra Drive. The entrance was lined with stately palms, their shiny fronds fluttering in the fall breeze against a sapphire sky. The mountains in the background looked close enough to smell the chaparral, but all I smelled was the fragrance of flower beds lining the driveway.

I drove past the valet parkers and found a space in the guest lot, right next to a blue vintage Mercedes-Benz. Bingo. Locked my car and walked back to the front entrance, which a uniformed attendant held open for me. I was dressed in shiny brown loafers, tan slacks, and a red shirt with a green alligator on my chest, so I guess he thought I was a golfer.

I didn't bother with the registration desk. I was running out of lies. I followed signs down the hall to the left, which led straight into the one room in the joint where I expected he'd be known. The Good Sport Bar and Grill. Dark wood panels, a wall-sized fireplace, paintings of famous golf courses, rich dark wooden tables and chairs, a long luxurious bar, and wooden stools with red leatherlike upholstery fastened to the seats by brass tacks.

The Good Sport was empty except for the woman behind the bar. I took a stool and sighed as if I'd been on the road for four hours—which I had. The bartender flipped a coaster in front of me and smiled. She wore a starched white shirt with a black clip-on bow tie, and a name plate that said "Roxie." She said, "Howdy. What can I get you?"

"Samuel Adams?"

"Tap or bottle?"

"Draft."

"You got it."

When she brought me my beer I said, "Roxie, I got a question for you. That's your name, right? Roxie?"

"That's right, guy. What can I do for you?" She wiped the bar down while she talked, but there was nothing to wipe. She just wanted to look busy. Still smiling, though. Her short hair was streaked with bleach and her face was leathery, but both effects might have come from life under the desert sun. Her eyes crinkled as if she enjoyed a good laugh whenever she could find one.

"You know a man named Fritz Marburger?" I asked.

She stopped wiping the bar. She also stopped smiling. "What about him?"

"He been in here lately?"

Roxie said, "What's up, my friend? Mind clueing me in?"

I took a sip of Sam Adams. "Nothing, really. I have a lunch appointment with him, and I'm a little early. Just wondered if this was a good place to wait for him." I guess I wasn't out of lies after all.

"He won't be coming in here," Roxie told me. "He a friend of yours?"

Clearly he was not a friend of Roxie's. "Business associate," I answered. She nodded, like go on, and I went on. "He's trying to put me out of business, and I drove all the way here to tell him to stuff it." Which was true, sort of. And also sort of a lie.

Roxie laughed out loud. "Well, you can tell him the same for me. Actually, I already have, so don't bother. Anyway, you won't find him here in the bar. He's still a member of the club, and he's still allowed to stay in the rooms and use the golf course and gym and eat in the dining room, but he's not allowed in the bar for six months, by which time I hope I've found another job. I'm not supposed to be telling you all this, I mean talking about the members and all that, but, well—" She shrugged. "Know what I mean?"

"What happened?" I asked. "Did he make a scene?"

"Shit. Excuse me. *Yeah,* he made a scene. The both of them. She was throwing glasses across the room, and he was yelling at her, words you wouldn't believe, and I've heard a lot of language."

"Do you remember when this was?" I asked. "How long ago?"

"Let me see." Roxie turned around and punched some numbers on her cash register. She turned back to me and said, "Saturday, September ninth. My last Saturday night, thanks to those two. About eleven p.m. They were both plastered, and by the time we got them hauled out of the bar, they'd pretty much cleared the room. I lost a lot of tips that night."

"The woman," I said. "Lorraine Evans?"

"That's right. The singer."

"I guess she's in Betty Ford now."

"That's what they say."

"Maybe I could go over there and have a talk with her? She's a pretty nice person, actually."

Roxie snorted. "Oh yeah, right. Go on over to Betty Ford and ask to speak to one of their celebrity inmates. Sure. Get real. Yeah, she is a pretty nice person, I guess, but that Fritz is a hemorrhoid. God. You want another beer?"

"I better not."

"You don't really have an appointment with Fritz, do you?"

"No. But I'm here to talk with him. He is staying here now, right?"

"I have no idea. But if he's here, he's out on the links. The guy's obsessed. How about you? Do you golf?"

"Miniature," I said.

Roxie shot me a smile. "Go on, man. You're not that small. Anyway, go on over to the pro shop. They got a list of who's out there swatting 'em."

◇◇◇

So I walked over to the pro shop. Sure enough there was a chalk board out front, with the names of the golfers and their tee times. There he was. Fritz Marburger, playing eighteen holes all by himself. I checked his tee time against my watch; he'd been out there for two hours. Not being a golfer, I didn't know how far that meant he'd gotten, but I figured I could catch up with him if I just started walking. I found the first tee and set off at a brisk pace down a gentle slope.

"Excuse me, sir! Can I help you?"

I turned around, and there was a golf cart bearing down on me from behind. The young man driving it wore wrap-around mirror glasses. He stopped the cart within a foot of my legs and stepped out. Tall and blond and tan as a football, he wore pressed slacks and an olive blazer with the Missing Links coat of arms stitched to the pocket. "Can I help you?" he repeated.

"I have to go talk to somebody who's out on the golf course," I explained. "Thanks, but I don't need a ride."

"Sir, you can't just walk out on a golf course," he said.

"I can't?"

"Hop in, sir. I'll take you back to the pro shop."

"But listen—"

"Hop in, sir."

"But—"

"I said get in."

"No."

The young man pulled a cell phone out of its holster, opened it up, and pulled out the antenna. "Security," he said.

"Wait." I took a deep breath. "Jesus, wait. I need to talk to Fritz Marburger. It's urgent. He'll be glad to see me, I promise. I need to give him an important message."

The bouncer sighed. "Okay," he told the cell phone. "What cart is Mister Marburger using? Thanks." Then he punched a series of numbers on his keypad. He looked at me and said, "Your name?"

"Mallon. Guy Mallon."

"Yeah, Mister Marburger? Sorry to bother you, but there's a Mister Mallon who wants to see you, says it's urgent?" He listened to what sounded, even to my ears, like blistering abuse, then said, "Thank you, sir. I'll bring him right over." He closed his phone and shoved it into its holster on his belt, then looked at me and said, "Get in. Sir. He's on the fourteenth fairway. I'll take you there."

"So he's expecting me?" I asked as we bounced along over green hills and valleys.

My chauffeur shrugged.

"And how did you know how to reach him on the phone?"

"All the carts have mobiles," he answered. "Safety precaution. We have a lot of older members."

Fritz was on the green of the fourteenth hole, lining up a putt. The young man stopped just short of the green, and he and I both watched Fritz miss an easy shot. Fritz wheeled around and faced us as I stepped out of the golf cart. His golf shirt was pulled out of his jackass slacks, and there were dark pools under his armpits. As usual, his hair was a thicket of gray that couldn't get along with itself.

"Okay, Mallon," he said. "What's so god damned important?" He turned to the young man and said, "Okay, okay you can take off. I'll bring him back with me."

"Thank you, sir."

"Yeah," Fritz said. We watched the cart hum away in the direction we'd come from, and Fritz turned back to me. "So?"

"Well, Fritz," I said, "I guess you're off the short list."

"Fuck are you talking about? What short list?"

"It appears you weren't in Santa Barbara the night of September ninth, so I guess you didn't burn my warehouse down."

"My warehouse, you mean," he said. "What's all this short list shit?"

"It was down to you or Roger Herndon," I said. "In case you weren't aware, that fire was no accident."

"So that leaves Herndon, is the way you figure it? Well, the way I figure it, it could have been you. Or your wife."

"Not me," I said. "I have an alibi. I had a date that night with Helen of Troy."

Fritz chuckled. "You are one weird duck. Your wife, then. Or was she part of your date?"

"I'm not married. If you mean Carol, of course she didn't do it."

"How do you know that, if you were off someplace else doing God knows what?"

"Carol Murphy is no barn burner."

"Well, it wasn't me, but I could give a shit about that building. That lot's worth more to me than the building. If it was Herndon who burned it down, then I have him to thank, but first I have to find him, which is where you come in. Where is Herndon, Guy? Tell me that. Where is Herndon? You were supposed to be finding that out. Where is he?"

"I have no idea. You're not the only one who wants to know."

"I told you to find him!" Marburger was squeezing the handle of his putter so hard the blade was shaking. His glittering blue eyes twitched.

"And why do you expect me to do that for you, Fritz," I asked. "As a favor? What? Why do you need him so much?"

Marburger sighed. "The man owes me a great deal of money. Why else would anyone in his right mind want to to see Roger Herndon?"

"What kind of money?"

"None of your fucking business."

"If you want me to help you, you'd better start talking."

"Fuck off."

"Okay. I'll walk." I turned. I could see a foursome in the distance, waiting at the tee of the fourteenth hole for us to get out of the way.

"Wait."

I turned back.

While I was waiting for him to speak, we heard a member of the foursome behind us shout, "Hey! Mind if we play through?"

"Ignore him," Fritz told me.

"What kind of money?" I repeated.

"Okay," Fritz said. "I don't know how much money Herndon collected on the contracts he sold, but most of the customers paid the whole thing up front. Herndon bragged to me over the summer that he had sold over thirty contracts, all for over twenty thou, and most of them paid in full, up front. So we're talking over half a mill, minimum, and it could be a lot more by the time that warehouse burned down. He has the money deposited offshore, and seventy-five percent of it is mine. Okay?"

"But how are you going to meet your obligation to publish all those books? Even if you are in on Roger's scheme to produce only one copy per title, most likely the production disks were destroyed in the fire, not to mention the DocuTech. You'd have to—"

"Tough shit. The money's still ours. There's an acts-of-God clause in the contract."

"That's not ethical."

"Grow up, kid. Now. What did you really want to see me about? You didn't come all the way to the desert to talk to me about Roger Herndon. What's on your tiny little mind?"

I took a deep breath and looked up into his face. "Last spring you said you wanted to acquire Guy Mallon Books. You wanted all our assets, you said, in exchange for which you'd pay all our liabilities."

"Yeah, I remember that," Fritz said, "but it's all ancient history by now, kiddo. You don't have any assets anymore, remember? Your inventory burned up, your bank account is zilch, even your office was broken into."

I had him. "How did you know about that?"

"I read the damn paper, for Christ's sake. Anyway, it's a moot point. I have no interest in paying your bills. Now if you don't mind, I want to sink this putt."

"Moot point it is," I agreed. "I can't sell you the company anyway, because it's half Carol's and Carol is incommunicado. Listen, Fritz, you and I both know you never wanted my inventory. You didn't even want those twenty thousand copies of Lorraine's novel. That's not why you made the offer, and that's not why you broke into my office. You wanted my poetry collection. Right? So okay, I'll sell. That's my property, and I need money. I'm afraid I'm desperate."

"I wanted your *what?*"

"First editions? Post-War Western American poets? Limited, signed, numbered...."

Fritz Marburger stared at me with an incredulous grin as I ran out of gas. Then he guffawed. "Jesus, you deluded little doodlebug! Broke into your office? What? And what would I want with a bunch of jerkoff poetry books?"

"That's not what you wanted?"

"Guy, get real. Jesus Christ, poetry books! I wanted your good name, your standing in the publishing community. Why? As a beard, that's all. A cover. So I could make real money financing Roger Herndon's POD operation in the back room—in exchange for seventy-five percent of the profits. Which he agreed to. In writing. You and I don't have a damn thing in writing, and it's going to stay that way. Okay? I don't need your good name anymore, because number one, I'm taking my cut and putting Roger out of business, once I find his ass, and number two, your name isn't worth shit anymore. Okay? Now keep your mouth shut while I sink this putt and play the last four holes. You can ride along with me and watch, but don't try to talk to me about poetry books or the fucking publishing business. I've had it up to here. I play golf to relax, and talking to you is turning into a major chore."

He turned to sink his putt, and I turned and walked away from him, toward the foursome waiting impatiently at the fourteenth tee.

Chapter Seventeen

"Well, in case you're interested, I found out where Fritz Marburger is."

Rosa looked up from her desk, her eyebrow creased with annoyance. "How many times—"

"Relax," I told her. "I tracked him down so I could talk to him about a personal business matter. But while I was at it, I learned that he didn't burn the warehouse down or kill Robert Worsham. Lorraine Evans didn't either."

"Guy, Guy, Guy," Rosa wailed. "Would you please stop watching cop shows on TV?"

"Can't," I told her. "I don't own a TV."

"Okay. And thanks, I guess. So what's their alibi?"

I told her what I had learned in Rancho Mirage. She took notes. I finished with, "But there are still a few unanswered questions."

She smirked. "Oh? Such as?"

"Such as where is Carol Murphy? Where is Roger Herndon? Where is Grace Worth?"

"I don't know yet, but I will. I have Missing Persons on all three."

"Where is Carol's car? Where is Commander Worsham's yacht?"

"I have to assume the car's with Miss Murphy. That's a matter for the DMV. But the yacht turned up. It's accounted for."

"Where, for God's sake?"

Rosa shook her head. "I don't have to tell you that."

"Rosa, have I ever actually interfered with your investigation, or are you just being territorial?"

She squinted at me. "Why do you want to know where this yacht is?"

"Just curious," I answered. "Why don't you want me to know?"

"Okay, okay," she said. "I just don't want you to go play detective again. Can you agree to that?"

"Okay," I said.

"That's a promise?"

"Where's the yacht?"

"It was found abandoned in the Ventura Marina. Worsham's widow has paid the back rent and is having it brought to Newport Beach, where she plans to sell it. She wanted to put her husband's ashes on the boat and have the boat set adrift outside the Channel Islands, but the Coast Guard and the Pentecostal Church of Jesus Christ both told her that was a bad idea."

"Ventura Marina? That's like fifty miles south of here."

"That's right."

"Oh, and another thing. Who the hell trashed my office?"

"We're working on that."

"Isn't that related to the—"

"Guy, we're working on it, I said," Rosa said. "Leave it to us, okay? Please?"

My landlord told me to have the glass door repaired and send him the bill, but I didn't bother. I went to the office for a few hours every day, where I listened to my phone messages and returned calls to book wholesalers and retail stores, telling them all that *Naming Names* was out of print and would not be printed again. I told the media and film companies the same thing. Lorraine had made her wishes clear. No more books, no movie. The only people to profit from *Naming Names* were the collectors lucky enough to have copies of the first printing. The prices on those were rising daily.

All my other titles were also out of print forever.

I also spent a couple of hours each day wrapping and boxing my collection of first editions of post-war Western poets. I knew it was just a matter of time before I would be giving up the office for good, and I wanted to have the books ready for the move.

It had been well over a week since I'd last spoken with Rosa Macdonald. I was finishing up for the day, about to take off for the beach, when the phone rang. I don't know why I answered it.

"Guy Mallon."

"Guy?"

Familiar voice.

"Guy, you there?"

"*Carol?* Is that you?" I sat down at my desk. Carefully, so I wouldn't scare her away. I slipped off my loafers and curled my toes and waited.

"Hello, Guy."

"Carol!"

"How are you, Guy?"

"Carol, where are you? When are you coming home?"

"I am home, Guy. I've found a new home. I just called to see if you were okay."

"Oh, I'm fine," I said. "New home?"

"Oh Guy, I'm sorry. I love you, but I have to do this."

"What about our partnership?"

"I want you to have Channing draw up papers," Carol said. "I'm giving you my half, no strings."

"Hmmm."

"It's the best I can do. And there's something else I want you to do for me, if you wouldn't mind."

"Where are you, Carol? I mean *where are you?*"

"I've moved to Jefferson City," she answered. "Jefferson County. I've fallen in love with this place, Guy. Wait till you see it."

I let that go by. "What was it you wanted me to do for you?"

"I want you to put my house on the market," she said. "Guy, I know how hard this is for you. I love you, Guy, I really do. But you're married to the publishing business, and I hate the publishing business. I can't stand what it's done to you. And Santa Barbara isn't the sweet little town I once fell in love with."

"Whereas Jefferson City—"

"You'd love it up here," she said. "Won't you—"

"I'm pretty busy."

"I'd come home and take care of the sale myself," she said, "but I can't get away. I have a job now."

"Doing what?"

"I'm in charge of the Californiana section in a beautiful antiquarian and used bookstore. Best bookstore in Jefferson County. And you know what? Their poetry section is a mess. They really need someone like you to take over."

"I'll call Vance Halliday and have him list the house for you. How can he get in touch with you? You have a phone number?"

"He can call me at the store. It's Scarecrow Books, 707-555-4261."

"Okay. Just one more question, if you don't mind."

"Yes?"

"As I understand it, you were in Santa Barbara the night of the fire. Why didn't you give me a call? We might have had dinner or something."

"What fire? What are you talking about, Guy?"

"Are you telling me your car wasn't parked in the warehouse parking lot at ten-thirty, Saturday night, September ninth?"

"I don't know," she said. "I honestly have no idea where my car is. It was stolen from my motel the day after I got to Jefferson City. That's why I'm still here. I was planning to go on up into Oregon, but when I realized I had no wheels I decided to take a look around. And…well, here I am. For good. I miss you, Guy. I do." I could hear a tear in her voice.

"Okay."

"I wish you'd come see me. Please."

"What about all your stuff?"

"I haven't worked that out yet. I'll have to sell the house first, I guess."

"I'll give Vance your number."

"Don't let him sell to a developer. I don't want them to turn our house into condos."

"Okay."

"This is very hard for me to say, Guy," she said.

"What is?"

"I'm sorry. And I love you."

"Good-bye," I answered.

"You'd really love it up here, you know."

"Good-bye, Carol."

We had another Santa Ana wind that night. I drove into the mountains, high, high up until I reached La Cumbre, which means "the peak." I parked at a lookout spot, got out of my car, and gazed out over the city I'd loved so much for nearly twenty years, nearly half my life. It was about eight-thirty, and lights were twinkling below me like a basket of jewels tossed on a bedspread of black velvet. Far out on the horizon the Channel Islands looked like a lazy school of planet-sized whales, backlit by the last azure light of day.

There, with the hot wind on my back and the air before me dry, sharp, clear, and hot, I knew it was time to take care of business. I pulled out the yellow pad in my mind and composed lists.

Call Channing Bates
Call Vance Halliday
~~Clean my house~~
Clean Carol's house
Pack
Call my office landlord
Move into Schooner Inn
Call Kitty
~~Call Rosa~~
~~Call Rosa~~
Call Rosa. Yes, call Rosa.

Thinking about Rosa Macdonald made me appreciate how important her job was. Any damn fool, standing up on the La Cumbre peak, with just a gallon of gasoline and a pack of matches from Mel's Tavern and a hot Santa Ana wind at his back, could say good-bye to all his troubles. Pull a Samson and bring the world down on top of his head, killing thousands in the process.

I got back in the car, put country music on the radio, and coasted down to the city I loved, to spend my last night in that bungalow in the East Side *barrio*.

"Channing Bates."

"Channing, this is Guy Mallon."

"Guy, how are you?"

"I am full of hope. I would like you to dissolve the business partnership I have with Carol Murphy."

"Well, I can't do that, Guy. I can draw up papers, if that's what you want, but only you and Carol can dissolve the partnership. Are you sure you want to do this?"

"Actually, I'm sure I don't want to do this. But Carol wants out, and I won't stand in her way."

"I see. Well—"

"Make it simple. Carol wants to give everything to me and walk."

"Give everything to you?"

"I don't mean to be greedy, and I know how much she has contributed to the success of the business, but—"

"What kind of everything are we talking about?" Channing asked.

"My personal book collection," I answered. "Other than that, everything went up in smoke. My debts exceed my bank account. I'm in the hole."

"So by walking away from the partnership, Carol's effectively sticking you with a lot of bills."

"That's true. And since I don't have any inventory, there's no way I'll be able to pay those bills."

"I can't believe Carol would do this to you," Channing said. "I know Carol, and—"

"She hasn't heard about the fire," I said. "She probably thinks I'm sitting on a gold mine. I'd like to leave it that way. Let her think she's doing me a favor."

Channing was silent for a thoughtful while. Then he said, "You don't have to do this. I love you and Carol both. But as your lawyer, it's my obligation to tell you that you don't have to dissolve this partnership. You don't have to accept all the problems."

"Yes I do," I said.

◇◇◇

"Halliday Realty. May I help you?"

"Vance, this is Guy Mallon."

"Hello, Guy. How's books?"

That's one of the reasons I like Vance Halliday: he likes books. That's how I know him, in fact.

"Books suck," I said.

"Sorry about that fire," he told me. "I heard you weren't insured."

"Where did you hear that?"

"You want to know the gossip, ask a realtor," he said. "Actually, Fritz Marburger told me."

"Yeah, well. Listen, Carol wants to sell her house, and she wants you to list it. Will you do that?"

"Really? What are you two going to do?"

"I have no idea what either one of us is going to do," I said.

"Either one?"

"I'm afraid so."

"I'm sorry."

"Yeah, well. So, will you sell the house for her?"

"Of course. But what about you? Do you have someplace to—"

"I'm moving into the Schooner Inn until I can figure out what's next. As of tonight."

"What about your books?" Vance asked. "I guess you'll be keeping that office, so—"

"Only till the end of the month. After that I'm going to rent some storage space until I know what's next."

"Let me give you some advice," Vance said. "Get some insurance on those books."

I told Vance how to get in touch with Carol and he wished me luck.

◇◇◇

"Rosa, this is Guy."

"Guy. Hello."

"I just want you to know that Carol's okay."

"That's nice," Rosa said.

Nice? "I just thought I should tell you so you could stop worrying about her," I said. "Oh, and by the way, she wasn't in Santa Barbara at the time of the warehouse fire. Her car was, but she wasn't. Somebody stole her car, is what happened."

"We know about the vehicle," she said. "At least we know where it is."

"You what?"

"Her car's impounded. It's in police custody."

"What?"

"We have the car. You can tell Miss Murphy to give me a call so we can—"

"How long have you known this?" I asked.

"About a week," she answered.

"And you didn't tell me? God damn it, Rosa, can't you see how much I've worried about that car? And you couldn't even tell me—"

"Guy, I have other things to take care of, too, you know. Now if you'll just have Miss Murphy contact me—"

"Where was the car?" I said. "Where did you find it?"

"It was towed to Love's Auto Storage after it had been parked for two weeks at the Santa Barbara Marina. Apparently it was abandoned there the morning after the fire that destroyed your warehouse."

"And you didn't put two and two together?"

Silence.

"Huh?" I asked.

"Mister Mallon, I want you to know I know what I'm doing. Just because I don't tell you everything I'm doing, doesn't mean I don't know."

"Well, I don't have to tell you everything I'm doing either, then, Detective Macdonald. Fair enough?"

"Guy."

"What?"

"Be careful."

Chapter Eighteen

That afternoon I finished wrapping my poetry books individually and packing them into boxes. Then I went to the house I had called home and vacuumed all of Carol's rugs, swept all of her floors, dusted her furniture, and washed her counters and windows. As the last light was leaving the sky, turning the eucalyptus giants across the street to dancing silhouettes, I went out into the garden behind the house, where I turned on the floodlights and swept up the carpet of wine-red bougainvillea petals that covered the redwood deck. Then I went back inside and packed all my clothes and stuff into two suitcases and a couple of cardboard boxes from the garage. I carried everything I owned out to my car. It was a refreshing discovery: I owned very little stuff, and I was owned by even less.

I finished about eleven. It was another warm, clear, breezy evening. I hadn't eaten and I wasn't tired.

So I locked up Carol's house and went back out to the street and climbed into the car. I drove to Arnoldi's, where I sat at the bar and ordered garlic bread and a bowl of steamed clams. Jim, the bartender, bought me a couple of drinks, after I'd already had a couple of drinks, and I bought him one and he and I played cribbage. He whipped my ass.

"So what's this I hear about you and Carol?" he asked.

"You tell me," I answered. "What have you heard?"

"How were the clams?" he asked.

"Jim, I want to tell you something."

"What's that, Guy?"

"I know who burned down the old DiClemente Avocado warehouse."

"Who?"

"Wouldn't you like to know," I said.

"Not really," Jim said.

I drove to the Kountry Klub and parked in back of the building, next to Kitty's pink Datsun. The back lot was brightly lit, which didn't stop the bouncers and the babes from coming out between dances to share a joint and a breath of hot wind. I kept my head down. I knew I might have to wait a long time.

The more I thought about it, the more obvious it was. A no-brainer.

Then there she was, she and the guy named Terry, standing outside the back door of the Kountry Klub, under the glow of the parking lot light, passing a paper bag back and forth between them, taking sips. Kitty wore a green fluorescent dressing gown; Terry sported his orange Kountry Club tee shirt.

I got out of my car and closed the door.

They both looked across the lot at me.

In for a penny. I stepped forward a few paces.

Terry covered the distance in no time. He grasped the front of my shirt with his left hand and lifted until I felt the cotton bite into my armpits. He held that bottle-stuffed paper bag in his right hand like a club.

"I gotta see Kitty," I said.

"Go home and jack off," he told me. He turned me around and shoved me toward my car. I hit the car and bounced back. I turned and said, "Listen, all I want—"

Whummmph. The butt-end of the bottle, right in the belly. I gasped for breath, then went down on my knees, then fell forward, the heels of my hands grinding into the asphalt.

"Terry, stop!"

I looked up and Kitty was pulling the bruiser back. She squatted down beside me and said, "Guy, honey, you little fool, get the fuck out of here before Terry beats the shit out of you. Okay?"

"I have to talk to you, Kitty," I wheezed.

Her robe parted a bit, giving me a flash of her left nipple and her shaved pudendum. She stroked my head and said, "No you don't. You think you do, but you don't. You're just lonely, Guy, that's all. And I'm just trouble. Not a good combo. Now go on home."

"I don't have a home."

"That's not my problem, okay? Now I gotta go in there and show my titties to a bunch of nice gentlemen. It's been real, Guy, but go away. If you don't, Terry here will kick your butt all the way to Goleta, right, Terry?"

"You got it, doll."

I lay back on the asphalt and looked up into the bright floodlight, trying to focus on Kitty's sweet, troubled face.

"I'll help you find Gracie," I said. "I know where she is."

Kitty turned around and faced the bouncer. "Step back," she said. "Go on back inside. I'll take care of him."

"You sure?"

"I can handle him."

"I'll wait over by the door," he said. He walked away, leaving Kitty with me.

She helped me to my feet and propped me against the back of my car. She tightened the dressing gown around her body and said, "Okay. Where is she?"

"Jefferson County," I answered.

"Gracie's in Jefferson County?"

"No, Carol is."

"I could give a fuck about Carol, Guy. Where's Gracie?"

"I don't know."

"You said—"

"But we'll find her," I promised. "You and I. We'll find her."

"When?" she asked.

"Tomorrow. First thing. We'll get started on it. Maybe have breakfast and—"

"How about tonight?"

"You have to work tonight," I reminded her. "And I have to go check into my hotel. I've moved out of Carol's house."

She turned around and called across the parking lot, "Terry, tell 'em I'm taking off for a few days. Starting now."

Terry walked over to us and glared at me. He put his hand on Kitty's shoulder and said, "Everything's cool?"

Kitty smiled. "He's going to help me find Gracie."

He glared at me some more, then turned on his heel and walked back across the lot and into the club.

"You can just walk off the job like that?" I asked.

"It's not like they pay me to dance," Kitty explained. "I do it for the tips. You can stay at my place. Wait here while I change and get my stuff."

◇◇◇

"So," she said, "welcome to the humble abode." We walked into her Bath Street studio apartment and she switched on the light, which was a soft pink bare bulb in the ceiling of the living room. It was typical low-rent furnished-apartment furniture: wall-to-wall dirt-colored industrial carpeting, a sofa on short peg legs, a coffee table made of imitation oak, a pole lamp, two chairs from different eras and different thrift stores. On the coffee table were a book of matches and several cigarette burns, an open, empty peanut butter jar with a spoon standing in it, and a mirror, face up. Against the opposite wall a metal stand held a television set; on the floor next to it was a boom box. I set my overnight bag down next to the coffee table. The room smelled faintly of kitchen garbage and unemptied ashtrays.

"You can sleep in the bedroom with me if you want," Kitty said.

"You have an extra bed?" I asked.

"Gimme a break."

"Well, I don't want to impose."

"The bed's big enough for two people, and Gracie's not coming home tonight," she said. "Apparently." She turned her attention to the door of the apartment, which she closed, locked, and double-locked, then chained.

"I'll be comfortable on the couch," I assured her.

"Suit yourself." She plopped herself down on one of the chairs and said, "So you want to do a couple of lines?"

Ye gods. "Show me around the place," I said.

"Not a whole lot to see." She rose and led me to the end of the living room, which turned the corner into a kitchenette: two-burner stove, one-bowl sink, and a short formica counter in between with a toaster oven on it. The walls had cupboards and there was a half-sized refrigerator. "This place isn't much, I admit," she said, "but big enough for me and Gracie, and Roger pays the rent." Then she led me back to her bedroom, which was barely big enough for a king-size unmade bed and two end tables that matched the coffee table in the living room. A closet door with a full-length mirror and an unfinished pine chest of drawers.

"Bathroom's in there. If you have to go in there in the middle of the night, be quiet coming through my room, okay? And sit down if you have to pee or whatever, no offense."

"Nice of you to put me up," I said. "I'll be very comfortable here."

"No problem," she said. "You and me have a job to do. You want to order a pizza?"

"I'm not really hungry," I said. "But if you—"

"Me neither. We're really going to find Gracie, right? You and me?"

"That's the plan."

"Yeah, but what's the plan?" she asked.

"Let's go in the living room and sit down," I said. "That's as much of a plan as I can come up with, but it's a good start. Kitty, do you have anything to drink?"

"Just Diet Doctor Pepper," she said. "But we could do a couple of lines, or a doob."

"That's okay. I mean you go ahead if you want, but I need to stay clear."

We went back into the living room and I sat in a chair. She sat on the couch and put her feet up on the table. Somehow she produced a joint out of thin air and picked up the matches. She lit a match and sucked at the flame through the joint, and suddenly the room smelled like college, like my first marriage, like fun. She held the joint out in my direction.

I waved my hand, shook my head, then changed my mind and took the joint, said, "What the hell," toked, coughed, grinned, toked again, and handed the joint back to her, watched her inhale, which was a beautiful sight, let my breath out slowly, whoa that was good stuff, took a long, long look at this sweet slutty porn queen in her Kountry Klub tee shirt so tight I could read her rib cage, and another deep breath while she scratched the underside of her left breast.

"Down boy," she said, grinning. "We got work to do. Your turn."

"I've had plenty."

"Tell me about it." She set the joint, still lit, on the surface of the coffee table and said, "Major planning session. Your turn."

"Okay," I said. "Do you have any idea where Roger Herndon is?"

She squinted at me through the cloud and said, "Newp. Let's talk about Gracie."

"Okay. So where was Gracie the night of the warehouse fire? I expected to see her at the Klub, but she didn't show up."

"You didn't see enough pussy?" Kitty asked, a mock pout on her lips.

"Where was she, Kitty? Any idea? Have you seen her since then?"

Her pout trembled. "Fucking bitch," she said. "She told me she was going to go do a number on that Commander Fucknose guy. She never came home."

"Commander Worsham," I said. "What does that mean, do a number?"

"A private show, maybe the works, and then turn it around so he'd feel like shit. I figured she was going to go to his yacht and promise him the moon, then give him the shaft. She was going to charge him for every feel and make him want to spend a thousand bucks, then walk off with every penny in his wallet. She does this thing with handcuffs, see. I won't go into details."

"Are you aware that Worsham's body was found, well-done, under the ashes of the warehouse fire?"

"I read it in the paper. But I swear to God she didn't kill him. Gracie wouldn't kill anybody. She's, like, nonviolent."

"So you don't think Gracie burned down the warehouse."

"No way. She loves you, Guy. We both do. Everybody loves you."

"Maybe not everybody," I said.

"Aw."

"Enough of that." Carol was the last person I wanted to think about.

"Come on, let's go to bed," she said.

"Enough planning for tonight?"

"I want you to come to bed with me, Guy. I could use a hug. You know?"

"Kitty, I don't really think I could do, well I mean I really like you and you're the prettiest thing since Snow White, but shit, I just don't think I'm up for what I think you might be talking about."

She reached across the corner of the table and laid a perfectly shaped hand on my knee. "You shush," she said. "You got a little problem, and I see a lot of it. We call it guilt wilt. I know how to fix it." She stood up and held out her hand.

And what do you know, I stood up, too and took it.

I made breakfast the next morning, stretching the only egg in the fridge into two omelets with Cheerios, some aerosol cheese, and what was still edible of a couple of bananas. I plated the omelets on top of toasted Wonder Bread and served them with

Tang and Maxwell House instant. I brought the meal to the coffee table in the living room and we took the seats we'd sat in the night before. I wore boxer shorts and she wore panties and a loose tee shirt. Just like old married folks.

"This is fucking delicious," Kitty said. "You're a good cook."

"Carol does most of the cooking," I said. "I just…aw shit. Yeah, this is pretty good, I got to admit." I was that hungry.

"Sorry about last night," she said.

"Why should you be sorry? If I remember correctly, I was the one who couldn't get it up."

"Yeah, I know," Kitty said, "but I could at least have given you a—"

"Let's talk about Gracie," I said. "What kind of car does she have?"

"Pink Datsun," she said. "Just like mine."

"Is that some kind of girl thing?" I asked. "I mean, that's fine, but—"

"It's Roger's trademark," she explained. "Cheapest shit car on the market, but he has them painted pink to make them special. All his movie stars get them. It's like his trademark. The cars are actually company property. Roger's company."

"Caslon Oldestyle Press?"

"No. His other company, XXX-Tra Credits. Company doesn't exist anymore. Roger's retired from the movie business."

"How many women are driving around in these classy automobiles?" I asked.

"Just me and Gracie now," she answered. "Roger's downsizing. Some of his old girlfriends may still have their cars, but chances are they've moved on to bigger spenders."

"What kind of car does he have?"

"Roger? He doesn't have a car. He just drives Gracie's. He's a first-class mooch."

"I already knew that," I said. "Except for the part about first class. Why do you and Gracie hang out with that asshole?"

"Roger's not so bad," Kitty said.

"Why do you say that?"

"He's just…never mind."

"Come on. We're working here. And I'm getting very, very, I mean *very* tired of secrets."

"Let's just say Roger has a good retirement package. Really, Guy, I'm not supposed to be talking about this. You want some more coffee? I can make it."

So I drank another cup of instant and she smoked a Salem and we didn't talk for about fifteen minutes while I put the puzzle pieces I had together. They were almost all there. There were still some missing pieces, and Kitty probably had one or two of them, but for now I worked with what I had.

When I came to the end of my coffee I took the dishes into the kitchen and washed them while Kitty got dressed. When I got done drying the dishes and putting them in the cupboards, I walked back into the living room and then into the bedroom looking for something to read. Anything, even *Cosmopolitan*, but no dice. I almost turned on the television. The answers were starting to form, and I didn't want to force them.

Kitty came out into the living room wearing flip-flops, cut-offs, and a sleeveless purple tee shirt. Her bleached and streaked hair was wet and limp, defenseless. "Your turn," she said. "I left you a dry towel."

While I showered it came to me.

"Ready?" I asked when I appeared in the living room, wearing clean clothes out of my overnight bag.

"Where are we going, Sherlock?" she said.

"DMV," I told her.

◇◇◇

The clerk behind the window at the Department of Motor Vehicles turned away from his computer and looked me straight in the eye. "Do you own that vehicle, sir?" he asked.

"No," I said. "We're looking for its owner, actually."

"We could give a shit about the car," Kitty added, and I bumped her leg with my knee to get her to shut up.

"I'm sorry," the clerk said. "I'm not authorized to give you any information about this vehicle unless you can present proof that you are its legal owner."

I picked up a business card from the tray on the counter. Irving Thomas. I handed the card to Kitty and said, "Listen, Mr. Thomas, I'm asking you to do me a favor. We know who the owner is; it's Roger Herndon, who happens to be a business associate of ours, and we're worried that he may be in trouble. So—"

"I'm sorry, sir," Irving Thomas said. "I'm not allowed to give out such information." Then he turned his attention to Kitty, who was gently nudging me to move out of her way.

I ignored Kitty and held my ground while I reached into my wallet and brought out Rosa Macdonald's business card. I slid it across the counter and said, "I'm gathering information for a police investigation."

He picked up the card and read it, then handed it back to me. "You should inform Detective Macdonald that she'll have to call Sacramento. I'm not authorized to give out this sort of information to her, let alone you."

"My turn," Kitty said.

I turned and looked at her and she was giving Irving Thomas the diamond smile. She nudged me again. This time I took the hint and moved to the side while she stepped up to Irving's counter, which was just the right height for her to rest her breasts upon. "Irving," she said, "where did you get those cool suspenders?"

"They're braces," Irving said, reddening. "Not suspenders. There's a difference."

"No shit?" Kitty said. "Did you know the English people call garters suspenders?"

"Yes, I do know that," he said, his glance rising briefly to her face, then dropping back down again to the comfort zone.

"So I wear suspenders, too," she said. "In my job." She reached into the hip pocket of her cutoffs and pulled out two business cards of her own. She gave me one, and I looked it over as she slid the other one across the counter to Irving, who picked it up as if it were the Queen of Spades. The card had a color photo of Kitty's face in its wickedest grin, with the caption, "I'm Pussy. Want to see more of me?"

Irving and I turned our cards over at the same time.

FREE PASS—ADMIT ONE.
THE KOUNTRY KLUB
Entertainment for Gentlemen

"So?" she said. "How about it? Come and see me wear my suspenders? If you're a good boy you can watch me take them off."

Irving reddened even more.

"Don't you want to?" Kitty persisted. "It's a free pass, man. You can't tell me you're not interested. Hmmm?"

Irving read the card again, smiled shyly and said, "Thanks."

But Kitty reached out and plucked the card from his pudgy fingers. "Irving, baby, first tell this nice gentleman what he wants to know about that sweet little pink Datsun. Okay?" She brushed the card over her nipples, one at a time. And again.

Irving Thomas cleared his throat and looked back at his monitor. "The registration on this vehicle expired two years ago," he informed us. "It was registered in the name of a Nevada corporation that has apparently gone out of business, leaving no forwarding address. If you want to claim the vehicle, you'll have to—"

"Can you tell me where the car is now?" I asked.

The clerk consulted the computer monitor again, then wrote a phone number on the back of yet another business card and slid it across the counter to me. "It's impounded," he said. "By the police department of Jefferson City, up in Jefferson County. Apparently it was abandoned, parked in a red zone where it collected tickets for seven days before being towed. In order to claim that vehicle you'll have to present proof of current ownership, pay the back registration to the Department of Motor Vehicles, pay parking fines, towage and storage charges, and—"

"Thank you, Mister Thomas," I said. "You've been very helpful."

"Jefferson City?" Kitty asked. "What—"

"Let's go," I said. "Good-bye, Irving. Say good-bye, Pussy."

Kitty glared at me, then flashed the clerk one more dazzling smile. "See you, honey. It was nice playing cards with you." She flipped the free pass across the counter, and he caught it in midair.

◇◇◇

I took Kitty to my office and we sat across from each other at the conference table. "Are you ready for this?" I said.

"Are you trying to tell me that Roger and Gracie are in Jefferson City? That's bullshit."

"No, they're definitely not in Jefferson City," I told her.

"Right," she agreed. "Because that's bullshit."

"Look," I said. "You have to be ready for the truth, or at least what I honestly believe is the truth. Okay?"

"Okay." She twisted a bunch of hair around a forefinger and frowned. "What the fuck are they doing in Jefferson City. God damn it, if they're—"

"Kitty?"

"What?"

"Shut up and listen."

"Okay." She quit twisting her hair and folded her twitching hands on the table in front of her. "Okay."

"And another thing. From now on, you stop holding out on me. You tell me everything you know. You can't expect us to find Gracie together if we keep secrets from each other. Okay?"

She pursed her lips.

"Okay?"

"Okay, I said."

"Okay." I took a deep breath. "First of all, forget Jefferson City. They're not in Jefferson City. Gracie was never up there. That's where Carol is."

Kitty rapped on the table with her knuckles. "So that's what this is all about, huh Guy? Finding Carol?"

"No," I said. "I already knew Carol was up there. She told me. I've been wondering how her car got down here to Santa

Barbara in time for the warehouse fire, and now I know. I figured it out while I was taking a shower, and this trip to the DMV confirmed it."

"So where's Gracie?"

"I'm getting to that. When Carol left town, Roger followed her. I don't know how he did that without her knowing about it, with that garish piece of junk he was driving, no offense, but somehow he did. He followed her all the way north to Jefferson County, where he stole her car and left his own pink Datsun, or Gracie's anyway, on the street. He drove Carol's car back to Santa Barbara, where he connected with Gracie. You're not going to like this. Roger and Gracie were working together. They had it all planned. They lured Worsham to the warehouse the night you were dancing for me. They murdered the man, Kitty. Not because Gracie didn't like him, but because he was going to blow the whistle on Roger's vanity press scam. Then, with Carol's car parked in the warehouse lot, they torched the building, hoping the car would be spotted."

Kitty was weeping.

"Then, as soon as they knew the building was about to be history, they got into Carol's car and drove to the marina. I guess they'd taken Worsham's keys and wallet and whatever else you need to steal a yacht. And they sailed off into the sunrise."

Kitty sobbed, then choked, then bawled.

"I'm sorry, Kitty," I said. "Maybe I'm wrong, but—"

"They didn't wait for me," she whimpered. "Why didn't they wait for me?"

Chapter Nineteen

I opened a bottle of 1992 Buttonwood Farm Syrah and poured two glasses. It wasn't even noon, and we hadn't eaten since the makeshift omelet, but I was ready for a drink, and Kitty looked even thirstier. She made a pretense of sniffing the bouquet, then swallowed half the glass.

"Your turn," I said.

She shrugged. "What?" she said. Not like what did you say, more like what are you talking about.

"Your turn," I repeated. "Didn't wait for you to what?"

She drank the rest of her wine, as if it were a glass of iced tea, and said, "Forget it. I don't even care where they went."

"But you know where they went," I said.

"Maybe."

"Where?"

"Who cares? Do you care? I don't."

"Where?"

She put her hand out toward the wine bottle and I moved it out of her reach. "I want to know where they went," I said, "and you said you wouldn't hold back. I've lost a lover, too, Kitty. Your turn."

Kitty looked at me with those sapphire eyes, now shiny with tears, and nodded, holding the glass out again. This time I filled it, and she pulled it back across the conference table toward herself, but didn't lift it to her lips. She took a deep breath and began.

"Roger has this place, this island off the coast of Honduras. It's called Polly's Key. I've seen pictures. It's really pretty, like a movie, all jungly and, like, tropical."

Her nose was a mess. I stood up and walked over to my desk to get a box of Kleenex. I sat back down and slid the box across the table to her. "So you think that's where they went? Polly's Key?"

She ripped three tissues out of the box and let fly with a loud honk. She shrugged. "We were all going there. Together, God damn it. And not till Christmastime. Now here I am, all alone, stuck with the rent, all alone with a dead-end job and a shit apartment, shit...." She began crying again.

When she snuffled to a pause I asked her, "Do you know where this island is, exactly?"

"Not really. It's teeny, like maybe a couple of acres. It's actually off the coast of another island, a bigger island, which is off the coast of Honduras."

"Do you remember the name of the bigger island?"

"No. I'd recognize the name if I heard it, probably."

I went to a bookshelf and got down an atlas. I set it down on the table and opened it up to Central America. "Probably one of these Bay Islands," I said. "Roatan? Morgania? Utila?"

"Morgania, that's it. Morgania. It's named after that rum guy, Captain Morgan."

"He was a pirate," I said.

"Whatever." She looked carefully at the map and said, "That's it, all right. In the Caribbean, just like at Disneyland. Roger says pirates used to hang out on his island. There are still pirates down there, he says, with all that coke traffic. Roger thinks it's all so cool, the fucker. And I was supposed to get to go! We got passports and everything." She wagged her head slowly back and forth. "If I ever see Gracie again, I'll kill her, I swear to God."

"Is Roger Herndon into coke traffic?"

She didn't answer me.

"Kitty?"

"What? How would I know?"

"Is he? Come on, now."

"Jesus. Of course, Guy. What did you think?" She took a deep breath. "It's no big deal, he just buys and sells. Don't you dare tell him I said so, or we're both dead, all right?"

"Worry not," I told her. "What a creep."

"That's another thing I've lost, I guess," she said. "Free cocaine. I guess I'm going to have to work extra hours. Fucking drag."

"Tell me more about the island."

"These Spaniards come up from Nicaragua and Panama and sell him a bunch of shit," she continued, "and then these dudes from Miami or somewhere come down and buy it off him. He's only ever done it a couple of times, just setting the business up, making the right contacts, doing what he calls building trust. He's been going down there three or four times a year, while he was getting his act together. Starting the first of the year he planned to do it big time, dump the business and move down there for good. So I guess he's already made his move, him and Gracie both, those little fuckers. He probably has enough cash by now anyway. He's been stashing all the money from the film business and the book business in a bank in the Caymans. That's what the publishing thing was all about. Sorry if that shocks you."

"You mean I'm supposed to be surprised?" I asked. "That this first-class low-rent mooch, this pornographer, this vanity press swindler, this car-stealing, yacht-thieving, arsonist murderer—"

"That's another thing," Kitty grumbled. "If they're taking that yacht all the way to the Caribbean, they'll have to go through the Panama Canal. Shit. I always wanted to see the Panama Canal. Those buttholes."

"Don't worry," I told her. "They're not going to see the Panama Canal. Worsham's boat was abandoned in the Ventura Marina."

"That figures," Kitty said.

"Why do you say that?"

"That's where Roger lives," she said. "In his film studio. He hasn't made any movies for over a year, but he still keeps it as a crash pad and an office. All his business records, his personal stuff, stuff like that. What a pig sty. That guy has no class, let me tell you."

I thought a minute, then shoved the cork back into the Syrah bottle. I got up from the table and put the wine in the cabinet, then carried our glasses to the sink in the bathroom. I rinsed them out and dried them and put them in the cabinet too. I sat back down and smiled sadly across the table.

Kitty said, "Guy, why are you doing this for me?"

"Because, as I told you, I've lost a lover too," I answered. "We've both been left behind."

"At least you know where your lover is."

"I also know where she's not, which is why I'm so eager to think about something else these days."

"Like finding Gracie?"

"Like revenge. Like finding Roger Herndon and whipping his ass," I said.

"He'd probably like that," Kitty said. "He's way into stuff like that."

"Let's go have lunch," I said.

"Lunch?"

"And then you and I are going for a drive."

"Guy, do you think Gracie and Roger might still be there? In Ventura, I mean?"

"Probably not," I said, "but it's the only lead we've got."

Why was I not surprised? When we arrived at the world head-quarters of XXX-Tra Credits, the first thing I saw was a fire truck in the parking lot. The next thing I saw was three police cars, one of them from the city of Santa Barbara. The parking lot was full of people, and two fire hoses stretched from a fire hydrant on the curb, across the parking lot, and in through the front door of the building. Smoke was hissing out of the broken windows at one end of the concrete structure. The sky over the building was orange-brown, and the air smelled of burning trash.

"Fuck," Kitty muttered. "Typical."

She parked on the street, right behind a parked powder-blue Mercedes-Benz, and we walked across the lot until we came to a policeman who was keeping people away from the building. He was the size of a Buick standing upright on its hind wheels. "Can we go in?" I asked. "We know how this fire was started."

"Off limits," the Buick told us. "Please step back."

For the second time that day I fished Rosa Macdonald's business card out of my wallet and handed it up to the cop. "Is Detective Macdonald inside?" I asked.

"She's very busy, sir." He handed back the card. "Now if you don't mind."

"Would you tell her Guy Mallon has some information for her? I know how this fire started, and I'm sure she'll—"

"Please step back, sir. I'm not going to tell you again." I had to believe him. He weighed more than Kitty and me put together.

"Guy!"

There she stood in the doorway, Rosa in her yellow jump suit, wiping her face with a red bandanna. She walked toward us. The cop said, "You know this man?"

"Yeah," she answered. "He's a giant pain in the ass." But she was smiling, and anyone who calls me a giant is forgiven. She turned to Kitty, gave her the toothy smile, and held out her right hand. "I'm Detective Macdonald," she said. "You must be Miss Murphy?" I could see Rosa looking Kitty over, top to toe. The detective in her, I assumed.

Kitty did not smile back, nor did she take Rosa's hand.

"This isn't Carol," I said. "Rosa, meet Kitty Katz. Kitty, this is the police officer who's been so helpful."

Kitty shrugged.

Rosa chuckled. "So you brought Miss Katz here to confirm your alibi for the night of September ninth? Really, Guy, that wasn't necessary."

"Looks like Roger Herndon burned down another business," I said.

She nodded. "Looks that way. Not much business left in there." She turned to Kitty and said, "I gather you worked for Mister Herndon?"

Kitty took a good ten seconds to decide to speak. She turned to me and I nodded. "He was my agent," she answered. "Still is, as far as I know."

"Maybe he still is," Rosa answered. "If we can find him."

"Do you know where Gracie is?" Kitty asked. Begging. "Grace Worth? Anything about her?"

Rosa turned to me and said, "She's the other one you told me about? Also works at the Kountry Klub, also works for Herndon?"

"That's right," Kitty said. "Do you know where she is?"

"Have you tried Missing Persons?"

Kitty rolled her eyes and gave me a look that said, we're outta here.

I said, "Rosa, you've got work to do. I just thought you might be interested in what we know about the business Roger had in that building, and why he burned the place up. But if we're in your way—"

"Can you make it fast?" Rosa asked. "I'm taking care of a lot of details right now."

Kitty said, "Take us in there. I know all there is to know."

Rosa nodded, turned on her heel, and marched back across the parking lot, leading the way through the cops and the maze of fire hoses.

The inside of the warehouse smelled sooty. "Roger only has that end of the building," Kitty said. "The one that isn't there anymore."

We followed Rosa into the large open area that had once been Roger Herndon's home and office and the studio for the XXX-Tra Credits Film Company. Heavy-duty fans were set up at the near end of the room, blowing the smoke and smell toward the windows at the rear. The fire site was contained to an area about twelve feet by fifteen in the middle of the room. What remained in that spot was a pile of soaking, scorched rubble. The ceiling above the fire zone was black, fading out to gray till it met the walls, which were also gray. A gray oil covered the floor and every piece of furniture and equipment in the space: chairs, dresser, movie cameras, desk, filing cabinets....

Filing cabinets. "Have you gone through the papers?" I asked.

Rosa said, "What papers? Nothing left in the filing cabinets, bookshelves, desk drawers, anything. All gone. He must have built himself quite a pyre, right there in the middle of the room. I take it that was his bed? He slept there, in the middle of the room?"

"His bed, also his movie set," Kitty said. "He made loops. That's mostly what he made was loops. You don't need much scenery for that."

"You were part of that operation?"

"I'm an actress," Kitty answered. "I can show you my résumé. I made a couple of feature films, too."

"Well, it looks as if he also used that bed to destroy all the evidence that he had ever made loops or anything else," Rosa said. "Our friend was quite the firebug. Attila the Hun could have taken lessons from him." She turned to Kitty, not the hint of a smile left on her face, and said, "Miss Katz, I need you to tell me where Roger Herndon is. This is crucial. Where is he?"

Kitty stared right back at her and said, "I have no idea. No idea whatsoever. I wish I knew. I'm worried about Grace Worth."

"Well, the man has destroyed two buildings in less than a month. It's time we slapped him behind bars to await a very serious trial. Murder, too, you know."

"No idea," Kitty repeated.

"Any bodies this time?" I asked.

"No. And no motive. Assuming it was Herndon. Any ideas? Either of you?"

"He wanted out," I said. "Both fires. Burning bridges."

"I thought you said he had a gold mine in that publishing business of his."

"He was in over his head. He had taken first deposits on more books than he could possibly produce, so he took the money and ran."

"Ran where?" Rosa asked.

"We already told you we don't know," Kitty said. "Shit."

"And why did he set this fire here?" Rosa persisted. "Miss Katz?"

"All his business records, all his finances, his contracts, his whatever, were in those filing cabinets."

"So he set fire to the whole shebang?"

Kitty shrugged. "Cheaper than renting a shredder, I suppose."

Rosa nodded and looked at her watch. "Okay for now," she said. "I have to write up my report. Can you two come to my office this afternoon at four? I want to get a statement from each of you."

Kitty said, "We're busy this afternoon."

I said, "We'll see you there."

Before we got back in Kitty's car I took a closer look at the Mercedes parked in front of it. I'd seen that car before. And I'd seen the clothes tossed in the back seat, too. Those jackass slacks.

"What's that smell?" Kitty asked, standing behind the Mercedes. "Something stinks. Like, bad."

"You don't mean the smoke?"

"No. I don't mean the smoke. Like gag me."

I rushed back across the parking lot and walked right past the upright Buick into the building. Rose turned around and raised her eyebrow at me.

"You'd better come have a look in the trunk of the blue Mercedes parked on the street," I told her. "And bring—"

My voice started to choke on a torrent of saliva.

"What?" Rosa snapped. "Guy, what? Bring what?"

"Bring along some of that mentholatum stuff for your nose."

She nodded. "Let's go," she said. On our way out of the building she gestured to the cop, and he joined us as we trotted across the parking lot. When we got to the Mercedes Rosa wrinkled her nose and asked the cop, "Can you get that open for us, Clarence?"

"No prob. Be right back." Clarence trotted across the lot to his squad car, then returned toting a tool kit. He squatted behind the car and got to work.

The trunk popped open and Rosa and Clarence peered inside, wearing expressions of curious revulsion. "What would you say, Clarence? A week?"

"Five days, at least."

I turned away, holding my nose, in time to watch Kitty vomiting on the curb.

It took a lot of persuasion, but I finally got Kitty to change into long pants and a grown-up blouse and go with me to Rosa's office at four. I convinced her to think of Rosa as an ally in our search for Herndon and Gracie. I wasn't convinced myself of that, but it was the only straw I could see to grasp.

"Welcome," Rosa said when we walked through her office door. "Thanks for coming. We have some stuff to discuss."

"Marburger?" I asked. "In the trunk of his car?"

"Yes, that, for one. What was all that about? Don't bullshit me now, Guy. I'm tired of secrets, and it seems to me you know more than I do. Let me repeat: I'm tired of secrets. What was Fritz Marburger doing in Ventura, outside Roger Herndon's studio?"

"If I tell you—"

"Shut up and talk."

"Marburger knew what Herndon was up to," I said. "When I talked to Marburger in Rancho Mirage, he told me he was looking for Herndon, because Herndon owed him a lot of money. They were in bed together on a scam publishing operation, and Herndon had collected over half a million dollars. Marburger was afraid Herndon was skipping town with his share. Which, as it turns out, may have happened for all we know. In any case, Herndon doesn't have to share with anybody, as of five days ago, at least."

"Okay, tell me about this scam operation they had. What do you know about that? Were you involved?"

"How about you answer a question or two for us first?" I asked. "I think that's fair."

"Such as?"

Kitty walked right across the office, leaned forward, and put her fists on Rosa's cluttered desk. "You know where they are? Roger and Gracie?"

Rosa smiled at her. "I don't know where Roger Herndon is exactly," she replied. "He was last seen—"

"Where's Gracie?"

"Sit down, Miss Katz. You too, Guy. Just listen for a few minutes, okay?"

Kitty and I both sat on metal folding chairs and Rosa said, "Thank you." She smiled again at Kitty. "Let me start with Herndon," she said.

Kitty nodded.

"He flew out of LAX this morning at four twenty-two, American Airlines," Rosa continued. "It was a nonstop flight for Miami, Florida, and it arrived on time. We don't know his exact whereabouts at present, but we can assume he's someplace in or near Miami. The local authorities have been informed, and we've got people checking hotels and car rentals. That's the best I can give you on him."

I could see that Kitty's face was about to go Medusa on us, so I asked the question for her: "Was Grace Worth on the plane with Herndon?"

Rosa took her time, then answered, "No. Grace Worth is in the Los Angeles County Jail. She is being held without bail, awaiting arraignment, which is scheduled for Wednesday, October eighteenth."

"*What?*" Kitty cried. "What are you talking about?"

"Miss Worth was apprehended at LAX. She was found to be traveling with an invalid United States passport, and she was carrying about five thousand dollars' worth of cocaine. Her ticket was for Miami also."

Kitty broke into tears. I rose from my chair and rushed to her side and put an arm about her shoulders, but she gave me a violent shrug that sent me back where I'd come from. I was stunned; she was clearly heartbroken.

When she regained her composure, she asked, "And that fucker Roger just got on the plane and left her there?"

Rosa shook her head. "They weren't traveling together, Kitty. She was arrested yesterday about noon. I only just found out about it when I came back to the office and checked with Missing Persons. They had the arrest on the computer. Then I checked with the jail and found out she had intended to go to Florida, so I checked with the airlines and found out that Roger Herndon flew to Florida this morning, as I said. Grace has been in custody since early yesterday afternoon, which is lucky for her in one sense."

"Why's that?" I asked.

"It's a pretty good alibi," Rosa answered. "She obviously didn't set that fire in Ventura."

Kitty rose to her feet and started pacing. "When can I see her?" she asked. Her voice was loud and brittle.

"Visiting hours are two to four p.m. You can see her tomorrow."

"And you don't know where the asshole is, you say?"

"We're working on that. Of course any tips you might have for us—"

"I got no idea," Kitty said, once more. "No idea whatsoever. Guy, I'm out of here. See you back at my place."

With that she left, and Rosa asked me, "Do you believe her? What's she hiding?"

"She's hiding a broken heart," I said. "Not very well, either."

"We'll need more information from her when she calms down. Meanwhile, what's this scam Herndon and Marburger were operating? Sit down, Guy. Let's have it."

So I sat and gave Rosa Macdonald a lesson in the business of Print On Demand.

Chapter Twenty

Late the next morning I took Kitty to Sambo's on the beach for breakfast. We had been up long into the night, making huge plans. Plans for her, plans for me.

Then we had gone to bed together, but this time we were both more realistic about what we really wanted from each other, and after a brief hug that meant nothing more than good-night, we slept. At least I slept. Kitty twitched a lot, and once when I woke up to pee I found her sitting on the edge of the bed weeping. But she shrugged me away when I put a hand on her shoulder, and in the morning she was, or at least she appeared, alert and as ready as ever to keep her quest going.

We sat across the table from each other, sipping our coffee and waiting for our short stacks and tiger butter.

"So," I said. "You still up for it? You're really going to do this trip?"

She nodded. "You?"

"I have to," I answered. "Can't just sit around Santa Barbara."

Kitty said, "What's taking them so long with our pancakes?"

I shrugged and said, "I guess I just want to take a trip. I'm out of work at the moment. How about you? Your trip is going to be a whole lot scarier. Why do you want to do it?"

"I don't know yet. I'll know better this afternoon. But I want to. Why won't you come with me, Guy? Aren't you supposed to take care of me?"

"I would if you'd wait till I get back from my own trip. It will only be a few days."

"Forget it. I'm leaving tomorrow. I don't need a body-guard."

"So you're going down to L.A. this afternoon?"

"I'm going to have to haul ass. I want to be there at two sharp. I'll leave here about eleven-thirty, if they ever bring us our food, and I'll stop at In 'n Out for lunch. You want to come?"

"No. There's a lot of stuff I have to do here. Why don't you come pick me up at the office when you get back to town. I'll get my travel agent to make all your arrangements."

"You sure you can afford this?" she asked.

"What's money for?"

"Here comes our breakfast."

After breakfast I dropped Kitty off and drove over to Carol's house, where a Halliday Realty sign was planted in the front yard. I parked my car in Carol's garage. There was nothing left for me in the house. My suitcases were now at Kitty's place, and my books and the remaining fragments of my business were at the office. I wouldn't need the car for a while.

From there I walked to work, through the sweet flowered streets of Santa Barbara's East Side. Amazing to live in a place where the streets are flowered even in October, even with the first nip of fall in the air. The air felt fresh and alive, with a hint of the ocean in its scent, and the sky beyond the glimmering fronds of the tall, dancing palms was dazzling blue. How could Carol want to leave a town like this, I wondered.

Unless of course you stopped to notice the condos going up on nearly every block. The price of the cars parked on the street. The For Sale signs. The renovations and reconstructions. More and more of them as I got closer and closer to State Street.

The traffic on State Street.

But still—the palm trees, the flowers!

◇◇◇

When I got to the office I sat down at my desk and made a list. I wrote a check to my office landlord to pay for another month, and I put it in outgoing mail. Then I lifted the phone and called the police department and asked for Rosa Macdonald.

"Good morning, Guy. How's Kitty doing?"

"She's better, thanks. She's going down to see Gracie this afternoon."

"Good. If she learns anything about where the suspect is, I hope she'll call me. Or come to the office."

"So how are you, Rosa?"

"I'm okay. What can I do for you?"

"I'm going away for a few days, and I want to know if you think my office is going to be safe. I mean is it more or less likely to get broken into now that there's a plywood door? I don't think my landlord's likely to get the door and lock replaced while I'm away. What do you think?"

"You're probably less likely to get hit with a plywood door, is my guess," she answered. "At least you can't break plywood as easy as glass. Where are you going?"

"You don't still have any surveillance on the building, I suppose?"

"No, Guy. Where are you going?"

"Well, I guess it's not very likely Herndon would come all the way from Miami to break in again."

"Herndon?" she answered. "Guy, it wasn't Roger Herndon who broke into your office."

"No? I've got two enemies?"

"I don't know how many enemies you have," she said. "But that wasn't Herndon. Why would he do that?"

"Because he's psycho?" I offered.

"He may be psycho, but he's not stupid. No, that was a young man named, let's see…Skip Webber. Transient. Talk about psycho. He was picked up two nights ago after he smashed in the front window of Earthling Books. He'd hit the Book Den the night before. Skip has a thing for books, it appears."

"How do you know—"

"Prints match. And we have a signed confession. All three jobs."

"You knew this and didn't tell me?" I said. "Rosa, why?"

"I was going to call you today, as a matter of fact. You're on my list. But this really isn't my department. Skip Webber's no arsonist, just a gentle soul practicing random chaos and senseless acts of violence. He'll be all right if we can get him back on his meds."

"I guess I'm relieved," I said.

"Tell me something, Guy," Rosa said. "Where are you off to for the next few days? You're not going to do anything stupid, are you?"

"Maybe it's stupid," I said. "I don't know if it's stupid. I thought I'd go up to Jefferson City and try to patch things up with Carol. See if she can still stand me."

"You sound conflicted."

"My heart's stuck in a Cuisinart," I said. "I don't know if she'll be kind enough to turn it off, since I'm the one who turned it on. Does that make sense?"

"No, but I wish you luck," Rosa said. "Tell Kitty to call me."

I called my travel agent and made reservations for Kitty and reservations for myself. Then I went to the Sojourner for lunch, then over to the P.O., then back to the office.

I spent the entire afternoon typing into my Macintosh a complete list of my Post-War Western American poets. My first editions. Friends to the end, some of whom had been with me for twenty-five years. Each one had a story. I copied down all the information I had written on 3x5 index cards: title, author, publisher, date of publication, binding, edition number, limitation on the edition, present condition, and whether and how the book was autographed.

I set the list up in twelve-point Baskerville with fourteen-point leading. Then I designed a cover sheet:

Modern Poets of the American West
The Guy Mallon Collection
Guy Mallon Books
Santa Barbara, California
Contact:

I checked my watch: five-fifteen. Kitty would be back from Los Angeles soon. I held my breath and lifted the phone again.

"Scarecrow Books, may I help you?"

"Carol, is that you?"

"This is Carol, may I—Guy!"

"Hi, Carol. How's the book business?"

"Guy, where are you?"

"I'm in my office," I answered.

"Oh, Guy, I wish you were *here*. So much!"

"I know what you mean," I answered.

"Now you're trying to make me feel guilty," she said.

"No, listen—"

"Guy, I've found my true home. I'm not going to give that up and go back to Santa Barbara just because I feel sorry for you."

"Right. So how are you?" I asked.

"Good," she answered. "A little lonely, I guess. But I still love it up here, Guy. More every day."

"Well, your house in Santa Barbara is on the market," I said.

"I know. Vance called me. Thanks for setting that up. Where are you staying?"

"And our business partnership is in the process of being dissolved. Channing will be sending you something to sign."

"He already has," Carol said. "It's in the mail, back to him. I really appreciate your help, Guy, and be sure Channing sends his bill to me, not you."

"Now I have a favor I want to ask of you," I said.

"Anything, Guy. You know that. Anything."

"You're in the book business, right? The antiquarian book business?"

"Is this a trick question? You know I am."

"Carol, I want you to see if you can find a buyer for my poetry collection. The Post-War Western—"

"Guy, no!"

"It should be pretty easy to move," I said. "I'd like to keep the collection together, but if you have to sell the books off to cherry pickers, that would be okay I guess."

"What the hell is this all about, Guy Mallon?"

"Carol Murphy, I need the money," I answered. "That should be obvious."

"What are you talking about?"

"The last time we had that collection appraised, back when we took out that loan, it was valued at sixty thousand. But that was a bank appraisal, so you should be able to do better. You should be able to move it for seventy, maybe seventy-five, keep a commission—"

"Don't be a fool, Guy."

"You won't do it for me?"

"I will if you really want me to. I mean, don't be a fool about me taking a commission. I'd never do that. But I wish you weren't selling those wonderful books!"

"Yeah, well."

"Really, Guy, isn't there some other way we can—"

"It's not a matter of we, Carol."

"Okay." Her voice was beginning to fall apart.

"I've written a complete list, annotated," I told her. "I'll bring it to you."

"Bring it? Oh, Guy—"

"Mail it, I mean." Just like that I changed my travel plans. If talking on the phone was so difficult, I knew I'd never be able to handle a face-to-face. "Make any deal that sounds good. Go ahead and finalize the best deal you can find. You don't need me to okay the terms or the buyer. I'll put that in my cover letter. You won't be able to reach me anyway. I'll be out of town for the next couple of weeks."

"Where are you going?" she asked. Her voice was now soft and high-pitched, the voice of a sad little girl.

Plan B.

"Honduras," I told her.

"Get serious."

"I'm serious."

"Skipping town?"

"You did."

"Okay," she said quietly. "I'll sell your books. Don't worry, I'll get a good price. Have a nice trip. Bye."

I called my travel agent again and changed my reservation.

I typed Carol's name and phone number on the cover sheet of my book list. Wrote a cover letter. Addressed a manila envelope. Licked stamps.

I opened a bottle of wine and poured myself a glass. Another. I had finished the bottle by the time Kitty showed up, and I still hadn't numbed the pain.

Part Three

Chapter Twenty-One

"That creep is staring at me," Kitty whispered to me. "He keeps staring at me."

"What creep?" I asked.

"That one right there."

"He's not even facing this way."

"Just watch."

We were standing in one of those long back-and-forth lines like they have at Disneyland, but this was at the American Airlines check-in counter at LAX, lined up for the seven a.m. flight to Miami. We'd been there since six, after a two-hour drive from Santa Barbara and a half-hour long-term parking process with a shuttle that drove us by a sign that said LIVE NUDE GIRLS, which Kitty had looked at with disgust. "Tacky," she had said. "No class."

"You got the tickets?" she asked me now.

"Don't need tickets." I fished in my jacket pocket and pulled out a sheet of paper my travel agent had faxed to me. "This is our confirmation. They'll give us our tickets when we check our bags. And our seat assignments."

"They better let us sit together," she said. "I'm not sitting next to that creep." She wasn't whispering anymore, but she was speaking softly and her lips were barely moving.

The creep still hadn't looked our way, so far as I could tell. He wore a Hawaiian shirt and was rolling a plaid suitcase. His head was bald on top and gray around the sides, but he stood up straight. Tall, good-looking. His carry-on was plaid too. Maybe that's why Kitty thought he was a creep. Plaid luggage? Maybe he was Scottish.

"Relax," I told her. "Got your passport?"

She fished it out of her purse and handed it to me. "It's a shitty picture."

"That's what makes it official." I opened it and looked at a plain, unsmiling, brown-haired young woman named Catherine Williams. "This is you? Catherine Williams?"

"Guilty, your honor."

"How did you go from Catherine Williams to Kitty Katz?"

"I was always called Kitty," she said. "Roger gave me the Katz. Said it was a good fit, marketing-wise."

"And Pussy?"

"No comment. Look, I'm not ashamed of what I do for a living, okay?"

"Okay," I said. "Okay."

"Speaking of which."

I looked up and the man with the plaid bags had rounded a corner. He was facing us now, and sure enough, he was checking us out. Checking Kitty out. I stepped in front of her and faced the man. I smiled and said, "Hello. Pretty early in the morning, huh? Going to Miami?"

The man smiled back. Tan, weathered face and bright white teeth. Yeah, bald, but so's Sean Connery. "I've been watching you two," he answered. "Honeymooners?"

"No, business," I said. "You?"

"Pleasure. Strictly pleasure. Have a good flight."

"Same flight as yours," I commented. "You have a good flight too."

"I plan to sleep through the whole thing."

I turned around and whispered to Kitty, "He's harmless. Nice guy."

"He was ogling me," she insisted. "Believe me, I know."

"So aren't you used to being admired?"

Kitty shook her head at me as if I were a dumb kid. "They better have coffee on this flight," she said. "Then I'll start acting like a human being. I'm not exactly what you'd call a morning person."

There was coffee on the flight, and shrink-wrapped sweet rolls. The bald man traveling for pleasure was seated several rows behind us, across the aisle, and Kitty looked back often to be sure he wasn't still ogling her; true to his word, he slept all the way.

As we began flying over the United States, Kitty and I quizzed each other on Spanish vocabulary, using a Berlitz phrase book I had picked up in the bookshop at LAX. The words that interested her most were *"taco," "Dos Equis," "dos mas tequilas, mi amigo," "¿Dónde está el baño, por favor?,"* and *"No, gracias, señor."* I learned how to say, "May I have an ashtray on the table, if you please?," "Do you accept Master Charge?," and "It is raining today but not as windy as yesterday. Yesterday was very windy. Where is the hotel?"

We got tired before we'd crossed the Mississippi, and we decided to continue the lesson on the next leg of the trip. Meanwhile, Kitty told me what she'd found out from Gracie the day before.

"She looked like shit. They had her dressed in this yellow canvas suit made her look like fucking Big Bird, and no makeup. Of course Gracie never wears makeup except when she's working but she looked drab and gray, and her eyes were swollen and red from no sleep and crying for two days straight. They could at least have given her a little lipstick or something, and a brush to take care of her hair. Her hair was all greasy and knotted, shit. Poor girl. Oh, that poor girl! Gracie never did anything bad to anybody, and look what those assholes did to her.

"Like Rosa said, they nabbed her at noon when she tried to check in for the flight to Miami. They asked for a picture ID, and she handed them her passport, which it turns out was invalid because it had a bunch of holes punched out of it. I guess that's what they do to passports when they don't want you to use them anymore. I asked Gracie how come her passport was all fucked up like that and she said she had no idea, but it had to be that asshole Roger who punched those holes. Because I asked her about the coke in her carry-on and she broke down and said she didn't know how that coke got in her carry-on, because she'd never owned that much coke in her life before, well maybe in her life but not all at one time, and she was framed, but by who she says. Who, she says. Duh?

"I just let her sit there sniffling for a minute and and then I put my hand across the table, I didn't care if I wasn't supposed to touch her, there were guards all over the place, and said, Honey think about it, who's the only asshole you know who carries that much dope? She knew who I was talking about but she wouldn't believe it. She's all, You mean Roger? Like Roger's some kind of good guy, some big hero, some saint. She's all, Roger wouldn't do that. Oh right, I said, and she's like, But why? Why would he do that? He's the one who's going to get me out of this mess.

"Oh yeah? I go, Right. When he comes back from his vacation? His Caribbean cruise? So she breaks down and says, What's he going to think when he gets to Miami and I'm not there to meet his plane? He'll be stranded. And I just sit there and and then I say, real soft and nice, Gracie, Honey, who's stranded?

"That got her. She's a puddle of tears now, and you know Gracie, she doesn't cry a lot. She's shaking her head back and forth, back and forth, tears streaming out of her eyes, and she says, But why? Why would Roger leave me behind like this? Why?"

By now Kitty was crying, too, gently, wiping tears from her lower eyelids before they could wreck her makeup. "And I squeezed her hand, a little harder than I should of, and looked her right in the eye, and said, Yeah. I said, Why? I said, looking straight at her, Why would somebody leave somebody behind, Gracie? Huh?

"I mean, she left me behind too, right? And was I supposed to pretend I wasn't totally pissed off? Oh man. Oh man. I didn't know whether I was bummed or pissed or stressed or what, or was I just so sorry for this poor baby, my Gracie, just sitting there looking pitiful, the bitch, the poor sweet girl. She's all choked up, she's like, We were going to send for you, we were going to send for you. Well, so okay, I give her the benefit of the doubt, like maybe she thought that was the plan, but I told her, You maybe, but Roger wasn't going to send for me any more than he's going to get you out of this mess. Roger left for Miami yesterday morning, sweetheart. You heard from him yet? Huh? Heard from him yet, because I sure haven't. I'm like, He did this to you, Gracie. He did this to you. Paper-punched your passport, put a bunch of toot in your tote. You're a fucking victim, and how does it feel?"

Kitty peered back to be sure the baldheaded fellow in the Hawaiian shirt still had his eyes closed.

"Don't you think you should have told some of this to Rosa Macdonald?" I asked her.

"Oh yeah, right. Like she's going to do anything about it. She's got the hots for me, by the way."

"Rosa has the hots for you?" I asked. "How do you know?"

"There's ways. You wouldn't know, and I couldn't teach you. It's a girl thing."

"So why not let her in on this stuff about Roger and Gracie? Wouldn't that help Gracie out to have her know?"

"Fuck that," Kitty said. "I'm going after Roger myself. I'm going to give him one more chance to make good on his promise to both of us. Me and Gracie both."

My turn to say: "Yeah, right. Set you both up for life in a tropical paradise, mangoes and bananas you can pick right off a tree, not to mention free rum, free cocaine—"

"Oh shut up, Guy."

"Well?"

"I don't expect him to be kind to us because he's a kind kind of guy, Guy. You know? He only does favors for people when it's really them doing a favor for him, okay? So I'm going to do him a favor. I'm going to not bust his ass, and he's going to help me get Gracie out of this mess, and then we'll call it quits. Okay?"

"Any idea how you're going to not bust his ass if he cooperates, or how you're going to if he doesn't?"

She shook her head fast, as if to clear out the gnats. "It sounds like we both need to get some sleep."

With that she closed her eyes in a manner that was all business.

"Shit, he's on this plane, too."

It was true. He was sitting two rows in front of us this time, and he'd smiled at us as we passed him in the aisle. "Just don't pay any attention to him."

"That's easy for you," Kitty said. "You're not the one he's stalking."

"Buckle up," I told her. "We've got a long flight ahead of us, and we're going to learn some Spanish."

"Did you see the way he was looking at me?"

"*¿Puede enseñarme en el mapa dónde estoy?*"

"I mean, what are the chances of our both being on the same American Airlines flight from Los Angeles to Miami and the same El Salvador Airlines flight from Miami to fucking San Salvador?"

"*¿Que tipo de mariscos tiene usted?*"

"I don't know what the fuck you're talking about."

"Same here. I mean, I understand the Spanish, but there's no phrase book for what you're saying about that poor innocent tourist. Just enjoy the trip, Kitty. How often do you get to travel to the Caribbean?"

"I'm not traveling for the fun of it."

I nodded. "Me either, come to think of it."

Kitty reached into my lap and grabbed my hand as the plane started taxiing down the runway. As we lifted into the air, she lifted my hand to her lips and kissed my knuckles, one by one. She finally gave me her first smile of the day. "You're a sweetie pie, Guy Mallon," she said. "Too bad we're both hung up on different people."

"Damn shame," I admitted.

She put my thumb in her mouth and did something delicious and obscene to it with her tongue, then put my hand back in my lap. "I just want you to know I appreciate you doing this for me."

"Aw, well," I said. "I'm really doing it for me, you know."

"Always wanted to see the Caribbean?"

"No. Well, yeah, but that's not why I'm on this plane. I'm on this plane because Roger Herndon stole my soul. Well, I guess he didn't, really. I was careless with it and left it lying around. But he took it, and I want him to give it back. It will be fun going after him without Rosa Macdonald always getting in the way. We'll nail his ass one way or another, Catherine Williams. I don't know exactly how or exactly why, but it's something to do when you're out of other options. He'll give us satisfaction or we'll turn him over to the war on drugs."

"I got no use for the fucking war on drugs," Kitty said. "I just got a war on Roger."

"It might get dangerous. You're going to be careful, right?"

She grinned at me. "Am I the one who's always getting beat up?"

"Necesito un médico rápidamente."

"I got to pee," she said. "I wonder where the bathrooms are on this crate?"

"Un momento. Veré si lo puedo encontrar en este libro."

"Damn, it's up front. I'm going to have to walk right by that guy."

"Relax," I said. *"Está tranquilízate."*

"Well, he's going to be looking right at my butt."

"You're wearing loose sweats, Kitty."

"I could care less. That man gives me the creeps."

While Kitty was out of her seat, and after she'd returned, complained about the bald ogler, and then fallen into a drooling snooze, I had some time to myself to ponder. Why the hell *was* I making this trip? Did I really hate Roger Herndon all that much? Thinking back over the past few months I realized the thing that made me maddest was that he'd walked into the warehouse the evening we first met him and helped himself to our pizza without being invited and never even thanked us for it. Carol had been furious about that and had expected me to say something, and I never did.

So.

The point is: here I was. I was on the plane. I was doing this thing, this dangerous, expensive, exhausting thing, partly to help Kitty out but mostly to hear Roger Herndon apologize for being a jerk, and to hear him say thanks for the pizza. Anything else would be gravy.

To Kitty's vast relief, Old Baldy wasn't on the Taca Airlines flight out of San Salvador. My relief too, because her paranoia was beginning to freak me out. We relaxed, forgot most of the Spanish we had learned over the past five thousand miles, and gazed down on green jungles. As we descended into San Pedro Sula, the jungles turned to plantations, just as green but with all the thousands of trees in orderly rows. Then the dirty city rose to meet us and we bounced to the ground and bumped along the pitted runway to a stop.

We went through customs and immigration, grateful that all the people we had to deal with spoke English, then settled down for another wait, this time in a steamy, un-air-conditioned airport where the ceiling fans didn't do much to the air current besides stir up the flies a bit. Kitty threatened to take off her sweatshirt, but when I found out how much she wasn't wearing underneath I told her the jail was probably a lot hotter than the airport. She took her carry-on to the women's room and returned wearing a pink Kountry Klub tee shirt. As they say in the porn trade, she was barely legal, and the local men did a bunch of subtle, polite ogling that didn't seem to bother her a bit.

We waited the rest of the afternoon, about an hour and a half, until we were led across the tarmac to a baby airplane. We climbed the steps, entered the airplane, took our seats, and buckled up. Up and away again, this time over the darkening blue water and out toward the silhouette of a long disheveled island. We touched down on a dimly lit landing strip and rolled to a stop in front of a concrete terminal.

We climbed out of the plane and stretched on the tarmac. The air was warm and sticky and smelled like fuel and spice. We walked wearily into the terminal, where we stood and waited until our luggage was laid out for us.

"Let's shlep," I said, when we finally had our suitcases in hand. "See if we can find the taxis. Can you remember how to say, 'Please take us to Pirate's Paradise' in Spanish?"

Kitty gave me a worried look. "Can you?"

"I think you just smile and say 'Pirate's Paradise, *por favor.*'"

"Hey, Cap'n, Pirate's Paradise right this way. Come on, come on!"

We turned and faced a sweet gap-toothed smile on a fat black man with Louis Armstrong eyes. "Yes sir!" he chuckled. "Pirate's Paradise, coming right up. Come on, come on! Gimme those bags, my friend. And throw away that Spanish book, Cap'n. This here's Morgania. It's all English here. All English, Cap'n. All English. Yes sir. All English. I'm Oliver. Right this way!" He hoisted both of our bags and both our carry-ons into his mighty arms and strode off. We had to haul ass to keep up.

Chapter Twenty-Two

Oliver wore a "Dive Morgania" tee shirt, cutoff khaki slacks, and flip-flops. His breathing had a wheeze to it, and his soft chuckle rumbled like far-off thunder. A giant of a man, he barely fit behind the steering wheel of his taxi cab, a rusty old Plymouth Fury with a push-button gear shift on the dash. The back seat where we sat was cracked and patched with duct tape. Oliver drove at a steady speed of about twenty miles an hour, maneuvering around potholes and fallen palm fronds. The windows were open all around and we breathed in the damp and pungent air.

"This your first visit to Morgania?" he asked. "Our historic island?"

"That's right," I said. "It's a beautiful place."

Oliver laughed out loud. "You seein' it in the dark, Cap'n. You seein' it in the dark. Lots of things look pretty in the dark, you know what I'm talking about."

"It's not pretty in the daytime?" Kitty asked.

He chuckled. "Oh yeah. Oh yeah. Morgania is the prettiest place on earth, day or night, rain or shine, year in, year out, it's the prettiest place. You folks gone love it here, you hear? You divers?"

"No, we're here on business," Kitty answered. I elbowed her in the ribs. "Tourist business," she quickly added.

"Thass good," Oliver said. "Thass the kind business Morgania likes. Not funny business. Just nice tourist business. So you folks staying at Pirate's Paradise. You gone like that. Gone like the Pirate's Paradise. Nice place, Pirate's Paradise."

We drove into a tiny village where barefoot black children in torn tee shirts were playing soccer in the road, by the light of one dim street lamp. The shacks by the side of the road were lit by lanterns, and the smell of the tropical air was tainted by garbage and latrines. The kids parted as we drove through and they stared at us silently and solemnly until we were out on the dark country road again.

"So I assume Morgania is named after Captain Morgan?" I asked. "The pirate?"

Oliver grunted and chuckled. "No sir. Everybody thinks that, ain't been here. No sir. Morgania was named after Colonel Morgan, not Captain Morgan. Not Captain Henry Morgan, this island named after Colonel Morgan, Colonel Ben Morgan. Yes sir. Ben Morgan. Colonel Ben. Thass why we speak English, see. Southern English from the American South. Morgania was founded by Colonel Ben Morgan to be a colony of the Confederate States of America. He brought his whole plantation down here to start over after the South got sold out by Jefferson Davis and Robert E. Lee."

"He brought all his slaves?" Kitty asked.

"Colonel Ben treated us good," Oliver answered. "Treated us real fine. Still does."

"But that was a hundred and fifty years ago," I pointed out.

"They's always been a Colonel Morgan. Big house on the hill. Always been a Colonel Ben. The Morgan family still own all the businesses on this island. Everywhere people work, everywhere they spend their wages. Treat us good, yeah. Treat us good. Morgan Shrimp Company, Morgan Fruit Company, Morgan Grocery Store, general store, hotels, bars, it's all Colonel Ben's. First Bank of Morgania, that, too. Yes sir. Treat us good. We're not slaves no more, see. See those lights up ahead? Those lights, all bright? Thass Pirate's Paradise. Morgan family own that, too. Yep. Own that too. You gone love it. Y'all don't dive?"

"We're in the tourist business," Kitty repeated. "Thought we'd do some exploring. I hear there are some little islands around Morgania? Keys, they're called? That's what our friend said."

Oliver said, "Hmmm."

"Polly's Key?" Kitty persisted. I took her hand and tried to squeeze caution into it, but she was on a roll. "You been out there, Oliver?"

Oliver pulled over to the side of the rutted, lonely road and stopped the car with the motor running. He twisted his shoulders around and stared at us. His face was blacker than the night. "Who tole you about Polly's Key?" he asked.

"Friend," Kitty said. Her voice was faint, and I could tell she knew she'd pushed her luck.

"Who? Who's your friend, Missus?"

"Guy named Roger," I said. "We met him in a bar in Los Angeles a few weeks ago. Didn't learn his last name, never saw him again. He said Morgania was a beautiful island and we should come see—"

"Mista Raja," Oliver growled. "He's right. Morgania is a beautiful island, no thanks to his ass. He's funny business, not tourist business. You stay away from Mista Raja, you hear? Stay away from those keys, too. Dangerous out there. Snakes, spiders, poisonous plants, big bats, bad lizards, funny business. You hear me? No funny business. No funny business. Now I'm gone drive this car, but you tell me you're here on funny business, I turn right around and straight back to the airport. I'll have you on the next plane out. For your own safety. Okay? Next plane out."

"Tourist business, Oliver," I assured him. "Strictly tourist business."

His stare was so silent we could hear the air alive with insects. Then he nodded. "Good. Thass good. Tourist business." He turned forward again and got the car out onto the road. "Lots to see on this island," he said. "Plantations, harbors, shipwrecks, parrots, flowers, hills, waterfalls, sandy beaches, then they's diving. Y'all don't dive?"

"Don't dive. We could learn?"

"Yeah, they be glad to certify you at the resort, you learn to dive, rent quipment, dive and see the prettiest fish you ever. Yeah, pretty fish, Cap'n. You too, Missus. Pretty fish. Golf, we got golf, there's tennis, golf, lots of stuff. You want I'll show you all over the island. Whole day, cost you twenty dollars. Whole day, and we stop for lunch, you buy lunch and the beer. Whole day. Any time, you just call your friend Oliver. Yeah. Call Oliver. Well, you two, here it is. Here we are. Pirate's Paradise. Bess hotel in Morgania. Bess in the world. Best."

He drove his cab through estate gates and along a flagstone drive lined with palm trees. The palace before us was lit up like Disneyland, all white and pink, surrounded by floodlit gardens. He rolled to a stop in front of the glass and brass entrance, opened his door, and extracted his body from the front seat. He opened our doors and we climbed out of the back seat. He lifted our luggage from the trunk and placed it on the curb in front of the hotel entrance.

"This is it," he said. "Bess place you ever stayed, for sure." He reached into his back pocket and drew out a damp, bent business card. "OLIVER CAB," it read. "4211." "Thass the phone number. Any time you want a ride, you just call me. I know what you want to see, and I show you. You got that?"

"Got it," I said.

"Got it, Missus?"

Kitty nodded.

Oliver nodded back and handed me the card, then granted us his gap-toothed smile. "You two stay a long time here in Morgania and you have a great time, you hear? Great time. And you got a ticket out, if you need it?"

"Yes," I said.

"I take you to the airport. And if you need to get out faster than that, emergency, something like that, you call me, call me, call me. I get you out. I get you on the next plane."

He wiped his right hand dry on the tee shirt that barely covered his massive belly, then offered it solemnly. I shook the hand, then Kitty shook it. She gave him one of her smiles and his grin grew to reveal a couple of bright gold molars.

"How much do we owe you?" I asked.

Oliver chuckled and shook his head. "All paid for," he said. "Paid in advance."

"What do you mean? Who—"

"One more thing, Cap'n. You happen to run into Mista Raja? You tell him he still owes me for the ride I gave him that one time. That Yankee bastard stiffed me."

I set our suitcases down on the floor and flipped on the soft indirect lighting. "Ye gods," I said.

Kitty said, "Not bad."

Our room had two king-size beds, hardwood floors, teak furniture, paintings of tropical sunsets on the walls, an air-conditioning unit in the window, a cabinet with a large-screen TV and an array of little liquor bottles, a refrigerator, and a ceiling fan making lazy circles. A bottle of champagne was chilling on the round table in the corner of the room, next to a basket full of papayas, bananas, and oranges. We walked into the bathroom, which had a gold throne, two sinks shaped like seashells, a marble tile floor, and a walk-in shower.

Back out in the bedroom I said, "So who gets which bed?"

Kitty gave me a tired but wicked smile. "Oh don't give me that crap," she said. She put her hands on my shoulders and brought her friendly chest in contact with mine. "You know we're sleeping in the same bed. And it's going to be this one, closest to the bathroom, because you get up to pee so much."

"Well, I'm of a certain age," I said. I gave her shoulder blades a friendly going over. She had some knots in there that I planned to untie later. Just being friendly here, nothing nasty.

"So throw the suitcases on that other bed and we'll unpack after."

"After what. Now Kitty—"

"After dinner," she said. "Isn't anyone else around here hungry?"

"Come to think of it, I'm starved. The last thing we ate was that strange, tasteless item in the San Salvador airport."

"And I could also use a coupla three drinks," Kitty added. "That looked like a pretty cool bar. Now leggo. I got to go wash my face and do a few things."

"Oh shit. There he is again."

The Captain's Pleasure bar was on the outdoor terrace, a big circular bar surrounded sparsely by drinkers on stools, all braying like yuppies on holiday, comparing their day's adventures underwater. A team of brawny black bartenders in starched tropical shirts kept us all well poured while they bounced and nodded to the reggae. They also brought us plate after plate of complimentary hors d'oeuvres: nachos, ceviche, and peanuts dusted with cayenne to keep us thirsty. A jolly joint, and Kitty, decked out in a lavender miniature dress that clung to her torso like crepe paper, was on her second coco loco, a hollowed-out coconut full of ice, fruit, umbrellas, straws, and who knows how much rum. I stuck to Tanqueray, which made me think of Carol, but I was too weary to be sad about that. I was, in fact, getting mellower by the minute until Kitty said it: "There he is, Guy. That bald asshole."

Indeed he was, directly across from us. It was him all right, sitting by himself, with empty stools on either side of him. He'd changed into a fresh white guayabera, but there he was, blowing smoke rings at his martini glass. Kitty said, "I'm going to go ask him what the fuck he wants exactly."

"Wait a minute," I said. "Look, it's a coincidence, okay? Let the man have his drink in peace. It's been a long day for all of us, and—"

"Bullshit, Guy. He's stalking us. Not just me. It's not just my bod he's got his eye on. It's the both of us, and I'm going to find out what this is all in the hell about."

But just as she was starting to slip from her stool, the man looked up and caught my eye. He smiled, raised his eyebrows in a slight nod, held out his martini glass and toasted us across the distance. Kitty slipped back into the saddle and said out of the side of her mouth, "Now what. He's seen us."

It was out of our hands. The man stubbed out his cigarette and stood up. He brought his martini with him as he glided around the bar and approached the stool on Kitty's left. "Hello, fellow travelers," he said through a smile made of perfect teeth. "Mind if I join you?"

"Feel free," I told him. I slid a plate of nachos in his direction and said, "Help yourself."

"Thanks, but I'm saving room for dinner. They do this amazing red snapper here, the whole fish, with wine and almonds. My name's Lew, by the way. Lewis Pomeroy."

I held my right hand out in front of Kitty and said, "I'm Guy Mallon. And this is—"

"Catherine," she said. "Catherine Williams. What do you do, Mister Pomeroy?"

"Lew. I'm on vacation. I don't do much of anything when I'm on vacation. I come here for the diving. Do you folks dive?"

"I don't know why everybody comes here for the diving," Kitty said. "The pool doesn't even have a board. I checked it out. Guy, buy me another one of these coconut thingies."

Pomeroy's face broke into a surprised smile. "That's not the kind of diving everybody's talking about, Catherine. Have you ever been SCUBA diving?"

Kitty snorted coco loco out of her nose and slapped him gently on his strong and hairy forearm. "I know, I know. I was kidding, man. You think just because I'm gorgeous I'm stupid or something?"

Pomeroy relaxed his smile into all charm and said, "Of course not." He held up his left hand for one of the bartenders and waved his right over all of our drinks. The bartender beamed and nodded and got to work.

"So Lew," Kitty said. "Don't want to tell us what you do for a living?"

"Can't," he answered, still smiling as if his secret was a sex toy. "Company secret."

"CIA?" she guessed.

"If I were CIA I wouldn't tell you. But I'm not. I work for myself, and I work all the time, but when I come on vacation I refuse to talk about it. Real estate if you must know, but please, let's don't talk about that. I'm on vacation. How about you two? Guy, I believe you said you were traveling on business?"

"No," I said. "Well, maybe I said that. I think I just meant we're not honeymooners. Catherine and I work together and we decided to take a vacation together. We're tourists. The tourist business I guess you'd call it."

The bartender set drinks in front of us all.

"I bet you work for the war on drugs," Kitty persisted. "Am I right?" She took a long suck on her straw. "You work for that asshole Barry McCaffrey, right?"

Still smiling, Lewis Pomeroy said, "Never heard of him. He's probably not a diver. So. You two work together, huh? What kind of business?"

"I just retired," I said. "I used to be a book publisher. But let's don't talk about publishing either, okay?"

"No kidding. What kind of books?"

And we were off and running, chatting about poetry and bridge loans, points and typos, galley proofs and escrow, good neighborhoods and bad reviews, hardwood floors, balloon payments, warehouse space, fire insurance, printer's bills, and Fannie Mae. It lasted through two more drinks, by which time Kitty was ready to do a back flip off her stool. At long last, Lew Pomeroy put down a credit card, shoved my credit card back at me emphatically, and said, "Time for my snapper. Care to join me?"

"No, thanks," I said. "We've stuffed ourselves on hors d'oeuvres. Enjoyed chatting with you."

Kitty said, "Likewise, I'm sure."

Lew said, "Get a good night's sleep. You're going to love Morgania, take my word for it. Good night, Guy. Good night, Kitty."

We had rolled out of each other's good-night hug and I was halfway to dreamland, riding on a cloud of gin and lulled by the slow, soft click of the ceiling fan, when Kitty said, "How the hell did he know my name was Kitty?"

"Huh?"

"That Lew guy," she said. "He called me Kitty."

"That's your name," I pointed out.

"I introduced myself as Catherine. Which is my name. Where did he come up with Kitty?"

"Lot of Catherines are called Kitty. You know what? I'm really sleepy. How about—"

"Is our door locked?"

"Yes. Good night."

"He's working for Roger, I bet," Kitty said. "I'll bet you a million dollars."

"You don't have a million dollars."

"He's one of Roger's goons. Probably here to do a pickup, take a bunch of coke back to L.A. Or maybe Roger sent him out to California to keep an eye on me, make sure I didn't cause any trouble."

"Like what kind of trouble?"

"Like following him here to Morgania and busting his sorry ass for what he did to Gracie, that's what. See what I mean? That Lew dude is tailing us. He's working for Mista Raja."

"Hmmm."

"I'm really tired, Guy. Sorry but I'm falling asleep. Good night, Guybaby." Within seconds she was softly snoring.

I lay there twitching and listening to the click of the ceiling fan, which seemed to get louder and faster for what felt like half an hour before it faded into a soft background pattern and got gauzy, the rocking of an airplane flight, the gentle whirlies of gin, and there was Carol, smiling at me from her desk at the office, smiling and humming....

"Guy?"

I shook my head. "Huh? What the hell time is it?"

"Who do you suppose paid Oliver to pick us up at the airport?"

"Mmph."

"And how come that dude wasn't on our plane?"

Chapter Twenty-Three

"So here's how I figure it," Kitty said, when we had finished our third cup of coffee. The breakfast had been silent, probably because we were both so hungry, but probably also because we were both thinking nonstop about what the fuck we were doing in Morgania anyway. At least I was, all through the cantaloupe, papayas, bananas, sweet rolls, Spanish eggs, and coffee, lots of coffee. "You listening to me, Guy? Here's how I figure it."

I set down my cup and wiped my lips with a napkin. "How d'you figger it, Miss Kitty?"

"That loodood is working for Mista Raja."

"Loodood?"

"Come on, Guy. Stick with me here. It's not like we're on vacation. Lew. Lewis Pomeroy he calls himself. He's working for Roger Herndon. Right?"

"Doing what?" I asked.

"Keeping an eye on us. It's obvious." Her eyes were glittering.

"Kitty," I said, "have you considered how dangerous this is? What we're doing? This mission we're on? We're talking guys with guns. Coke traffic. Pirates are romantic and all, but nowadays they're all business. They're into vengeance and pain. Not to mention local politics, jails, tin toilets, disease....I mean—"

"You trying to back out on me, you little fucker?"

I looked at my coffee cup, wishing there were more coffee in it.

"Huh?"

I looked up into her face, which was on the point of crumbling, and said, "No, Kitty. I'm with you."

◇◇◇

After breakfast we went into the resort dive shop. "Everybody's all dive, dive, dive," she said. "The least we can do is snorkel, as long as we're here. Besides, I want to talk to whoever's in charge."

So we rented fins and snorkels from the weathered hippie who ran the shop. Kitty looked quite charming behind the faceplate of a neon-blue mask. As I was signing the MasterCard slip, she asked the old salt, "Lew Pomeroy been in this morning?"

"I don't know a Lew Pomeroy," he told us. "You folks are my first customers of the day."

"You never heard of Mister Pomeroy?" I asked.

"Newp. Course I doubt if he ever heard of me either," he said.

End of that road, I decided. "So how do we find the best snorkeling spot?"

The proprietor looked at his wristwatch. "You folks staying here at the resort, right? Okay, go get your swimsuits on. Be sure and put on a lot of sunscreen, okay? Okay, be down there at the marina at ten o'clock, that's like twenty minutes from now. I'll have somebody there to take you out, show you the spots, bring you back."

"How much will that cost?" Kitty asked.

"It's provided by the Pirate's Paradise. You might want to tip the man twenty bucks."

"How will we recognize him?"

The shop owner tossed us each a tee shirt. "Put these on over your swimsuits, and he'll recognize you."

"Good," I said. "How much do we owe you for these?"

He grinned at Kitty, then winked at me. "Not a dime. Having you two wear those shirts is better than any advertising I could buy."

◇◇◇

Twenty minutes later we stood on the dock wearing our flip-flops, bathing suits, and bright orange-and-purple "Snorkel Morgania" tee shirts, plus our touristy shades and sailor hats from the hotel gift shop. We looked out across a sparkling blue harbor full of gently bobbing yachts. Beyond that was a bay and on the distant side of the bay were a couple of small jungly islands. Halfway across the bay a spiny brown wreck rose from the surface like a band of Giacometti ghosts.

"Lookee them two," a voice behind us cackled. "Miss Catherine and Mister Guy, my friends already, from last night. Thass right!"

Kitty and I turned, and there was our Morgania cabbie, same Satchmo grin on his face. "Heard you folks want to go round the island, see the sights," he said. "All aboard, my friends, because Oliver's your man. Your main man. Yes, sir."

"Wait a minute," Kitty said. "It's good to see you and all that, Oliver, but we don't want a taxi tour of the island today. We're going snorkeling."

"Yeah, snorkeling. You came to the right island is all I can say, and you in good hands. Good hands. Less go, folks, right this way. Yep, the snorkel express. I'm your man," Oliver repeated, smiling like daylight. "You think I just drive an automobile? Thass my boat yonder. Right this way, folks. Right this way. You just stick with old Oliver. Yep, right this way."

Kitty and I shrugged at each other and followed. Oliver led us to the end of the pier and bowed us aboard a skiff rigged up with an outboard motor.

"Oliver's limousine service," he announced, untying the line that held the boat to the pier. "On land and sea."

When we were settled in the two forward seats, with our snorkeling gear, tote bags, and sandals in the bow of the boat, Oliver climbed into the stern and the boat tilted us up. He grabbed the engine rope and the motor fired up on the first pull. He grinned. "Tug tug chug chug," he pronounced. With that he opened the throttle and we wove our way out of the marina and into the harbor. Oliver guided us through the community of yachts and out onto the bay.

As we got closer to the rusty metal rising from the water, Kitty pointed and said, "Is that a shipwreck?"

"Thass right," Oliver shouted over the roar of his outboard and slapping of the waves. "Shipwreck. The captain was drunk."

"Was that a pirate ship?"

Oliver shook his head. "Shrimp boat."

"Can we get closer to it?" I asked.

Oliver nodded. "Closer, but not close. Too dangerous. Tetanus, sharp. Like a razor, every piece of it. And you gotta be careful where you steer in this bay. Gotta know the channels, yes sir. Stay in the channels. Otherwise, you're a shipwreck yourself. Look like that ugly boat."

It was indeed an ugly boat. The closer we got to it, the larger and scarier it loomed. All that remained was a complex skeleton of ragged rusted metal, about sixty feet long and thirty feet high. The whole thing listed to the side and sat in its reflection, a spiny pool of shimmering blood.

Kitty said, "Gah lee."

"Gah lee," Oliver repeated. "Thass right, Miss Catherine. Gah lee is exactly right. Less get moving. Can't snorkel around here, no ma'am. Can't snorkel here."

With that he turned his boat away from the wreck and headed west, parallel to the shore.

Kitty pointed back to the two silhouettes of jungle behind the shipwreck. "Is one of those islands Polly's Key?" she shouted.

"You don't want to go out there, no, sir. No, ma'am."

"Does Roger Herndon live on one of those islands?"

Oliver ignored the question.

"How does he get to shore?" she persisted. "He's got to buy groceries, right?"

Oliver cut the motor and we bobbed on the suddenly quiet bay. "Miss Catherine, you want to forget all about that man and that island. You hear me? You better off climbing on that old rusty shrimp boat than climbing on that island. You hear?"

She took off her shades and gave him a sparkling smile, with the late-morning sun lighting her teeth like silver-white pearls. "Just wondering," she said. "No biggie."

"Biggie," Oliver insisted. Then he smiled. "Less find you a place to snorkel."

Tug tug, chug chug, and we were skipping west again over the water. Turning south, we left the bay and continued, staying about a hundred yards from the shore. Fifteen minutes later Oliver steered us toward a small cove with a sandy beach. Behind the beach, on all sides of the cove, was a forest of palms. Oliver slowed down and brought his boat close to the beach, then cut the engine just before the bottom touched the sand. We hopped out into the warm water and he and I dragged the boat closer to the water's edge.

"Thass good," he said. "It ain't goin' nowhere. Here you go, Mister Guy." He reached into the boat, behind his seat, and pulled out an Igloo cooler. Then he put it back. "Full of sodas and beer," he told me. "Sodas and beer, Cap'n. You gone get thirsty, thass for sure. Snorkeling is thirsty work. Sodas and beer."

"Thanks, Oliver. You think of everything."

"You got plenty of sunscreen?" he asked.

"We're all lathered up," Kitty said. We peeled off our "Snorkel Morgania" tee shirts and threw them with our sailor hats and sunglasses into the boat. Kitty wasn't wearing a top, and Oliver instantly turned away and looked out to sea.

"I got more sunscreen for when you need it. You can snorkel out there in this little bay. Lots of nice coral, beautiful, yeah, coral. Beautiful." Then he turned around but kept his eyes on the water lapping gently against his shins. "Coral. Fishes, too. And squid."

"It's okay, Oliver," Kitty said. "You can look."

Oliver shook his head and said, "Y'all have a good time out in the water. I'm going over there to the trees and find us some nice coconuts. Then when y'all get hungry, we'll go on back to the harbor and you can sample some local shrimp. Snorkeling is hungry work. After lunch, we'll go the other direction. Yeah.

Other direction." He splashed through the water and onto the dry sand, then trudged across the beach, leaving a wet trail with his broad bare feet.

Kitty and I took the flippers and masks out of the bow of the boat. "You ever done this before?" I asked.

"No, you?"

"Never."

"Then I'll show you how to do it." She snapped the flippers onto her feet and put her face into the mask, then dropped to her knees in the water, fell forward onto her face so that her rainbow-colored hair floated like a nimbus around her head, then stretched her body out toward the open water and began wiggling. Graceful as an otter, she scooted out to sea, her purple snorkel pipe pointing to heaven. My God, she was young.

Nowhere near so young, I struggled with my flippers, falling twice into the water. Finally I got myself into the equipment and followed her lead. Turns out snorkeling is the easiest thing in the world.

And the loveliest. Before long we were gliding over fan corals bright as a garden of summer flowers. Little yellow and blue fish swam with us, surrounding us for a closer look. A cloud of silver minnows flashed back and forth before our eyes, catching the sunlight and tossing it this way and that. And clinging to the rocks on the ocean floor only five or six feet below, cobalt blue starfish glowed in the dappled light. Lazy parrot fish, green and orange, blue and yellow, nibbled at the coral and vanished like magic when we got close enough to tickle them.

We popped our heads above the surface and took off our masks while we treaded water. By now we were far from shore. "Ready for a beer?" I asked.

"You bet."

So we donned our masks again and flapped our flippers toward the sandy cove. When we got close enough, we took off the flippers and masks and walked the rest of the way to shore.

When we were almost there, wading through water up to our thighs, we heard a squawk from the dense palms on one side of the cove. Suddenly two brilliant, blazing macaws flapped out of the trees and flew directly over us on their way to the other side. When they were right above our heads, Kitty tilted her hips, stretched her right hand high into the air and pointed, her smile lifted to the noontime sky. The pose lifted one breast a couple of inches higher than the other, and drops of saltwater dripped from her puckered nut-brown nipples. Her navel was stretched vertical, like the door to a tiny cavern behind the glistening skin of her belly. I saw rapture on her shining face as she watched the birds disappear into the forest behind me. When she looked at me her eyes were moist and bluer than the sky.

"Guy," she sighed, "have you ever seen anything so beautiful in all your life?"

◇◇◇

We were back in the bay, but still far from the harbor when Oliver told us, "You folks got to put your shirts back on now."

"How come, Oliver?" Kitty asked. "We put on more sunscreen."

"I don't mind how much sunscreen you got on, Miss Catherine. Fact is, you gone upset folks if you don't dress nice, hear what I'm sayin."

"Aw."

I got into my tee shirt and said, "Better do as he says."

"There's nothing dirty about my body," she said, pulling the tee shirt over her head and down over her skin. "I'm an ecdysiast, Oliver."

"Well ma'am, you can act easy-ass up north. Down here folks don't appreciate it. I'm trying to get you to some lunch, and if you want lunch—"

"Fine," Kitty conceded. "You said the magic word. Where are you taking us?"

"Colonel Ben's," he answered. "Colonel Ben's Bar and Grill. Serves the best shrimp you ever tasted. Also snapper, also hamburger, also cheeseburger, also peanut butter and grilled cheese, but I do strongly recommend the shrimp salad for lunch. Shrimp salad. Morgan Shrimp Company's finest. The finest."

Oliver brought the engine down to a gentle putt-putt as he negotiated the channels of the bay. He wove his way among the yachts, then headed to the other side of the harbor from the Pirate's Paradise resort. We tied up at a dock at the base of a steep hill, alongside several other dinghies. "This here's the parking lot," he said. "Parking lot."

We stood on the dock and stretched our legs. "Who owns all these dinghies?" I asked.

"Yachties," he answered. "Folks on the yachts. They come here for lunch and dinner. And to drink. Right this way. Yes, they do like to drink."

He pointed to a weathered wood staircase and we shouldered our tote bags and followed him up. At the top was a flagstone terrace with a dozen picnic tables. Each table had a giant umbrella advertising Heineken, but no customers sat outside.

"They's all indoors," Oliver explained. "They serve lunch inside, where it's air-conditioned. Y'all wait here a second, I'll be right back."

He went inside and we took a seat at one of the tables, under the shade of the umbrella, and looked out across the harbor to the small islands in the distance. "We have to get out there, Guy," Kitty said. "I'm having fun snorkeling, but that's not why we came. We have to go confront that stinking sack of shit. That's why we're here."

I nodded. "Oliver isn't going to take us there. That's clear."

"We'll rent a boat. Do you know how to drive an outboard motor?"

"No. You?"

"No, but it looks simple. Starts like a lawn mower."

"What about the channels in the bay?" I asked.

"Channels, my ass," she answered.

"Not to mention we don't know which island it is, and, and Christ, Kitty, we don't even have a plan worked out. I mean—"

"We got this far, and I'm not turning around. I'm not abandoning my Gracie, and you're not abandoning me. Right?"

For her it was all so simple. She loved Gracie, Roger had fucked Gracie over, and she was going to fuck Roger over or die trying, which was more than likely. You don't really need a plan to die trying. Fine for her.

Okay. Fine for me too. I was bumping along on borrowed money that I had no way of repaying. I knew this downfall was my own fault. I had been stupid in business, a dumb risk-taker, vain enough to fall for the scams of Fritz Marburger and Roger Herndon. Marburger was good and dead, but Herndon was still alive, Herndon who cheated dozens of authors out of hundreds of thousands of dollars, who burned down my warehouse and murdered two men, who stole Carol's car and stole Worsham's yacht, who framed Gracie and left her to rot in prison, who welched on every promise he ever made and who still owed me for four slices of pizza. Plus he was a drug-runner. Was I with Kitty? What choice did I have?

"Right," I said. "Of course. I'm with you all the way."

"Good. I knew it. How come Oliver made us wait outside?"

I didn't have a chance to guess the answer to that question, because right then Oliver burst out the door, letting it slam behind him. "Come on, you two. We're going someplace else. Someplace good."

"What's wrong with this place?" I asked.

"No good," Oliver said. "No good. I went in to check on the shrimp, see how it smelled. No good. Smelled bad. No good. Come on, less go. Less go."

"Wait a minute, Oliver," Kitty said. "I have to go use the ladies' room."

"No time for that, Miss Catherine," he told her. "No time. We have to get moving here."

"Oliver, calm down," she said. "I have to pee, okay?"

"Miss Catherine, I think—"

"I should have peed in the ocean, I suppose," she said, "but it didn't seem like a nice thing to do. So if you don't mind waiting for two minutes, I'll be right back."

He did not step aside for her, but she walked around the table and sidestepped him. She reached the door of the restaurant before he did, and then she vanished into the dark inside.

Oliver turned back to me with a scowl. "Cap'n, that woman's going to get you into a lot of trouble. Unless you're trouble, too. Is that what it is? Are you trouble? You told me last night no funny business. Now you tell me right now, are you trouble? Are you funny business?"

I didn't get a chance to answer that one either. Kitty stepped outside the restaurant door and called across the patio, "Guy, get in here. Get in here now."

I stood up and said, "Oliver, I'm afraid—"

He pointed a finger at my throat. "You on your own. I ain't going in there with you. You understand me? You go in there, you on your own."

Kitty walked across the terrace to us and said, "Oliver, we won't be needing a cab anymore. We have a ride back to the hotel. Give him a twenty, Guy."

I fished in my tote bag for my wallet, but Oliver held up his palm like a traffic cop. "Keep your money." He turned on his heel and strode toward the wooden staircase, and we could hear his heavy feet clump down and out of earshot.

I took Kitty by the shoulders and made her look me in the face. "Now you can tell me what you're up to," I said. "What's going on?"

"Come with me," she answered. Her fists were clenched, her eyes were squinty and her nostrils flared, her shoulders were hunched, and she was moving her lips fiercely across her teeth. "Showtime, gentlemen, showtime. Please put your hands together for Miss Pussy Katz."

"So he's—"

"Not just him," Kitty said. "Fuckin both of them."

Chapter Twenty-Four

Oliver was right about at least one thing. It smelled bad inside Colonel Ben's Bar and Grill. I didn't smell any bad shrimp, but I smelled griddle grease, spilt beer, and tobacco smoke in spades. Not that I mind smells like that as a rule; some of my pleasantest memories involve smelly taverns. But I was nervous, and my defenses were turned up to nine. Ready to bolt. It was that kind of smell.

Kitty was all business. She strutted through the lunch crowd, ignoring the swiveling heads and lusty glances, while I followed in her wake. She marched right to a wooden booth in the back corner, then stopped, turned to me, put a hand on my cheek, and whispered, "Guy, you're going to hate me for this. I'm so sorry!" Then she let me see her face morph from angry to surprised and overjoyed. She winked at me twice, once with each eye. She spun around again and faced the two men who were just looking up from their platters of shrimp gumbo, shock on their faces.

"Roger!" she cried. "Roger *baby!* God, *shit!* I've been looking all over for you!" She plopped down on the bench beside him and planted kisses on his flummoxed face, first on the cheek, and then a long wet one right on his mouth. "God! Good to see you, lollipops! Shit!"

Huh? I shook my head to get the gnats out of there, then turned to the bald man. "Howdy," I said.

Lew Pomeroy gave me his Sean Connery smile and said, "Guy. Fan*tas*tic. We were just talking about you. Sit down, sit down. Have you tried the shrimp gumbo here? It's outrageous. Sit down." He wore an impeccable, starched white guayabera.

He moved over a bit and I did as I was told. That put me diagonally across the table from the one and only, whose guayabera was wrinkled and stained and had obviously been washed in the same load with red socks. Kitty was snuggling up to his arm and he was grinning at me with his eyebrows sailing high on his forehead.

"Hey, Guy," he said. "Hey, hey, hey!"

"Hello, Roger," I said. "Burned any good books lately?"

Kitty scowled at me and said, "Guysie, be nice."

I hate being called Guysie. Hate it.

Roger said, "Great to see you. Both of you. Welcome to paradise. I was going to send for Kitty—in fact I was just now making travel arrangements for Kitty and Gracie, right, Lew?—but I didn't expect to see you, Guy. What brings you to Honduras?"

"I came to collect Carol Murphy's car," I answered. "So if you have it, just give me the keys and I'll drive off into the sunset and leave you lovebirds alone."

Lewis Pomeroy said, "This is going over my head a bit."

Roger said, "Whoa, Guy. Back off a bit, okay? Chill out. Have a beer. What'll you have?"

Lew Pomeroy said, "If you folks will excuse me, I should be running along. Guy, Kitty, I guess I'll see you two back at the resort?"

Kitty said, "Aw, don't leave, Lewbaby."

He smiled graciously, then turned to Roger and said, "I'll be in touch. What do I owe you for the lunch?"

Roger waved him away and said, "I got it covered." Was this the Roger I knew? The new Roger? Roger redeemed?

I got up and let Pomeroy out of the booth. He clapped me on the shoulder, saluted Roger, and blew a kiss at Kitty, who answered it with batting eyelashes. I sat back down and seethed across the table at the phonus balonus lovebirds. What the fuck *was* I doing in Honduras? Colonel Ben's was smelling worse by the minute. I watched Pomeroy cross the restaurant and speak quietly to the waitress, a black woman built like a halfback. Then he looked back at us, lit a cigarette, and left the restaurant.

"Well," Kitty said. Her voice was full of giggles. "I finally made it. Gracie couldn't get away, but she'll be here as soon as she can, she told me."

"That's great," Roger said, waving a spoonful of gumbo in front of his face. "It'll be great having my girls back with me. I'm a lucky man, wouldn't you say, Guy?"

"You've gotten away with it so far," I answered.

Roger slowly put down his spoon and wiped his mouth on the flap of his guayabera. The trademark toothy con-artist smile was gone. "Guy, I think we need to have a few cards on the table here," he said. "It's always a pleasure to see you, but it's time for you to tell me who the hell invited you? Exactly why are you here is exactly what I want to know."

Kitty fielded that one. "I asked him to come, Rog. I needed his help. Well, I mean he paid for my ticket is what I'm saying." She turned to me and said, "I guess I used you, Guy. I'm sorry. But we had a pretty good time, right?" Back to Roger: "This little man's a stud. He could be in pictures." Back to me: "Huh, Guysie?" All the time with the big, phony shit-eating grin.

Roger said to her, "How much does he know?"

"He knows you've got this beautiful vacation home. He knows me and Gracie get to come here and spend time with our favorite man in all the world."

Roger nodded. "And?"

"And nothing," Kitty said. "He brought me here, and—"

"Nope," I said. "I know a lot more than that."

Kitty gave me a look. Brief but all business.

Roger squinted. "Such as?"

At this point the waitress arrived at our table with two steaming bowls of shrimp gumbo, which she set in front of Kitty and me. "Y'all enjoy. Beer?"

"Beer's good," Kitty answered.

"Just water," I said.

The waitress nodded. She picked up Roger's and Lew's empty bowls, then left the table. We were silent until she had come back and delivered our drinks. When we were alone again, Roger said, "Eat your shrimp. It's good. And between bites, tell me what you know. I'll be very interested."

The shrimp was good. Delicious. I was halfway done with it before I spoke. Then I laid down my spoon and said, "I know, for starters, that you killed Fritz Marburger."

"Marburger's dead?" Roger asked, his face a false surprise. "That's good news."

"And Commander Bob Worsham. You killed him too."

"That's not true," Roger said.

"And I assume that's why you're on the run."

"Not true."

"So you're on the run for some other reason, is that what you're saying?"

"It's not true that I killed that asshole Worsham. I'm not sorry he's dead, but I didn't kill him. Marburger either. I mean that. I don't kill people. I've never killed anybody in my life."

"Then who did?" I asked. "Maybe it doesn't matter who killed Worsham, I hated the guy, but—"

"Gracie," Roger answered. "Grace Worth killed Commander Robert Worsham. And she did it for you, by the way."

Kitty told me, "It's true, Guy. She told me that last time I saw her." Meaning, I guess, when Kitty visited her in jail. "She didn't actually mean to kill him. So it wasn't, like, murder."

I tried to take a bite of my shrimp, but I wasn't hungry anymore. Kitty had stopped eating too. "Anybody want to fill me in on this?" I asked. "As long as we're telling secrets?"

Roger was chuckling to himself. Then he shared his mirth: "Gracie and her god damned handcuffs!"

Kitty explained it to me. "That night you came to the Kountry Club? Well, Worsham had been around earlier that evening, and he wanted Gracie to give him a private. She told him she couldn't do it in the club, but she'd do it for him over in the warehouse. That was the first time he realized that this stripper he was panting after was the same girl he'd been stalking that day you first met him. So anyway, I drove the two of them over there and dropped them off and came back to the club. I guess Gracie took him back to Roger's office and handcuffed the stupid asshole to the chair. Then she did her thing."

"Her thing?"

"Yeah, well she does a pretty sensational lap dance where she, it's kind of hard to explain, but she's nude, right? His hands are cuffed behind the chair, so he can't get weird on her, and she kind of gets really close to the guy's face, I mean like, you know, close. So she had him in this position, this holier-than-thou, self-righteous Jesus freak, and I guess the commander probably thought he'd died and gone to heaven, which as it turned out was exactly what happened. The dying part anyway. I guess he had a heart attack or a stroke or something, I don't know, but the point is he died while she was dancing for him."

"Dancing?" I said. "You call it dancing?"

"Whatever."

"You never told me this before."

"Whatever."

We were silent until Roger contributed his role in the show. "And that's how I found him. By the time I got there, the poor man was dead, with his tongue hanging out of his mouth and his fly open. Gracie was dressed and crying. She was a mess."

"Then what?" I asked.

Roger shrugged. "We had to get out of there. I mean the poor girl was in trouble, and she was, well, in trouble. I take care of my girls, right?" He put his arm around Kitty's shoulders and gave her a squeeze.

"So you burned down the warehouse?" I said.

"Maybe not a smart idea," Roger admitted, "but Gracie was in trouble. I was taking care of business. I gave up a lot by burning that place down. I had a good business going there. But I take care of my girls. We had to get Gracie out of there, and we couldn't leave any evidence."

"So you stole Worsham's keys and wallet."

"Well what the fuck? He wasn't going to use them anymore," Roger said.

"And left your belt behind, right? So people would figure the dead guy was you? Left your belt buckle behind? No evidence? Yeah, right."

Roger chuckled. "I miss that belt buckle. Solid Monel."

"And jumped into Carol's car," I said. "And drove down to the marina."

Roger shrugged.

"Carol's car," I repeated. "Which you stole."

"Aw shut the fuck up," Roger shot back at me. "Mister Do-No-Wrong. That was between me and Carol Murphy, nothing to do with you. I didn't steal *your* car."

"But you did steal Carol's."

Kitty said, "Guy, give it a rest."

"Fuck that," I said. Fuck Roger and fuck Kitty too.

Roger reached in front of Kitty and grabbed what was left of her beer. He drank it dry, then slammed the bottle on the table. "You don't know jack shit," he told me.

"Okay," I said. "Tell me jack shit. I'm all ears."

"I know you love that menopausal bitch," Roger said. "The divine Miss Murphy. But she'd been busting my balls since day one. Day one. Okay?" His freckles were florid, and his upper lip was twitching with anger. "Every step of the way, calling me names, making these snide remarks about the way I do business. Well, I put up with it. Neighbors and all. Why not. And then I realized she was busting your balls, too, man. You poor pussy-whipped little fart, she was taking you for a ride on the nutcracker seat, and you didn't even know it. Okay, so I took her car, but shit, man, I was practically doing you a favor. You know what happened? Okay, I'll tell you what happened. I guess you told her about the business deal we had, where I was going to produce that book for you, one copy? So Carol calls me up and threatens me. Says if I do that DocuTech job for you she'll make me sorry. Expose my ass to the world. Tell all my clients I'm a crook, shit like that. I told her to fuck off, the business deal was between you and I, and she had nothing to do with it. She said okay then, fuck the both of you, meaning the both of us, you and me, pal. She had no use for either one of us. Said she was leaving town, and neither one of us crooks—she called us both crooks, what a bitch!—would ever see her again. Listen, Guy, listen to me. I was, like, doing you a favor. Okay?"

The waitress showed up. "You folks doing okay?"

"Beer," I said. "Whatever you got."

Roger said, "Me, too. Kitty?"

"Yeah."

"Beers all around," Roger said.

The waitress nodded, left, returned, and placed three bottles on the table. I noticed that we were the only ones left in Colonel Ben's Bar & Grill.

"Okay?" Roger asked, holding out his bottle for me to clink. "Friends?"

I ignored the offer. "That doesn't explain why you drove six hundred miles to steal Carol's car."

Roger nodded. "Good point. Well, I was following her, and that was the first chance she gave me. Look, I was pissed, okay? Pissed off. Maybe it was a dumb thing to do, but—"

"Or maybe it was smart. Maybe you were planning to burn down the warehouse anyway, make a run for it. Maybe you wanted Carol's car to be seen in the parking lot at the time the fire was set. Maybe you were glad to leave Carol's car in the marina parking lot when you stole Worsham's yacht."

He grinned back at me. "I'm not saying you're right, but think about it, Guy. The bitch had a lot of motives for burning that warehouse to the ground. She hated that warehouse from day one. As far as I could see, she hated your company, she hated the publishing business, and—I'm sorry to say it, but it's true—she hated you, too. She hated your sorry ass. My friend, you're not going to like this, but I was doing you a favor. Carol Murphy was bad news, and you're lucky to be rid of her."

Minutes passed silently. For all I could tell, Kitty was giving Roger a hand job under the table. At some point I realized that

I had finished my beer and the waitress had replaced it with another.

Kitty spoke, "Well. So Rogerbaby, what are we going to do about Gracie?"

Roger nodded, his face grave. The concerned fatherly bit. "Pomeroy told me what happened to poor Gracie. You heard? She got caught carrying some blow in her purse or something. Poor girl. I told her not to travel with drugs, but I guess she didn't listen or didn't hear or I don't know what. Jesus, poor dumb Gracie. Well, no problem. Lew's going to take care of it. I'm sending him back there to L.A. with plenty of money to bail her out. Then we'll get her down here, and no problem. I'll have my girls back with me again. No problem."

"So you have plenty of money to bail her out?" I asked. "I heard she was being held without bail."

"That's not what Pomeroy told me. He said a hundred thou would do it."

"You have a hundred thou?" Kitty asked.

"I will have tomorrow. I have some irons in the fire."

"That's a lot of money," I observed.

"Nothing's too much for my girls."

Kitty kissed his cheek. "I love you, Daddy," she said. "I love you to death."

He grinned.

"Me and Gracie are going to make you so happy," Kitty said. "So happy. You'll see."

"So Guy," Roger said to me. "How long you sticking around here in Morgania?"

"I'm leaving tomorrow," I said. "I've about had it." I looked across the table and they both seemed pleased to hear my plans. *Both.* "What about you, Kitty? I'm going back to the Pirate's Paradise and pack. Kitty, are you coming with me, or…what?"

"I guess I better come with you and get my stuff," she answered. "I'll spend the night in the resort, then Roger can pick me up tomorrow morning. Okay, Rog?"

"You got it, babe."

"I hope you're not mad at me, Guysie," she said. "I mean I really did enjoy spending time with you, and shit I'm so grateful to you for bringing me here, but now I have to stay with Roger. He's going to get Gracie out of jail."

"Right."

"You're not mad?"

"Let's go," I said.

"How are we going to get there?" she wondered. "Oliver left us stranded."

"I'll take you over there," Roger said. "I have a skiff tied up down below. No problem."

The waitress appeared. "That be all?"

"That'll do it," Roger told her. "Just put it on my tab, Dolly."

"I can't do that, Mista Raja," she said. "Colonel Morgan says your tab's too high."

"Aw, come on, Dolly, Christ's sake, give me a break."

She shook her head. "The Colonel says you have to pay it off before you get any more credit." She held out her big pink palm and said, "Cash. I told you this the last time, Mista Raja," Dolly said. "Yesterday in fact."

Roger threw her an irate glance and muttered, "Pay the lady, Guy, and let's get out of this dump."

"Forget it," I said. "You still owe me for four slices of pizza." I stood up and walked across the empty restaurant to the door and stepped out into the bright sunlight of late afternoon. They joined me a few moments later. I don't know how Roger talked his way out of that one.

As we descended the rickety wooden staircase, Roger pointed out across the harbor at the green islands on the horizon. "The one on the right," he said. "There she is, folks. Polly's Key." He put his arm around Kitty's shoulder. "Our little piece of paradise."

She squirmed with joy against his rib cage.

I wanted to shove the both of them down the stairs, but I held my fire.

Roger's skiff was not as classy as Oliver's, but it was floating, and we needed a ride. We climbed in and put our tote bags in the bow. We sat on a seat together, facing Roger, who got the outboard motor started after four violent pulls on the frayed rope. He gave the engine too much gas, and we took off like a rocket, caroming off two other skiffs until we were out in the harbor.

When we were halfway across the harbor, before we reached the community of yachts, Roger said, "I'd like to stop by my place first, if you don't mind."

I said, "No, thanks."

"I insist. I'd like to show you guys around." He grinned and reached out to lay a freckled hand on Kitty's knee. "Your new home."

"Wait a minute."

"I'm in the driver's seat," Roger reminded me. "Sit back and relax."

Chapter Twenty-Five

"So Guy," Roger said, "you ready for another?"

"Okay." I held up my empty glass and he walked across the deck to take it from me.

"You want some Coke with it this time?" he asked. "Rum and Coke?"

"No. On the rocks is fine."

Kitty, sitting in the other deck chair, the one next to Roger's deck chair, said, "I, on the other hand, would just love to have some coke, if you have any."

Roger threw his head back and laughed.

"Oops," Kitty said. "Maybe I should keep my voice down?"

"Don't worry, babe," he told her. "Nobody hears a thing out here. Not a damn thing. You could have a brass band out here and nobody would know it. Fire a bazooka, whatever. That's what I love about this place. Privacy. You two sit tight and I'll go inside and get some more refreshments."

"Thanks, Lollipops. You're so sweet!"

While Roger was inside I stood up and walked over to the rail and looked down on the jungle floor. Roger's house was on stilts, so I was looking down twenty feet to a bed of natural color, dark red and purple flowers growing amok, with no names and no tending, just feasting on the wet earth and filtered sunlight of late afternoon. A warm, damp breeze was picking up, and the world smelled of glorious rot. Puke.

Kitty approached me and put her hand on my shoulder. "You hate me, don't you, Guy?" she said. "Please don't hate me. I had to do this."

I turned to her and shook my head. "I don't understand," I said. "I thought we were friends."

She smiled sadly, but without tears. "I belong here with Roger."

"Why? What do you see in that cheap, low-rent con man?"

"You don't get it, do you, Guy?"

"No. Tell me. What does Roger Herndon have that's the least bit appealing to you? *What?*"

The smile left her face and her answer was clear and no-nonsense: "Cocaine. I happen to like cocaine. Okay?"

"What about Gracie?"

"What about her?"

"You're just abandoning her? She's going to go to trial and live the rest of her sad life in—"

"Oh don't be ridiculous," she snapped. "Roger will get her out. He's waiting for the money to get here tomorrow, and then he's sending Lew back to L.A. to bail her out and bring her here. No problem."

"And you believe that."

"Shut up, Guy."

"Stupid," I said. "You're being stupid."

"I said, shut up. You *shut up.*"

We walked back to our deck chairs and sat down. "And what about me?" I asked.

"I like you a lot, Guy Mallon, and I'm really grateful to you for bringing me here. But it's time for you to go back to L.A. tomorrow with Lew Pomeroy. And you can forget all about me, and about Gracie and Roger, and just think about something else, okay? Think about Carol. Maybe you can find her and get her to come back to you. Whatever."

Roger came out on the deck and said, "Refreshments are in the house. I made us some treats. It's getting too breezy out here on the deck. I'm afraid one of the treats might get blown away."

He grinned and Kitty gave him a little squeal. We followed him into the house.

We sat in the kitchen-living room, our chairs drawn up to a steamer trunk which served as a coffee table. On the trunk were our refreshments: rum on the rocks for Roger and me and a plain Coke for Kitty, a paper plate with a few Vienna sausages and a sprinkling of Fritos, and a mirror face-up with four neat and generous lines of white powder. And a straw.

"Well, you do know how to entertain," I said. "You're in the entertainment business, first class."

Kitty sat down on the steamer trunk and bent her head down over the mirror. Pinching one nostril, she deftly sucked a line of powder up into her brains. She looked up and gave Roger a full, adoring smile. "You have plenty more of this, I hope?"

Roger grinned. "I have assets, babycakes. In fact right now your babycake ass sets on a gold mine."

Her eyes widened. She put her palms down on the surface of the trunk. "In here?"

"Full," he boasted. He reached forward and flipped the padlock affectionately. "But most of it's being shipped out tomorrow. My associates are coming to pick it up."

"And pay you for it," she said. "So you'll have money to spring Gracie and—"

"You got it, doll. Go ahead, do another line and pass Guy the mirror."

She did as she was told but I passed the mirror to Roger. "No, thanks," I said.

Roger took the straw and snorted up one of the lines, then put the mirror back on the trunk. "So, Guy. Like my spread? My digs?"

"You own this place?" I asked.

"It belongs to the business," he said.

"XXX-Tra Credits? Caslon Oldestyle?"

"No, my new business. I'm only a part owner, but I get to live on the island for free." He turned to Kitty and said, "With my girl here."

Kitty said, "And Gracie. Huh, Roger?"

Roger nodded.

"What's the name of your new company, Roger?" I asked.

Kitty said, "That's none of your business. Right, Roger?"

"I'm not worried about Guy telling anybody," Roger said. His face was darker now. The whole room was darker. Twilight comes quickly to the jungle. Roger stood up and walked around the room, lighting kerosene lamps.

I said, "I think I should be getting back to the resort. Before it's too dark. So Roger, if you don't mind, let's go on over there. Kitty can grab her stuff and come back with you. I assume you want to do that, Kitty?"

Roger sat back down, inhaled the other line of coke, stood up, and said, "Let's take a walk. I want to show you something."

"Well—"

"Don't worry. I can handle the skiff in the dark. I do it all the time. I want you to see the sunset through the palms. It's outrageous."

"Roger, I'm ready to leave now. This is making me—"

"Aw Guy," Kitty said. "Come on. Just a little walk, right, Roger?"

Roger went over to the kitchen area of the room and opened a drawer. He pulled out a pistol. And something else, which he put in his pocket before I could see what it was.

Kitty said, "Roger, honey, what are you doing?"

For some reason I didn't feel frightened. Just numb at the prospect that I might very well die in the jungle, soon, in the company of a couple of two-bit pornographers. And angry that I might never get to see Carol Murphy again. Angry.

"Don't worry, folks," Roger laughed. "The gun's not for people. I don't kill people. I already told you that."

"Then—"

"Bats," Roger said. "They come out every evening. I'm trying to shoot 'em out of the sky. Little fuckers are hard to hit, but I've gotten a few. God, I hate bats. Come on. Let's go."

After a few long seconds, I stood up and said, "Lead on, Macduff."

Kitty said, "Who's Macduff?"

Roger said, "You first."

So we went out of the house and down the steps. "It's the path to the left," Roger said, so that's the way we went, me in front, with Roger behind me and Kitty bringing up the rear. "Be careful on the path," Roger warned us. "You guys just have flip-flops on, and the path gets kind of rocky. I always wear tennis shoes on this island. Safer that way."

It was getting so dark it was hard to see the path before me, but I followed the corridor between the parted plants. Roger was right about the bats. They were darting and swooping through the darkening sky over our heads, silent and spooky, dozens of them, maybe hundreds. Then suddenly through the forest of palms and ferns I saw the light up ahead. A brilliant ball of blazing gold filling the sky and reflecting on a still sea, some two hundred yards in front of us through the dense silhouette of jungle.

"Stop here," Roger said. "Isn't that something?"

"God, it's so beautiful," Kitty said.

Well, it was. A pyromaniac's dream. I turned back and saw Kitty and Roger, their arms around each other's waists, smiling into the sunset, their teeth glowing gold. They were about ten feet behind me on the path.

"Yup," I said. "Thanks for showing us that. Now I think it's time—"

"It's time," Roger said.

"Huh?" I moved aside slightly, just enough to let the last of the sun's light shine on Roger's face. He was still smiling. Kitty was not. Roger was pointing his gun directly at my chest.

"I told you I don't kill people," he said. "I want to keep it that way, so just do what I tell you, okay?"

I kept my mouth shut.

Roger brought the gun up and fired it into the air. The sound was immense. A bat flew off into the trees. "Shit," Roger said. "Missed him. So like I said, do what I tell you, okay? Okay?"

I held my tongue again. Roger fired again and missed another bat. My ears were ringing, my mind a Mixmaster.

"Don't make me ask you again," Roger said. "I only have four shots left, and I'm not wasting them on bats."

Kitty said softly, "Do what he says, Guy. Do what he asks you to do."

I nodded.

"Okay," Roger said, his pistol once again pointed at my chest. "That's better. Okay, Guy, I want you to go over and stand next to that palm tree. No, that one. That one. Face me. Right. Just stay there." He reached into the pocket of his dirty guayabera and fished out a pair of handcuffs, which he gave to Kitty. "Cuff him to the tree," he told her. "Hands behind the tree."

"But—"

"Do it."

Kitty nodded and approached me. "Sorry, Guy," she said. "Put your hands behind you. Either side of the tree. That's right."

I felt the cuffs snap in place, biting my wrists like the jaws of a large dog. My arms were pinned and stretched behind me. My chest was cramping up. There was about six inches of chain between the two cuffs.

"Atta girl," Roger said. "Here you go, Kitty. Come here."

She walked back to where he was standing.

"The key to the handcuffs. I'm giving it to you." He placed it in her palm. "Now I want you to throw that key as far as you can into the jungle. Do it. Do it now, Kitty. Now."

"But Roger, you said you don't kill people. You said—"

"I don't. I'll leave that to my business associates. They'll be here early tomorrow afternoon. They're good at killing people. It's kind of an art form for them. If the bugs and the bats and the iguanas don't eat him first." He laughed long and loud, then suddenly stopped laughing altogether. "Throw away the key, Kitty."

"Why don't you just shoot him?" Kitty cried. "It'll be kinder."

"Throw away the key."

"He's in pain, Roger. And he won't have anything to eat or drink, and—"

"He can eat bat shit," Roger said. "Drink bat piss. Throw away the key."

"Oh fuck!" She wound up and pitched the key. It was too dark now for me to see where it went, but I could hear it whistle off and land softly somewhere in the universe far, far away. She turned to Roger and said, "If you won't shoot him, let me."

"You'd kill your friend, your friend Guy?"

"He's not a close friend, Roger," she said. "It's just, well it would be kinder to him to let me kill him now, rather than spend the night out here and then get, I don't know, tortured or something, I don't know, I just, oh Roger, let me shoot the poor little fucker. Please! Then we can go back to the house and do some more lines, have a party. Come on."

"You kill him, you bury him. First thing tomorrow morning."

"Okay."

Roger handed her the pistol and said, "Now be careful. Don't waste any bullets. One shot is all you get."

There, in the darkening twilight, I saw my friend Kitty sighting at me down the barrel of Roger's gun. Her hand shook. "I want you to remember I'm doing you a favor, Guy," she said.

Then she lowered the gun to her hip. "I'm not sure I can do it," she said.

Roger said, "Forget it then. Give me the gun."

"No. I'll do it." She brought the gun back up and sighted again. The gun was shivering like a leaf. "Give me a reason, Guy. Make me mad enough to kill you. I need for you to piss me off real bad." There was just enough light for me to see her wink at me twice, first with one eye, then with the other. "Piss me off, God damn it!"

Everything slowed way down, and I had time to recall that for as long as I could remember, everyone was always giving me orders. Carol Murphy telling me what to do. Fritz Marburger, telling me what to do. Roger Herndon, Commander Bob Worsham, Rosa Macdonald, all telling me what to do. Now here was Kitty Katz, this stripper, this cokehead, this false friend, telling me what to do. I was going to die doing what other people told me to do. Well, okay, that's me all over. All over.

"Kitty," I said, "I can't stop you from killing me but if you think you're going to survive this adventure yourself, you are the dumbest, stupidest—"

"Don't call me stupid!"

"—stupidest girl on the planet. You're just a stupid stripper with a sense of humor and a good body, but all your brains are in your tits, and they're starting to sag. You're a coked-out dumbbell. A stupid, stupid...." There was a word in my mind but I couldn't force it to my mouth. "Stupid."

"Come on, Kitty," Roger said. "Pull the damn trigger."

She did.

She turned right around, took aim in a split second, and shot Roger in the right foot. The report echoed in the jungle and lived on in my ears.

"Holy Jesus!" Roger shouted. "God damn it, Kitty, *fuck!*"

"Right," Kitty said. "Hold still, Roger." And she shot him in the left ankle.

Roger went down on his knees and howled. "What the fuck do you think you're doing?" he roared.

"I know what I'm doing," Kitty said. She walked over to me, kissed me on the lips, then walked behind the tree and fired the gun again. I felt the heat as the shot left the muzzle. It burned my hands, but my arms were suddenly free. I still had steel bracelets on both wrists, but the wrists weren't attached to each other. My arms were cramped up but free. I took a deep breath, stepped away from the tree, and opened my eyes.

It was dark now, but I could see Kitty standing over Roger's crouched body. She lifted her foot and shoved him off balance, so that he lay whimpering on his side, clutching his wounds. "I have one more bullet left, Roger," she said. "Any requests?"

"You can shoot it up your ass, you stupid cunt!"

Ah. The word my mouth does not have an easy time saying.

"You shouldn't have said that, Rog," Kitty told him. "Nobody calls me stupid. Guy, take his shoes off. Take off your shirt, Roger."

"What?"

Kitty pointed the gun at his temple. "You heard me. Take off your shirt and put your hands behind your back. Now. Do it now."

Roger did as he was told. Using her teeth and her fingers, Kitty ripped the guayabera up the back, giving her enough cloth to work with. She knotted Roger's wrists together behind his back, while I removed his bloody tennis shoes and socks. Blood is sticky stuff. It smells, too, or maybe that was just the smell of Roger's feet.

Kitty and I stood up. "Thank you, Roger. Thanks for cooperating. I've never killed a man, and I'm glad I didn't have to start tonight. So thanks for being so stupid. Guy, give me those shoes."

I handed them to her.

"Ewww," she said. "Gross." She threw one shoe as far as she could into the jungle on one side of the path, then threw the other far off into the other side. "Okay," she said. "Let's go."

"Wait," Roger cried. "You can't just leave me here!"

"Some people will be around early tomorrow afternoon," I reminded him. "They'll take care of you. Meanwhile, eat bat shit."

◇◇◇

"God, can you believe he called me stupid?" Kitty said when we got back to the house. The lamps were turned up high and the house was cheerful and bright. "Roger, of all people, calling *me* stupid?"

"I called you stupid, too," I said. "I'm sorry about that."

"I didn't mind you calling me that," she said. "You're a lot smarter than I am. But Roger's dumb as shit."

"Okay," I said, "we'd better get going. Got your tote bag?"

"It's out on the deck. Just a minute, I got one more thing to take care of. One bullet left."

She carried the pistol to the steamer trunk in the center of the room and blew the lock off. Then she threw the empty gun on the couch and opened the trunk. "God," she said. "God."

"Kitty, let's go."

"Go get my tote bag," she said.

"No way. Close the trunk and let's get out of here."

"But Guy—"

"No."

"I'm not going to snort it, I swear. We're going to sell it, right? Make enough to bail Gracie out?"

"Forget it."

"But—"

"Who's going to bail you out of the jail in Honduras? Roger?"

"How about one toot for the road, then?"

"We don't have time."

She glared at me, then slammed the trunk shut. She walked to the kitchen table and picked up a kerosene lamp. She threw it across the room at another lamp, and the two lamps hit the floor together and became a flaming pool.

"Okay," she said. "We're outa here. I hope you can figure out how to drive an outboard motor in the dark."

"Me? What about you?"

"Me? Don't be silly. I'm just a stupid stripper, remember?" She picked up the one remaining lamp and led us out the door, across the deck, grabbing her tote along the way, down the stairs, and through the jungle to Roger's dock.

Chapter Twenty-Six

Trial and error, by the light of a kerosene lamp.

It took me half an hour to find the switch, pull the cord a million times, find the throttle, kill the engine, do it again, kill it again, do it again, then figure out the difference between backwards and forwards, right and left. But eventually I got the hang of it and we chugged out into the open channel, headed for the big island of Morgania.

The luck didn't last. First our lamp blew out, then I steered us out of the channel and into shallow water. I ran us onto a sand bar and killed the engine.

We sat there a few minutes, slapping at mosquitoes, until Kitty said, "Okay, smarty. What do we do now?"

"We get out of the boat and shove off into the channel. Come on."

"What about sharks?"

"There aren't any sharks in these waters."

"How do you know?"

"I don't."

We climbed out of the boat, and without our weight the boat lifted free of the sand bar and started to float away from us. I had to dive in and swim after it. Luckily the water was shallow enough for me to stand up and drag the boat back to where Kitty was waiting.

We crawled back into the skiff and I got to work yanking on the cord. I got us going again and we were back in the open channel, putt-putting nicely along without any idea where the channel would bend again and leave us running aground.

"Guy, look!"

I turned and looked back at Polly's Key, now about a hundred yards behind us. Flames were rising from a fire in the middle of the island, licking up and turning the sky above dark orange. The night got suddenly silent.

"Uh-oh."

"Well, it can't be helped," Kitty said. "And nobody knows we were out there. We'll get Oliver to take us to the airport first thing tomorrow morning and we'll be long gone before—"

"Kitty, that's not why I said uh-oh."

"What."

"Fuck," I said. "We're out of gas."

"Holy shit!" she cried. "What a flake!"

"How was I supposed to know—"

"Not you. Roger. He was always running out of gas. Okay, so now what?"

"I have no idea," I admitted. "We're drifting with a current of some kind, but I have no idea where it's taking us."

"Maybe you should set the emergency brake."

"Kitty—"

"Just kidding, Guy. God."

Whatever current we were traveling in was not taking us to the Pirate's Paradise. That was clear. Were we headed for the open sea, outside the reef? Then onward to the Gulf Stream for a brief eternal pit stop at the Bermuda Triangle? "At least it's warm," I said. "And the moon's rising. That's something."

"Fucking mosquitoes." *Slap.*

"Shit."

"Now what?" she asked again. Then: "Guy, look!"

Looming ahead of us, directly in our path, was the rusted wreck of the shrimp boat, lit up by the low-lying waning moon behind us.

"I guess that's something we can hold onto," Kitty said.

"Razor sharp," I reminded her. "That's what Oliver said."

"Any better ideas?"

"Nope, especially since—"

"What?"

"We must have scraped a hole in the bottom back there. We're taking water."

◇◇◇

There wasn't much left of Roger's skiff by the time we bumped up against the metal wall of the shrimp boat. Fortunately we were able to step aboard fairly gracefully onto the low end of a deck that was leaning at a thirty-degree angle. We let the skiff sink behind us as we crawled on all fours up to the high side of the deck, where we could pull ourselves up and hang onto a rail.

"How are your hands and knees?" I asked.

"Scraped up. Probably bleeding pretty bad, but I don't want to look. Yours?"

"Not so good. Well, if we die here we won't have to have tetanus shots. I hate tetanus shots. Speaking of shots, where did you learn to shoot a gun? You're a damn good shot."

"Not hardly. I was aiming at his kneecaps. Both times."

From our vantage point we could see firelight flickering through the trees on Polly's Key. We had to hold tight to the rail, which left us only one hand each for slapping bugs. Every part of my skin was on fire with bites.

"Guy," Kitty said, "I'm really sorry I got you into all this."

"Oh well, I wasn't really doing anything important at the time."

"And I'm sorry I was so pissy to you this afternoon. When we were in the bar I was faking it, you know. I had to. I had to pretend I was on his side, so he wouldn't think we were double-teaming him. You understand, don't you?"

"You could have let me in on it," I suggested.

"No way. You'd have blown it. You're a terrible liar, Guy Mallon. Don't ever play poker."

"I'll try to remember that. But you took a pretty big risk with both our lives, right?"

"Actually, by the time we were sitting out there on Roger's deck, I had changed my mind. All of a sudden it seemed like a pretty good deal—give up stripping and spend all day snorkeling with Gracie, snorting coke with Roger. I had myself convinced he was going to come through for me. I know, stupid. But see, you've never been addicted."

"I have been. Just not to coke. So what made you change your mind?"

"Well, when he got that gun out of the drawer, I woke up. Like, hello? Trust Roger? By then it was almost too late, but I knew I had to do something, anything I could to get that piece out of his hands. Fortunately my brain was on overdrive. I guess you can thank the coke after all. I mean, we got away with it, right?"

"Right. I guess. At least we got this far."

The moon rose higher and gave us more light for slapping each other's mosquitoes. It was like doing each other a favor. But after a while it seemed to me that Kitty was slapping harder than necessary.

"Kitty?"

Slap. "Did you mean that, Guy? About my tits sagging?" *Slap.* "Did you really mean that?"

"That's not what I said," I said. "I said your brains were sagging. But I didn't mean that, either."

"Okay, you're forgiven. I guess now my tits never will sag, huh?" She began crying and moved close to me, let go of the rail, and threw both arms around my neck. "Oh, Guy, I'm so scared!"

I let the bugs have their way and wrapped my free arm around her back. We hugged and stayed in that perilous embrace until we heard the chugging of an approaching outboard motor.

"Kitty, I think we're going to get off this disaster zone."

"You think?" Her face was buried in the hollow between my shoulder and my neck. "Tell me when you know for sure."

The motor grew louder, and a flashlight found us as the boat drew up alongside the wreck.

"You there!" the man in the bow of the boat shouted up to us. "Get down here. Come on, move it! Now!"

I whispered to Kitty, "Our luck has changed."

She tentatively pulled her head away from my neck and looked into my face.

"For the worse, I'm afraid," I continued. "But we don't have a choice. Be careful climbing down."

We held hands and stepped gingerly down the steep deck into the beam of the flashlight. When we reached the lower edge of the shipwreck, the boat pulled up close to us, and Lewis Pomeroy said, "Get in the boat. We're going for a ride."

Chapter Twenty-Seven

We stepped into the rocking boat and huddled together on the middle seat, facing Pomeroy. We were both shivering, and it was a hot night.

"Okay, let's go," Pomeroy told the dark mountain in the stern of the boat. We heard the throttle being opened and the boat putted backwards away from the wreck, then turned around and picked up speed as we went forward into the channel. Pomeroy didn't look at us, but kept staring off to the side of the boat, as if keeping an eye out for bandits.

Nobody spoke until we were halfway across the bay, approaching the lights of Morgania. Then Pomeroy shouted over the roar of the outboard, "Cut the engine."

Suddenly we were surrounded by throbbing silence, bobbing gently on the inky bay. The moonlight lit Pomeroy's face, which he now turned to us. "I don't mind telling you that I'm really pissed off," he said. "You two came very close to getting yourselves killed out there, which would have been a shame. Even worse, at least as far as some people are concerned, you may have botched a major drug raid. Do you understand what I'm saying?"

"No," I said.

Kitty said, "You mean you're not working with Roger?"

"I'm not going to answer a bunch of questions right now. We don't have time for that. But no, I don't work for Herndon, or with him. I'm in law enforcement. There's a sting operation scheduled for tomorrow afternoon, but if the Miami contingent shows up and things aren't right on Polly's Key, they're not going to stick around and fill their pockets full of evidence. Thanks to you idiots, things are not right on Polly's Key. As far as I could see from Herndon's dock, his house is destroyed, along with any evidence that was inside it. Now listen to me. Listen to me carefully. Don't ask questions and don't you dare argue.

"We're going back to the Pirate's Paradise. I will give you exactly fifteen minutes to get cleaned up, packed, and out of your room. No more. Fifteen minutes. While you're doing that I'll get you checked out at the front desk and I'll pay your bill. Then I'm going outside to the courtyard, where I'll wait for you in a cab, with the motor running. You paying attention? Fifteen minutes. I don't want to waste gas, and you don't want to waste time.

"We're going to make a quick stop in Morgantown. There's an all-night pharmacy there. I'm going to give you both tetanus shots. The side effects can be pretty uncomfortable, but there's no choice and you don't dare wait till you get back to the States. And some cortisone cream for those bug bites. Even in this light I can see you've been eaten alive. Then we're going to the airport. I'll have you on the next flight to San Pedro Sula. From there you're on your own, but I want you to catch the earliest flights available. Your return tickets are open-dated. Don't ask me how I know that. What the hell are those things on your wrists?"

"Handcuffs," I said, holding them up for him to see. "You like?"

"You're a lot of trouble, Guy Mallon. You're lucky I have skeleton keys that fit those things."

"You travel with skeleton keys?"

"Standard equipment in my line of work." He shook his head at me. "Okay, Oliver," he called to the man in the stern. "Let's get going."

"Oliver!" Kitty and I said it together, twisting around to look at the big man behind us. There he was, chuckling, grinning in the moonlight.

"Yes sir, Oliver's taxi service, at your service, on land, on sea. Mighty good to see you folks, yes sir. Mighty glad. On land, on sea. Mighty glad!"

◇◇◇

An hour later Kitty and I were in front of the Morgania airport, hugging Oliver good-bye. Then Lew Pomeroy walked with us into the airport, stood with us at the ticket counter, and made arrangements for us to be on the flight for San Pedro Sula that left at six a.m. The agent was able to book us on all our other flights and check our baggage through to Los Angeles, where we would arrive at four-eighteen that afternoon, Pacific Daylight Time. Lew paid our airport departure tax and walked with us to the waiting room. We sat on little gray plastic chairs and scratched our bug bites. Breathed.

Kitty grinned at Lew and said, "So. So you really do work for the war on drugs. Man."

Lew smiled back and said, "Doesn't matter who I work for."

"This soldier saved our ass, Kitty," I said.

"It's dirty money," Kitty said. "I'm grateful you saved our ass, Lew, but the war on drugs is dirty money."

"And drug traffic is clean money?" he asked. His tone was genial.

"I've been making dirty money myself," I quickly admitted. Anything to segue off the subject. "Vanity press publishing. Easy money. But I've quit."

"I'm glad to hear that," Lew said. "I don't know anything about publishing, but easy money is an addiction."

"So's the war on drugs," Kitty persisted. "Tell your boss Barry McCaffrey the war on drugs is stupid. It just goes after the victims. It's just another big business, like napalm or whatever, and it's dirty money."

"Why would I tell him that?" Lew asked. "If I worked for him, I mean. It's just a job for him. I should tell him to give up his career? He has a family to support, just as I do—"

"Dirty money."

"And stripping isn't dirty money? Taking your clothes off for horny old men?"

"Who told you I'm a stripper?"

Lew laughed. "Kitty, I'm not with the war on drugs. Honest. I'm a federal marshal working in cooperation with the Los Angeles Police Department. I was sent here to collar Roger Herndon for a number of crimes, only one of which was drug traffic, and I was also asked by Rosa Macdonald to keep an eye on you two and protect you. Now I'm sending you back, and that part of my assignment's over. But I have to stick around to lend a hand tomorrow. I owe the DEA a favor. Okay? Give my friend Rosa a big kiss for me when you get back to Santa Barbara."

"No kidding?" I said. "A federal marshal? You sure had me fooled. I was sure you were in real estate. You seemed to know a lot about it."

He nodded. "My wife and I bought a house in Encino last year. Talk about a crash course in lunacy."

"So how did you know we were coming here to Morgania, and, I mean, what's going on?" Kitty demanded. "Just how much do you know?"

"Grace Worth told the LAPD all about Roger Herndon's operation in Morgania. I have extradition papers prepared, and I'm taking him back to California tomorrow to stand trial for two murders and two arsons. He'll also be charged with fraud, tax evasion, drug traffic, and car theft. I wanted to collar him right away, but McCaffrey's team convinced me I should wait until they completed their sting. Then you two got in the way. But I'll still get him. And as soon as we have him behind bars, awaiting arraignment, Grace Worth will walk free."

"Maybe he died out there on the island," Kitty said. "We might have killed him."

Lew and I shrugged to each other. "No great loss," I said.

"But will Gracie still walk free?" she asked, a whine in her voice.

"Of course. Just a little more paperwork for me, that's all. She cleared her name by letting us know where to find Herndon.

I found him. She'll be outside in a few days, max. So you see, you really didn't need to make this trip at all."

Kitty nodded. "Shit," she said. "It would have been a lot easier. But I didn't know Gracie was going to tell on Roger. She didn't tell me she was going to."

"I needed to make the trip," I said.

"You?"

"Roger Herndon took something from me, and I wanted it back."

Lewis Pomeroy sighed. "Well, let's hope that attitude is out of your system, Guy. I hope you've learned to leave crime-fighting to the professionals. Rosa told me you've got a bit of a problem that way."

I shrugged. "I'll be good from now on," I promised. "Whatever that means."

Lew stood up. "I guess I'd better get back to my hotel. Big day tomorrow. You guys okay on your own?" Then he turned to Kitty and said, "By the way, I hope you haven't packed any of Roger's cocaine into your luggage. They're going to be going through your bags very thoroughly in Los Angeles, and—"

Kitty flared. "Don't be silly. What do you think I am? Stupid?" Then she grinned and hugged him. "Thanks Loodood. You're my hero."

He blushed and was gone.

Kitty turned to me and said, "Guy?"

"Hmmm?"

"You're my hero, too."

Her eyes were nearly swollen shut from all the bug bites, and tears leaked out and found a path to her trembling smile. I took her in my arms and squeezed her fragile body, knowing somehow it would be my last hug from this dear, fucked-up friend.

Epilogue

Kitty and I arrived in Los Angeles late Monday afternoon, October 9. We stayed overnight in the Hacienda Inn, near the airport, and on Tuesday morning we drove back to Santa Barbara through a steady rain. "Weather sure changed since we left town three days ago," I remarked.

"Lot of stuff has changed," Kitty said. "One more thing I want you to know. Gracie didn't kill Worsham. She handcuffed him, all right, and she did her lap dance, but he didn't have a stroke and he didn't have a heart attack. Roger came in, saw what was happening, and stuffed Worsham's underpants in his mouth and sealed his face with duct tape. Then he poured the gasoline and lit the match. Worsham died in the fire. He was burned alive. And Gracie didn't set that fire. She just watched, scared to death. And still she trusted him. Roger. Still she trusted that fucker, and so did I. Cocaine. Jesus. What was I thinking?"

"Well—"

"Shut up. I don't want to talk about it."

I stayed at Kitty's place the rest of that week. We barely talked, and we didn't talk at all about our adventure in Morgania. I spent my days at the office. She went back to work at the Kountry Klub, so she was gone every evening until all hours, and in the afternoons she cleaned house. She told me she took all the cocaine left in her apartment to the club and gave it to Terry, the bouncer. "But I'm keeping the weed," she insisted. "Don't expect me to give that up."

"I never said a word."

At the end of the week, Gracie called to say she'd been released from jail, and she was coming home. I moved out that day and checked into the Schooner Inn, where there was still a room waiting for me.

Santa Barbara was cool and fresh. The rains had washed the smog from the sky. I took long walks around the city every cool, crisp morning, always ending up at my office, where I'd stay until dark, except for short trips to the post office for mail and the Sojourner for lunch. I didn't have much of a business left, but I had paid the rent until the end of October. My poetry books were all packed up, sitting on the office floor in boxes, ready to be shipped to wherever Carol could find a buyer, or to Scarecrow Books if she wanted to hold onto them while they sold. I did some writing, and I read my way through the Sue Grafton oeuvre-to-date. I made arrangements to store my office furniture and equipment at Budget U-Stor, but that wouldn't happen till the end of the month. I ate breakfast every morning at Esau's and I had dinner every night at the Casa Blanca Mexican restaurant down the street, washing it down with one beer. That was all the drinking I did. It reminded me of how healthy I'd been in 1977, when I'd first come to Santa Barbara. Before I got into publishing. I realized I could live without publishing.

That was also before I knew Carol. I realized I could live without Carol, too, but I wasn't happy about that. Nobody is guaranteed happiness anyway. I would survive. Not in this town, though. Santa Barbara without Carol? I didn't think so. Come November, it would be time to move on. I had no idea where, but I had a few weeks left to think about it.

◇◇◇

One morning as I left Esau's, I found myself holding the door open for Maxwell Black, who was on his way in. He stopped, clapped me on the shoulder, and said, "Guy! I thought you were in Honduras, pardner."

"Howdy, Max. Who told you that?"

"Carol," he answered.

"Carol Murphy."

"Herself."

"You've been talking to Carol Murphy? She called you?"

"Yeah," he said, looking a bit nervous. "She's moving, you know. Selling her house and relocating."

"I know that."

"Yeah, well she called me and asked me—"

"Listen, Max, I'm in kind of a rush here. Late for the office. Have a good breakfast."

So I took an extra-long walk that morning, through the upper East Side, where the Riviera comes down to the Mission and everybody's wealthy and happy. I had a long talk with myself.

You've been in love before, right?

Right.

You've been dumped before too, right?

Right.

And it hurt.

Right.

But you got over it, right?

Right.

Survived?

Right.

So you can survive this one, too. Right?

Well....

Right?

Yeah. Right.

Right.

So I was in pretty good shape by the time I got back downtown, ready to spend another day alone in my office. *F Is for Fugitive.*

◇◇◇

I put the key into the lock on my office door and turned it this way, then that way, which locked me out. Turned it back where it was and let myself in. So what was going on? Why was the door unlocked?

My books! My chest flooded with adrenaline, but one look had me back to normal: there were the boxes, just as I'd left them. I carefully walked to the back office and peered through the open door.

She looked up from her desk and smiled. A shy smile.

I walked to my desk and sat down. Our desks were arranged so that we had no choice but to search each other's frightened, yearning eyes.

I spoke first: "You've come back?"

She shook her head. "I'm just catching up with the mail," she said. "You've left a lot of work on my desk."

"I was going to get to it eventually," I said. "I figure it's mostly orders for books we don't have."

"Vance told me about the fire," she said. "Guy, I'm so sorry!"

"It's okay," I said. "Who needs a warehouse?"

"So you're all right?"

"No."

"Neither am I," she said.

We stared hungrily across the distance between our desks. I could tell she was as nervous as I was, and, like me, she was trying to fight off a monster grin. We both gave up at the same time, and our smiles filled the office. We stood up from our chairs, walked around our desks, and danced into each other's calling arms. I held her firm, strong, trembling body, kissed her shoulder, her throat, and moved up to her open lips.

I said, "Jesus, I have—"

"—missed you so!" she answered.

"This is where the end began," I said. We sat at a table on the El Encanto terrace, overlooking the bowl of red-tiled roofs pouring down the hills and out into the harbor. The midday, mid-October sky was a dazzling blue, and a soft breeze danced through the graceful droop of eucalyptus branches on the lawn beside us. I had just filled her in on all the details of all that had happened: the fire, the dead Commander, the stolen yacht, the avalanche of books on my body, the Ventura studio fire, Marburger à la Mercedes, Gracie's arrest, and the trip to Honduras. Yes, I even told her about the night I went to the Kountry Klub, but I spared her the details.

"Fritz Marburger, may he rot in peace, and I sat at this table," I said, "and I steadfastly defended the honor of being a rinky-dink small-press poetry publisher, while he wrote me a check for thirty thousand dollars so I could turn his celebrity girlfriend into a published author."

"And—"

"And my soul flew out over the canyon and was gobbled by a condor, never to be seen again."

"Poor Lorraine."

"And poor Fritz," I said. "He died trying to cheat me out of everything, but I still will miss that pompous piece of—"

"And Roger? Will you miss Roger?"

"This has been an awful year," I said. "I loved the high of being a publisher of a book the public wanted to read for a change. But the rest of it—"

"I think you also enjoyed hanging out with Miss Kitty Katz," Carol said. "How was your trip, by the way?"

"I have a lot to tell you," I said. "A lot, a whole lot. About tropical fish and the sunset through the palm trees...."

"And about Kitty."

"I got to know Kitty pretty well. At least I think I did. I'm not really sure." I looked at her and realized I'd said the wrong thing. "You're not really jealous, are you? Jealous of Kitty?"

"Me?" she responded. "Jealous of a drop-dead gorgeous twenty-something, if that, porn star only two inches taller than you, with a bust like the Grand Tetons and a laugh like brook-water in the early spring? Jealous?"

I chuckled.

"Chuckle," she said. "Go on and chuckle. You had me worried there, Guy. I'd like to say I was worried for you, and maybe that was true, but mainly I worried that I'd never see you again, and that would be the end of my heart."

"How can I show you you had nothing to worry about?" I asked.

"You'll think of something. So how was Honduras? Did you have a good trip? Tell me."

We weren't finished with lunch until after three o'clock. I suggested we go down to East Beach and take a walk along Palm Park, but Carol said we had to go to the office first. We had business to conduct.

I sat down and put my arms in front of me on my desk. I still couldn't take my eyes off Carol, watching her sit down as if she still belonged in that seat. She said, "Look down."

I dropped my eyes to the surface of my desk and read the rectangle between my arms: "Pay to the order of GUY MALLON...Eighty-two thousand dollars and no cents..." From Scarecrow Books, Jefferson City, California.

I touched it. I picked it up and smelled it. It was real.

"You found a buyer! That didn't take any time at all. But all this money—"

"The books are safe with me, Guy."

"I—"

"What?"

"How much do I owe you?" I asked. "Have you figured out your commission?"

"Don't worry about it."

"No, it's important. Where's my calculator? My checkbook...."

She reached into the drawer of her desk where she kept the company checkbook. She stood up and brought it to my desk. "Don't write me a check," she said. "Write a check for forty thousand dollars to Samuel Welch. Put 'repayment in full' in the memo line. Then we'll walk it over to the post office together. And you'll be free."

"Free to what?"

"Free to love me again, dope."

"I never stopped loving you, Carol," I said as we took our late-afternoon stroll by the ocean. The sky was bright orange and the silhouettes of the palms were black; Halloween season was approaching. We held hands.

"How lovely it is here in Santa Barbara," she answered. "This town is still so easy on the eyes."

"You might come back?" I asked, then chewed my lower lip.

She squeezed my hand. "No. I don't live here anymore. I haven't told you all my news yet. I sold my house. I mean Vance sold it. And I've bought a house in Jefferson. I'm meeting the movers tomorrow morning. Art Summers and Max Black will be there to help with the lifting."

"Oh."

"What does that mean, oh?"

"So that's what brought you to Santa Barbara? To meet the moving van?"

"Partly. Also to give you your check and pick up the books. Also to hold your hand at this very moment. And to ask a favor of you."

"Anything."

"Would you help me move?"

"Tomorrow morning?"

"For starters."

We went to Arnoldi's for dinner. Jim saw us coming through the door and poured Carol a double Bombay on the rocks without asking. Sitting at the bar, waiting for our favorite booth, I asked her, "So, did you make a bundle in real estate?"

"I certainly did," she said. "The real estate market in this town is obscene. I sold the East Side bungalow with a hefty mortgage and bought a much bigger house by the ocean, free and clear, and made a profit. I never had this much money before."

"Let me guess," I said. "You bought my first editions, right? I mean you gave Scarecrow Books the money to buy them?"

"I'm a money-launderer," she confessed. "I can't lie to you, never could. But I only did it to keep those wonderful books in the family. I know how presumptuous that was of me. Are you angry?"

I was done forever being angry with Carol. "I'm glad they're in good hands," I said.

"Maybe you could come visit the books from time to time?"

"For starters, I could drive you north tomorrow. I don't have any other plans right now. We could go up together, get there before the moving van arrives. How's that?"

"And will you stick around for a while?" she asked.

"Well, I'm not sure. We could talk about it on the drive."

"Guy, can't you see how easy I'm trying to make this for you?"

"Make what?"

"Come be with me, Guy. Please, please, please! There's nothing holding you in Santa Barbara now."

"But I don't know what I'd do up there," I said. "How will I make a living?"

"I'm wealthy now, remember?"

"But I'm broke. I can't just—"

"Marry me," she said. "Please marry me. You love me, Guy Mallon, and we both know it. Marry me."

Jim said, "Your booth is ready."

"Marry you?"

"That's what I said." She opened the door and we walked into the house where we'd lived together for a decade. She flipped on the living room light. The floor held an array of cardboard cartons labeled "Dishes," "Linens," "Books," "Clothes," "Food," "Pictures," "More Books." I followed her into the kitchen, where she poured us each a glass of bedside water. I followed her into the bedroom, where she lit a candle and we took off our clothes.

We sat on the bed, her on one side and me on the other. Yes, I was nervous.

"You really want me to—"

"Marry me. Can't you see how easy this will be?"

"You'd, uh, you'd take me as I am?"

"As you are? Guy, you're all in the world I love."

"But I sold my soul," I said.

"Yes, but you've earned it back. With interest. Guy, one last time. No, it won't be the last time till you say yes. Will you marry me?"

I grinned. "But I'm so short."

"Oh, that." She pealed with Irish laughter. "You're going to have to give up being short."

Carol Murphy threw her strawberry curls back on the pillow and stretched her long body out in the center of the bed, reaching with her strong arms and naked legs to the four corners of the world. "Come to me, king of my heart," she crooned. "Climb aboard my body and my future, and I promise you the ride of your life!"

To receive a free catalog of Poisoned Pen Press titles, please contact us in one of the following ways:

Phone: 1-800-421-3976
Facsimile: 1-480-949-1707
Email: info@poisonedpenpress.com
Website: www.poisonedpenpress.com

Poisoned Pen Press
6962 E. First Ave. Ste. 103
Scottsdale, AZ 85251